THE GOLD-STEALERS

Edward Dyson

THE GOLD-STEALERS

A Story of Waddy

BIBLIOBAZAAR

THE GOLD-STEALERS

CHAPTER I.

THE schoolhouse at Waddy was not in the least like any of the trim State buildings that now decorate every Victorian township and mark every mining or agricultural centre that can scrape together two or three meagre classes; it was the result of a purely local enthusiasm, and was erected by public subscription shortly after Mr. Joel Ham, B.A., arrived in the district and let it be understood that he did not intend to go away again. Having discovered that it was impossible to make anything else of Mr. Joel Ham, Waddy resolved to make a schoolmaster of him. A meeting was held in the Drovers' Arms, numerous speeches, all much more eloquently expressive of the urgent need of convenient scholastic institutions than the orators imagined, were delivered by representative men, and a resolution embodying the determination of the residents to erect a substantial building and install Mr. J. Ham, B.A., as headmaster was carried unanimously.

The original contributors were not expected to donate money towards the good cause; they gave labour and material. The work of erection was commenced next day. Neither plans nor specifications were supplied, and every contributor was his own architect. Timber of all sorts and shapes came in from fifty sources. The men of the day shift at the mines worked at the building in the evening; those on the four-o'clock shift put in an hour or two in the morning, and mates off the night shift lent a hand at any time during the day, one man taking up the work where the other left off. Consequently—and as there was no ruling mind and no general design—the school when finished seemed to lack continuity, so to speak. As an architectural effort it displayed evidence of many excellent intentions, but could not be called a brilliant success as a whole—although one astute Parliamentary candidate did secure an overwhelming majority of votes in Waddy after declaring the schoolhouse to be an ornament to the township. The public-spirited persons who contributed windows, it was tacitly agreed, were quite justified in putting in those windows according to the dictates of their own fancy, even if the result was somewhat bizarre. Jock Summers gave a bell hung in a small gilded dome, and this was fixed on the roof right in the centre of the building, mainly for picturesque effect; but as there was no rope attached and no means of reaching the bell—and it never occurred to anybody to rectify the deficiency—Jock's gift remained to the end merely an ornamental adjunct. So also with Sam Brierly's Gothic portico. Sam expended much time and ingenuity in constructing the portico, and it was built on to the street end of the schoolhouse, although there was no door there, the only entrance being at the back.

The building was opened with a tea-fight and a dance, and answered its purpose very well up to the time of the first heavy rains; then studies had to be postponed indefinitely, for the floor was a foot under water. A call was made upon the united strength of the township, and the building was lifted bodily and set down again on piles. When the open space between the ground and the floor was boarded up, the residents were delighted to find that the increased height had given the structure quite an imposing appearance. Alas! before six months had passed the place was found to be going over on one side. Waddy watched this failing with growing uneasiness. When the collapse seemed inevitable, the male adults were again bidden to an onerous public duty; they rolled up like patriots, and with a mighty effort pushed the school up into the perpendicular propping it there with stout stays. That answered excellently for a time, but eventually the wretched house began to slant in the opposite direction. Once more the men of Waddy attended in force, and spent an arduous half-day hoisting it into an upright position, and securing it there with more stays. It took the eccentric building a long time to decide upon its next move; then it suddenly lurched forward a foot or more, and after that slipped an inch or two farther out of plumb every day. But the ingenuity of Waddy was not exhausted: a few hundred feet of rope and a winch were borrowed from the Peep o' Day; the rope was run round the schoolhouse, and the building was promptly hauled back into shape and fastened down with long timbers running from its sides to a convenient red-gum stump at the back. Thus it remained for many years, bulging at the sides, pitching forward, and straining at its tethers like an eager hound in a leash.

It was literally a humming hot day at Waddy; the pulsing whirr of invisible locusts filled the whole air with a drowsy hum, and from the flat at the back of the township, where a few thousand ewes and lambs were shepherded amongst the quarry holes, came another insistent droning in a deeper note, like the murmur of distant surf. No one was stirring: to the right and left along the single thin wavering line of unpainted weatherworn wooden houses nothing moved but mirage waters flickering in the hollows of the ironstone road. Equally deserted was the wide stretch of brown plain, dotted with poppet legs and here and there a whim, across the dull expanse of which Waddy seemed to peer with stupid eyes.

From within the school were heard alternately, with the regularity of a mill, the piping of an old cracked voice and the brave chanting of a childish chorus. Under the school, where the light was dim and the air was decidedly musty, two small boys were crouched, playing a silent game of 'stag knife.' Besides being dark and evil-smelling under there, it was damp; great clammy masses of cobweb hung from the joists and spanned the spaces between the piles. The place was haunted by strange and fearsome insects, too, and the moving of the classes above sent showers of dust down between the cracks in the worn floor. But those boys were satisfied that they were having a perfectly blissful time, and were serenely happy in defiance of unpropitious surroundings. They were 'playing the wag,' and to be playing the wag under any circumstances is a guarantee of pure felicity to the average healthy boy.

Probably the excessive heat had suggested to Dick Haddon the advisability of spending the afternoon under the school instead of within the close crowded room; at any rate he suggested it to Jacker McKnight, commonly known as Jacker Mack, and now after an hour of it the boys were still jubilant. The game had to be played with great caution, and conversation was conducted in whispers when ideas could not be conveyed in dumb show. All that was going on in the room above was distinctly audible to the deserters below, and the joy of camping there out of the reach of Joel Ham, B.A., and beyond all the trials and tribulations of the Higher Fifth, and hearing other fellows being tested, and hectored, and caned, was too tremendous for whisperings, and must be expressed in wild rollings and contortions and convulsive kicking.

'Parrot Cann, will you kindly favour me with a few minutes on the floor?'

It was the old cracked voice, flavoured with an ominous irony. Dick paused in the middle of a throw with a cocked ear and upturned eyes; Jacker Mack grinned all across his broad face and winked meaningly. They heard the shuffling of a pair of heavily shod feet, and then the voice again.

'Parrot, my man, you are a comedian by instinct, and will probably live to be an ornament to the theatrical profession; but it is my duty to repress premature manifestations of your genius. Parrot, hold out!'

They heard the swish of the cane and the school master's sarcastic comments between the strokes.

'Ah-h, that was a beauty! Once more, Parrot, my friend, if you please. Excellent! Excellent! We will try again. Practice of this kind makes for perfection, you know, Parrot. Good, good—very good! If you should be spoiled in the making, Parrot, you will not in your old age ascribe it to any paltry desire on my part to spare the rod, will you, Parrot?'

'S'help me, I won't, sir!'

There was such a world of pathos in the wail with which Parrot replied that Dick choked in his efforts to repress his emotions. The lads heard the victim blubbing, and pictured his humorous contortions after every cut—for Parrot was weirdly and wonderfully gymnastic under punishment—and Jacker hugged himself and kicked ecstatically, and young Haddon bowed his forehead in the dirt and drummed with his toes, and gave expression to his exuberant hilarity in frantic pantomime. The rough and ready schoolboy is very near to the beginnings; his sense of humour has not been impaired by over-refinement, but remains somewhat akin to that of the gentle savage; and although his disposition to laugh at the misfortunes of his best friends may be deplorable from various points of view, it has not been without its influence in fashioning those good men who put on a brave face in the teeth of tribulation.

'Gee-rusalem! ain't Jo got a thirst?' whispered Dick when the spasm had passed.

'My oath, ain't he!' replied Jacker, 'but he was drunk up afore twelve.'

It is necessary to explain here that the school committee, in electing Mr. Ham to the position of schoolmaster, compelled him to sign a formal agreement, drawn up in quaint legal gibberish, in which it was specified that 'the herein afore-mentioned Joel Ham, B.A.,' was to be limited to a certain amount of alcoholic refreshment per diem, and McMahon, at the Drovers' Arms, bound himself over to supply no more than the prescribed quantity; but it was understood that this galling restriction did not apply to Mr. Ham on Saturdays and holidays.

The noises above subsided into the usual school drone, and the boys under the floor resumed their game. It was an extremely interesting game, closely contested. Each player watched the other's actions with an alert and suspicious eye, and this want of confidence led directly to the boys' undoing; for presently Dick detected Jacker in an attempt to deceive, and signalled 'Down!' with an emphatic gesture. 'Gerrout!' was the word framed by the lips of the indignant Jacker. Haddon gesticulated an angry protest, and McKnight's gestures and grimaces were intended to convey a wish that he might be visited with unspeakable pains and penalties if he were not an entirely virtuous and grievously misjudged small boy.

'It's a lie,' hissed Dick; 'it was down!'

'You're another—it wasn't!

''Twas, I tell you!'

'Twasn't!

'Gimme my knife; I don't play with sharps an' sneaks.'

'Won't!'

Gimme it!

All caution had been forgotten by this time, voices were shrill, and eyes spoke of battle. Dick made at Jacker with a threatening fist, and Jacker, with an adroitness for which he was famous, met him with a clip on the shin from a copper-toed boot. Then the lads grappled and commenced a vigorous and enthusiastic battle in the dirt and amongst the cobweb curtains.

In the schoolroom above Joel Ham, startled from a dreamy drowsiness, heard with wonder fierce voices under his feet, the sounds of blows and of bumping heads, and saw his scholars all distracted. The master divined the truth in a very few minutes.

'Cann, Peterson, Moonlight,' he called, 'follow me.'

He selected a favourite cane from the rack, and strutted out with the curious boys at his heels.

'Now then, Peterson,' he said, and he paused with artful preoccupation to double his cane over and under, and critically examine the end thereof, 'you are a very observant youth, Peterson; you will tell me how those boys got under the school.'

'Dunno,' said Peterson, assuming the expression of an aged cow.

The master seized him by the collar.

'Peterson, you have the faculty of divination. I give you till I have counted ten to exert it. I am counting, Peterson.'

Very often the schoolmaster's language was Greek to the scholars, but his meaning was never in doubt for a moment.

'Eight, Peterson, nine.'

Peterson slouched along a few yards, and kicked stupidly and resentfully at a loose board.

'Might 'a' got in there,' he growled. 'Why couldn't you 'a' asked Moonlight?—he don' mind bein' a sneak.'

But Mr. Ham was down on his knees removing the loose board, and for two or three minutes after crouched at the opening like a famished yellow cat at a rat-hole, awaiting his opportunity. Meanwhile the fight under the school was being prosecuted with unabated fury. Dick and Jacker gripped like twin bull-terriers, rolling and tumbling about in the confined space, careless of everything but the important business in hand. Suddenly Mr. Ham made his spring, and a smart haul brought a leg to light. Another tug, and a second leg shot forth.

'Pull, boys!' he cried.

Moonlight seized the other limb, and a good tug brought the two boys out into the open, still fighting enthusiastically and apparently oblivious of their surroundings. Two soldier ants never fought with greater determination or with such a whole-souled devotion to the cause. Over and over they tumbled in the dust, clutching hair, hammering ribs, and grunting and grasping, blind, deaf, and callous as logs; and Joel Ham stood above them with the familiar cynical twist on his blotched visage, twisting his cane and making audible comments, but offering no further interference.

'After you, my boys—after you. There is no hurry, Haddon, I can wait as you are so busy. McKnight, your future is assured. The prize ring is your sphere: there wealth and glory await you. Peterson, you see here how degraded that boy becomes who forgets those higher principles which it is my earnest effort to instil into the hearts and minds of the boys of this depraved township. Cann, my boy, behold how brutalising is ungoverned instinct.'

But, wearying of the contest, the master made a sudden descent upon Jacker, and tore him from his enemy's grasp. The effort brought Dick to his feet, panting and still eager for the fray. He could not see an inch beyond his nose, and for a few moments moved about fiercely, feeling for his foe.

'D'you gimme best?' he spluttered. 'If you don't, come on—I ain't done up!' Then he flung the curtain of cobweb from his eyes, and the situation flashed upon him in all its grim significance. For a swift moment he thought of flight, but the master's grip was on his collar.

'Blowed if it ain't Jo,' he murmured in his consternation, and yielded meekly, like one for whom Fate had proved too strong.

The schoolmaster's white-lashed eyelids blinked rapidly for a second or so, and he screwed his face into a hard wrinkled grin of gratification.

'Yes, Ginger, my lad,' he said genially, 'Jo, at your service— very much at your service; and yours, McKnight. We will go inside now, boys. The sun is painfully hot, and you are fatigued.'

He marched his captives before him into the school room and ranged them against the wall, under the wide-open wondering eyes of the scholars, by whom even the most trifling incident of rebellion was always welcomed with glee as a break in the dull monotony of Joel Ham's peculiar system. But this was no trifling incident, it was a tremendous outrage and a delightful mystery; for the boys as they stood there presented to the amazed classes a strange and amazing spectacle, and were clothed in an original and, so far as the children were concerned, an inexplicable disguise. Fighting and tumbling about under the school house, Haddon and McKnight had gathered much mud, but more cobwebs. In fact, they had wiped up so many webs that they were covered from head to foot in the clammy dusty masses. Their hats were lost early in the encounter, and their hair was full of cobwebs; sticky curtains of cobweb hung about their faces, and swathed them from top to toe in what looked like a dirty grey fur. Each boy had cleared his eyes of the thick veil, but so inhuman and unheard of was their appearance that there was presently a suspicion amongst the scholars that the master had captured two previously unknown specimens of the animal kingdom, and consequently further astonishing developments might be looked for.

CHAPTER II.

Mr. HAM, with wise forethought, carefully locked the door and pocketed the key after disposing of the lads; and this was well, for Dick Haddon, fully appreciating the possibilities of the situation, was already plotting—plotting with every faculty of an active and inventive mind.

The master faced his prisoners, and stood musing over them like a pensive but kindly cormorant. Mr. Joel Ham, B.A., was a small thin man with a deceitful appearance of weakness. There was a peculiar indecision about all his joints that made the certainty of his spring and the vigour of his grip matters of wonder to all those new boys who ventured to presume upon his seeming infirmities. He had a scraggy red neck, a long beak-like nose, and queer slate-coloured eyes with pale lashes; his hair was thin and very fine in colour and texture, strangely like that of a yellow cat; and face, neck, and nose were mottled with patches of small purple veins. Today he was dressed in a long seedy black coat, a short seedy black vest, and a pair of now moleskins, glaringly white, and much too long and too large.

'Haddon,' said the master in a reflective tone, 'you are not looking as neat as usual. You need dusting. I will perform that kind office presently, and, believe me, I will do it well. Jacker, I intend to leave you standing here for a few moments to cool. You may have noticed, boys, that the youthful form when over-heated or possessed with unusual excitement has not that poignant susceptibility which might be thought necessary to the adequate appreciation of a judicious lambasting. Has that ever occurred to you, McKnight?'

Jacker shifted his feet uneasily, rolled his body, and, knowing that nothing could aggravate his offence, answered sullenly:

'Oh, dry up!'

Mr. Ham grinned at the boy in silence for a few moments, and then returned to his high stool and desk. Mr. Ham never made the slightest effort to maintain before his scholars that dignity which is supposed to be essential to the success of a pedagogue. In addressing the boys he used their correct names, or the nicknames liberally bestowed upon them by their mates, indiscriminately, and showed no resentment whatever when he heard himself alluded to as Jo, or Hamlet, or the Beetle, his most frequent appellations in the playground. He kept a black bottle in his desk, at the neck of which he habitually refreshed himself before the whole school; and he addressed the children with an elaborate and caustic levity in a thin shaky voice quite twenty years too old for him. His humour was thrown away upon the rising generation of Waddy, and might have been supposed to be the cat-like pawing of a vicious mind; but Joel Ham was not cruel, and although when occasion demanded he could use the cane with exceeding smartness, he frequently overlooked misdemeanours that might have justified an attack, and was never betrayed into administering unmerited cuts even when his black bottle was empty and his thirst most virulent.

In spite of his eccentricities and his weaknesses, and the fact that he was neither respected nor dreaded, Ham brought his scholars on remarkably well. There were three big classes in the room—first, third, and fifth—and a higher and lower branch of each; he managed all, with the assistance of occasional monitors selected from the best pupils. Good order prevailed in the school, for little that went on there escaped the master's alert eye. Even when he drowsed at his desk, as he sometimes did on warm afternoons, the work was not delayed, for he was known to have a trick of awakening with a jerk, and smartly nailing a culprit or a dawdler.

The school today was in a tense and excitable condition, now heightened to fever by the two cobwebbed mysteries standing against the wall, but the imperative rattle of Joel's cane on the desk quickly induced a specious show of industry.

'Gable!'

The individual addressed, a big scholar in the Lower Third, was so absorbed in the spectacle provided by Haddon and McKnight that he failed to hear the master's voice, and continued staring stupidly with all his eyes.

'Gable! This way, my dear child.'

Gable started guiltily, and then fell into confusion. He climbed awkwardly, out of his seat, and advanced hesitatingly with shuffling feet towards the master. It was now evident that Gable was not a large boy, but a little old man, slightly built, with a round ruddy clean-shaven face and thick white hair. But his manner was that of a boy of eight.

'Hold out, my young friend!' Joel commanded, with an expressive flourish of his cane.

Gable held out his hand; his toothless mouth formed itself into a dark oval, his eyes distended with painful expectancy, and he assumed the shrinking attitude of the very small boy who expects the fall of the cane. The situation was absurd, but no one smiled. Ham raised the extended hand a little with the end of the dreaded weapon.

'You are going the right way to come to a dishonoured old age, Gable,' he said, and the cane went up, but the cut was not delivered. 'There,' continued the master, 'I forgive you in consideration of your extreme youth. Go to your place, and try to set a better example to the older boys.'

The old man trotted back to his seat, grinning all over his face, and set to work at his book with an appearance of intense zeal; and Joel Ham turned his attention to the prime culprits. Having marched the youngsters from the front desk of the third class, he drew desk and form forward into the middle of the clear space, and then beckoned to McKnight.

'Jacker, my man,' he said cheerfully, 'bring your slate and sit here. I have a little job for you.'

Dick, standing alone, watched his mate seat himself at the desk, elated for a moment with the idea that perhaps Jo was not going to regard their offence as particularly heinous after all; but his better judgment scouted the idea, and he returned to his scrutiny of the wall. There was a weak spot near where Hector, Peterson's billy-goat, had butted his way through on a memorable occasion, and escape was still a comforting contingency.

The master approached McKnight with a pencil as if to set a lesson, but this was merely a ruse; Jacker was a hard-headed vicious youth whose favourite kick Ham wisely reckoned with on an occasion like this. To the boy's surprise and disgust he was presently seized by the neck and hauled forward on to the desk. His legs, being against the seat, which was attached to the desk, were quite useless for defence, so that he was a helpless victim under the chastening rod. It was a degrading attitude, and the presence of the girls made the punishment a disgrace to rankle and burn. Jacker, for pride and the credit of his boyhood made no sound under the first dozen cuts; but his younger brother Ted, from his place in the Lower Fifth, set up a lugubrious wail of sympathy almost immediately, and, as his feelings were more and more wrought upon by the painful sight, his wailing developed into shrill and tearful abuse of the master.

'You let him alone, see!' yelled Ted, when Jacker, unable longer to contain himself, uttered a dismal cry.

'Hit some one yer size—go on, hit some one yer size!' screamed Ted.

But Mr. Ham's whole attention was devoted to his task, and the younger McKnight's threats, commands, and warnings were entirely ignored, although the boy continued to utter them between his heart broken sobs.

'Mind who you're hittin'! You'll suffer for this, Hamlet, you'll see! We'll get some one what'll show you! Rocks for you nex' Saterdee!

Ted howled, Jacker howled, but the master caned on until he thought he had quite accomplished his duty in that particular; then he let the limp youth slide back into his seat.

Mr. Ham returned to his high stool to rest and recuperate. Thoughout the proceedings he had displayed no heat whatever, and when he addressed Jacker it was with his usual bland irony.

'You should thank me for my pains, my boy, but youth is proverbially ungrateful. You will think better of my efforts a few years hence; meanwhile I can afford to wait for the verdict of your riper judgment, Jacker—I can afford to wait, my boy.'

Jacker's only reply to this was a long wail expressive of a great disgust. That outburst was too much for the already over-wrought youngster in the Lower Fifth; starting up with a cry, Ted snatched one of the leaden ink-wells from its cell in the desk, and took aim at the master's head. The well struck the wall just above its mark, and scattered its contents in Joel Ham's pale hair, in his eyes, down his cheeks, and all over his white moles. Amazement—blind, round-eyed, dumb amazement—possessed the school, and for a few seconds a dead silence prevailed. The spell was broken by Dick Haddon, who discovered his opportunity, plunged like a diver at the weak spot in the wall, went clean through and disappeared from view. Ted McKnight, who had awakened to the enormity of his crime at the sight of the master knuckling the ink out of his eyes, and had gone grey to the lips in his trepidation, looking anxiously to the right and left for a refuge, saw Dickie's departure; jumping the desk in front he rushed at the aperture the latter had left in the wall, and was gone in the twinkling of an eye.

The master mopped the ink from his hair and his face with a sheet of blotting paper, and calling Belman, Cann, Peterson, Jinks, and Slogan, made for the door. Already Dick Haddon was halfway across the flat, scattering the browsing sheep to the right and left in his flight, and Ted was following at his best pace.

'After them!' cried the master. 'Two whole days' holiday for you if you run them down.'

The pursuit was taken up cheerfully enough, but it was quite hopeless. The breakaways were heading for the line of bush, and the sapling scrub along the creek was so thick that the boys would have been perfectly secure under its cover, even if the pursuers were not in hearty sympathy with the pursued, and the pursuit were not a miserable and perfidious pretence.

Mr. Ham, recognising after a few minutes how matters really stood, returned to the school. His approach had been signalled by a scout at one of the windows, and he found the classes all in order and suspiciously industrious, and Jacker McKnight still sitting with his head sunk upon his arms—a monument of sturdy resentment.

'My boys,' said the master, looking ludicrously piebald after his ink bath, 'before resuming duties I wish to draw your attention to the crass foolishness of which our young friends Haddon and McKnight are guilty. You perceive that their action is not diplomatic, eh?'

'Ye—yes, sir,' piped a dubious voice here and there.

'To be sure. Had they remained they would have been caned; as they have run away, they will receive a double dose and certain extra pains and penalties, and meanwhile they suffer the poignant pangs of anticipation. Anticipation, Jacker, my boy, the smart of future punishments, is the true hell-flame.'

Jacker replied with a grunt of derisive and implacable bitterness, but the schoolmaster seemed much comforted by his apophthegm, and stood for several minutes surveying the back of McKnight's head, and wearing a benignant and thoughtful smile.

CHAPTER III.

WADDY was soon possessed of the facts of the shameful acts of insubordination at the school and the escape of Dick Haddon and Ted McKnight, and nobody—according to everybody's wise assurances—was the least bit surprised. The fathers of the township (and the mothers, too) had long since given Dick up as an irresponsible and irreclaimable imp. One large section declared the boy to be 'a bit gone,' which was generally Waddy's simple and satisfactory method of accounting for any attribute of man, woman, or child not in conformity with the dull rule of conduct prevailing at Waddy. Another section persisted in its belief that 'the boy Haddon' was possessed with several peculiar devils of lawlessness and unrest, which could only be exorcised by means of daily 'hidings,' long abstinence from any diet more inflammatory than bread and water, and the continuous acquisition of great quantities of Scripture.

An extraordinary meeting of the School Committee was held at the Drovers' Arms that evening to confer with Joel Ham, B.A., and consider what was best to be done under the circumstances. The men of the township recognised that it was their bounden duty to support the master in an affair of this kind. When occasion arose they assisted in the capture of vagrant youths, and when Joel imagined a display of force advisable they attended at the punishment and rendered such assistance as was needful in the due enforcement of discipline. It was understood by all that the school would lose prestige and efficiency if Haddon and McKnight were not taken and at once subjected to the rules of the establishment and the rod of the master.

The meeting was quite informal. It was held in the bar, and the discussion of the vital matter in hand was concurrent with the absorption of McMahon's beer. Mr. Ham's best attention was given to the latter object.

'Bring the boys to me, gentlemen,' he said, 'and I will undertake to induce in them a wholesome contrition and a proper respect for letters—temporarily, at least.'

Neither of the lads had yet returned to his home; but the paternal McKnight promised, like a good citizen, that immediately his son was available he would be reduced to subjection with a length of belting, and then handed over to the will of the scholastic authority without any reservation. Mr. McKnight was commended for his public spirit; and it was then agreed that a member of the Committee should wait upon Widow Haddon to invite her co-operation, and point out the extent to which her son's mental and moral development would be retarded by a display of weakness on her part at a crisis of this kind?

Mr. Ephraim Shine volunteered for this duty. Ephraim was a tall gaunt man, with hollow cheeks, a leathery complexion, and large feet. He walked or sat with his eyes continually fixed upon these feet—reproachfully, it seemed—as if their disproportion were a source of perennial woe; he carried his arms looped behind him, and had acquired a peculiar stoop—to facilitate his vigilant guardianship of his feet, apparently. Mr. Shine, as superintendent of the Waddy Wesleyan Chapel, represented a party that had long since broken away from the School Committee, which was condemned in prayer as licentious and ungodly, and left to its wickedness when it exhibited a determination to stand by Joel Ham, a scoffer and a drinker of strong drinks, as against a respectable, if comparatively unlettered, nominee of the Chapel and the Band of Hope. His presence at the committee meeting tonight was noted with surprise, although it excited no remark; and his offer to interview the widow was accepted with gratitude as a patriotic proposal. There was only one dissentient—Rogers, a burly faceman from the Silver Stream.

'Don't send Shine to cant an' snuffle, an' preach the poor woman into a fit o' the miserables,' he said.

Ephraim lifted his patient eyes to Rogers's face for a moment with an expression of meek reproof, then let them slide back to his boots again, but answered nothing. The enmity of the two was well known in Waddy. Rogers was a worldly man who drank and swore, and who loved a fight as other men loved a good meal; and Shine, as the superintendent, must withhold his countenance from so grievous a sinner. Besides, there was a belief that at some time or another the faceman had thrashed Shine, who was searcher at the Stream in his week-day capacity, and for that reason was despised by the miners, and regarded as a creature apart. Ephraim, it was remarked, was always particularly careful in searching Rogers when he came off shift, in the hope, as the men believed, of one day finding a secreted nugget, and getting even with his enemy by gaoling him for a few years.

As Ephraim passed out from the bar he again allowed his eyes to roll up and meet those of his enemy from the dark shadow of his thick brows.

'Don't forget the little widow was sweet on Frank Hardy before you jugged him, Tinribs,' said the miner.

Tinribs was a name bestowed upon the superintendent by the youth of Waddy, and called after him by irreverent small boys from convenient cover or under the shelter of darkness. He found the Widow Haddon at home. She it was who answered his knock.

'I have come from the School Committee, ma'am,' he said, still intent upon his boots.

'About Dickie, is it? Come in.'

Mrs. Haddon was dressmaker-in-ordinary to the township, and her otherwise carefully tended kitchen was littered with clippings and bits of material. She resumed her task by the lamp a soon as the delegate of the School Committee was comfortably seated.

'Has Richard come home, ma'am?' Ephraim was an orator, and prided himself on his command of language.

The widow shook her head. 'No,' she said composedly. 'I don't think he will come home tonight.'

'We have had a committee meeting, missus,' said Ephraim, examining the toe of his left boot reproach fully, 'an' it's understood we've got to catch these boys.'

'What!' cried Mrs. Haddon, dropping her work into her lap. 'You silly men are going to make a hunt of it? Then, let me tell you, you will not get that boy of mine tomorrow, nor this week, nor next. Was ever such a pack of fools! Let Dickie think he is being hunted, and he'll be a bushranger, or a brigand chief, or a pirate, or something desperately wicked in that amazin' head of his, and you won't get a-nigh him for weeks, not a man Jack of you! Dear, dear, dear, you men—a set of interferin', mutton-headed creatures!'

'He's an unregenerate youth—that boy of yours, ma'am.'

'Is he, indeed?' Mrs. Haddon's handsome face flushed, and she squared her trim little figure. 'Was he that when he went down the broken winze to poor Ben Holden? Was he that when he brought little Kitty Green and her pony out of the burnin' scrub? Was he all a little villain when he found you trapped in the cleft of a log under the mount there, when the Stream men wouldn't stir a foot to seek you?'

During this outburst Shine had twisted his boots in all directions, and examined them minutely from every point of view.

'No, no, ma'am,' he said, 'not all bad, not at all; but—ah, the—ah, influence of a father is missing, Mrs. Haddon.'

'That's my boy's misfortune, Mr. Superintendent.'

'It—it might be removed.'

'Eh? What's that you say?'

The widow eyed her visitor sharply, but he was squirming over his unfortunate feet, and apparently suffering untold agonies on their account.

'The schoolmaster must be supported, missus,' he said hastily. 'Discipline, you know. Boys have to be mastered.'

'To be sure; but you men, you don't know how. My Dick is the best boy in the school, sometimes.'

'Sometimes, ma'am, yes.'

'Yes, sometimes, and would be always if you men had a pen'orth of ideas. Boys should be driven sometimes and sometimes coaxed.'

'And how'd you coax him what played wag under the very school, fought there, an' then broke out of the place like a burgerler?'

'I know, I know—_that's bad; but it's been a fearful tryin' day, an' allowances should be made.'

'Then, if he comes home you'll give him over to be—ah, dealt with?'

'Certainly, superintendent; I am not a fool, an' I want my boy taught. But don't you men go chasm' those lads; they'll just enjoy it, an' you'll do no good. You leave Dickie to me, an' I'll have him home here in two shakes. Dickie's a high-spirited boy, an' full o' the wild fancies of boys. He's done this sort o' thing before. Run away from home once to be a sailor, an' slep' for two nights in a windy old tree not a hundred yards from his own comfortable bed, imaginin' he was what he called on the foretop somethin'. But I know well enough how to work on his feelings.'

'A father, ma'am, would be the savin' o' that lad.'

Mrs. Haddon dropped her work again and her dark eyes snapped; but Ephraim Shine had lifted one boot on to his knee, and was examining a hole in the sole with bird-like curiosity.

'When I think my boy needs special savin' I'll send for you, Mr. Shine—

'It'd be a grave responsibility, a trial an' a constant triberlation, but I offer myself. I'll be a father to your boy, ma'am, barrin' objections.'

'An' what is meant by that, Mr. Shine?'

The widow, flushed of face, with her work thrust forward in her lap and a steely light in her fine eyes, regarded the searcher steadily.

'An offer of marriage to yourself is meant, Mrs. Haddon, ma'am.'

Shine's eyes came sliding up under his brows till they encountered those of Mrs. Haddon; then they fell again suddenly. The little widow tapped the table impressively with her thimbled finger, and her breast heaved.

'Do you remember Frank Hardy, Ephraim Shine?'

'To be certain I do.'

'Well, man, you may have heard what Frank Hardy was to me before he went to—to—'

'To gaol, Mrs. Haddon? Yes.'

'Listen to this, then. What Frank Hardy was to me before he is still, only more dear, an' I'd as lief everybody in Waddy knew it.'

'A gaol-bird an' a thief he is.'

'He is in gaol, an' that may make a gaol-bird of him, but he is no thief. 'Twas you got him into gaol, an' now you dare do this.'

Shine's slate-coloured eyes slid up and fell again.

''Twas done in the way o' duty. He don't deny I found the gold on him.'

'No, but he denies ever havin' seen it in his life before, an' I believe him.'

'An' about that cunnin' little trap in his boot-heel, ma'am?'

'It was what he said it was—the trick of some enemy.'

Mr. Shine lifted his right boot as if trying its weight, groaned and set it down again, tried the other, and said:

'An' who might the enemy ha' been, d'ye think?'

'I do not know, but—I am Frank Hardy's friend, and you may not abuse him in my house.'

'You have a chance o' a respectable man, missus.' Mrs. Haddon had risen from her seat and was standing over her visitor, a buxom black-gowned little fury.

'An' I tell him to go about his business, an' that's the way.' The gesture the widow threw at her humble kitchen door was magnificent. 'But stay,' she cried, although the imperturbable Shine had not shown the slightest intention of moving. 'You've heard I went with Frank's mother to visit him in the gaol there at the city; p'r'aps you're curious to know what I said. Well, I'll tell you, an' you can tell all Waddy from yon platform in the chapel nex' Sunday, if you like. 'Frank,' I said, 'you asked me to be your wife, an' I haven't answered. I do now. I'll meet you at the prison door when you come out, if you please, an' I'll marry you straight away.' Those were my very words, Mr. Superintendent, an' I mean to keep to them.'

Mrs. Haddon stood with flaming face and throbbing bosom, a tragedy queen in miniature, suffused with honest emotion. Ephraim sat apparently absorbed in his left boot, thrusting his finger into the hole in the sole, as if probing a wound.

'You wouldn't think, ma'am,' he said presently with the air of a martyr, 'that I gave fourteen-and six for them pair o' boots not nine weeks since.'

Mrs. Haddon turned away with an impatient gesture.

'If you've said all you have to say, you might let me get on with my work.'

'I think that's all, Mrs. Haddon.' The searcher arose, and stood for a moment turning up the toe of one boot and then the other; he seemed to be calculating his losses on the bargain. 'You hand over the boy Richard, I understand, ma'am?'

'I'll do what is right, Mr. Shine.'

'The Committee said as much. The Committee has great respect for you, Mrs. Haddon.'

Ephraim lifted his feet with an effort, and carried them slowly from the house, carefully and quietly closing the kitchen door after him. About half a minute later he opened the door again, just as carefully and as quietly, and said:

'Good night, ma'am, and God bless you.'

Then he went away, his hands bunched behind him, walking like a man carrying a heavy burden.

CHAPTER IV

DICK HADDON and Ted McKnight were still at large next morning, and nothing was heard of them till two o'clock in the afternoon, when Wilson's man, Jim Peetree, reported having discovered the boys swimming in the big quarry in the old Red Hand paddock. Jim, seeing a prospect of covering himself with glory, made a dash after the truants; but they snatched up their clothes and ran for the saplings up the creek, all naked as they were, and Jim was soon out of the hunt—though he captured Ted's shirt, and produced it as a guarantee of good faith.

That night three boys—three of the faithful—Jacker McKnight, Phil Doon, and Billy Peterson, stole through Wilson's paddock carrying mysterious bundles, and taking as many precautions to avoid observation and pursuit as if they were really, as they pretended to be with the fine imagination of early boyhood, desperate characters bent upon an undertaking of unparalleled lawlessness and great daring. They crossed the creek and crept along in the shadow of the hill, for the moon, although low down in the sky, was still bright and dangerous to hunted outlaws. Off to the left could be heard the long-drawn respirations of the engines at the Silver Stream, and the grind of her puddlers, the splashing of the slurry, and the occasional solemn, significant clang of a knocker. They passed the old Red Hand shaft, long since deserted and denuded of poppet legs and engine-houses, its comparatively ancient tips almost overgrown and characterless, with lusty young gums flourishing amongst its scattered boulders. Waddy venerated the old Red Hand as something so ancient that its history left openings for untrammelled conjecture, and the boys associated it with not a few of the mysteries of those grand far-off ages when dragons abducted beautiful maidens and giants were quite common outside circuses. The mouth of the shaft was covered with substantial timbers, save for a small iron-barred door securely padlocked. The pit now served a useful purpose as air-shaft for the Silver Stream, and the iron-runged ladders still ran down into its black depths.

The boys kept to the timber, and presently found themselves climbing down the rugged rocks where the hillside suddenly became an abrupt wall. From here had been blasted the thousands of tons of rock that went to the building of that grim prison in Yarraman, the town where Frank Hardy lay, a good half-day's tramp across the wide flat country faced by the township The quarry, too, was overgrown again; being almost inaccessible to Wilson's cattle its undergrowth was rank and high, and as it was sheltered from the sun's rays and watered in part by a tiny spring, it was often the one green oasis in a weary land of crackling yellow and drab.

After gaining the bottom of the quarry, Jacker led the way to the deepest end. Here the bottom, covered with scrub growth, sloped rather suddenly for a few feet up to the abrupt wall. Going on his hands and knees under the thick odorous peppermint saplings, Jacker ran his head into a niche in the rock amongst climbing sarsaparilla, and remained so, like some strange geological specimen half embedded in the rock. Within, where his head was hidden, the darkness was impenetrable. Jacker blew a strange note on a whistle manufactured from the nut of an apricot, and after a few moments a light appeared below him, a feeble flame, far down in the rock. This was waved twice and then withdrawn.

'Righto!' said Jacker in a hoarse piratical tone. 'Gimme the tucker, Black Douglas; I'll go down. You coves keep watch, an' no talkin', mind.'

Phil grumbled inarticulately, and Jacker's tone became hoarser and more piratical still.

'Who's commandin' here?' he growled. 'D'ye mean mutiny?

'Oh, shut up!' said Doon, bitterly. 'No one's goin' t' mutiny, but there ain't no fun campin' here.'

McKnight relented.

'All right,' he said, 'come down if you wanter. S'pose you'll on'y be makin' some kind of a row 'f I leave you.'

Jacker put the growth aside carefully, and going feet first gradually disappeared. Within there in the formless darkness he stood upon a ladder made of the long stem of a sapling to which cleats were nailed. The sapling was suspended in a black abyss. The boy, with his bundle hanging from his shoulder, started down fearlessly. Presently he came to where a second prop was fastened to the first with spikes and strong rope. Here he paused a moment, and called:

'Hello, be-e-low there!'

Jacker's character had undergone a rapid change; he was now quite an innocent and law-abiding person, a working shareholder in the Mount of Gold Quartz-mining Company.

'On top!' answered a cautious voice from the depths.

'Look up—man on!

And now, having observed the formalities, Jacker continued his descent, and in a few moments dropped from the primitive ladder and found a footing on a few planks thrown from one drive to another, across what was really an old shaft. At his back was a drive running into darkness; before him was a small irregular excavation lit with a single candle, and sitting in this, dressed, or, more correctly, undressed, like miners at their work, were Dick Haddon and Ted McKnight.

Jacker threw his bundle on the floor of the drive.

'Crib,' he said carelessly; and then, after examining the face of the excavation: 'S'pose we ain't likely to cut the lode this shift, Dick?

Dick shook his head thoughtfully.

'No,' he said. 'Allowin' for the underlay, we should strike her about fifteen feet in.'

The other boys had now joined their mates. Each on his way down had gravely followed the example of Jacker, who was supposed to be the boss of the incoming shift. As the fathers labour their sons play, and for months these boys had been digging in this old mine, off and on, with enthralling mystery. The excavation in which Dick and Ted were seated represented the joint labour of the members of the Mount of Gold Quartz-mining Company, though the very existence of the mine was unknown to a single soul outside the juvenile syndicate.

On the surface all signs of the shaft had long since been obliterated. The quarrymen blasting into the side of the hill years back had made a small opening into the disused pit at some distance from the top, and this opening was accidentally discovered by Dick and Jacker one day during a hunt for a wounded rabbit. Investigation proved the mine to be of no great depth, and, thanks to the pumps of the Silver Stream, as dry as a bone. A company of reliable small boys was formed with exceeding caution and a fine observance of rule and precedent; for Dick Haddon did nothing by halves, and forgot nothing that might give an air of reality to the creations of his exuberant fancy.

The original intention of the Mount of Gold Quartz-mining Company was to strike a reef five yards wide, composed entirely of gold, and to overwhelm its various parents with contrition on account of past lambastings by making them suddenly rich beyond the dreams of Oriental avarice. Time had served to dim the ardour of its hopes in this direction; but the mine was still an enticing enterprise when exciting novelties in the way of adventure were wanting, and would always be a hiding-place in which a youthful fugitive from injustice might defy all authority so long as the members of the Company remained true to their oath. Now that oath was quite the most solemn and impressive thing of the kind that Dick Haddon and Phil Doon had been able to discover after consulting the highest literary authorities.

The quarrel between Dick and Jacker McKnight that originated under the school was quite forgotten in the resulting excitement. It was a mere incident in any case, and would have made no material difference in their friendship. It had not kept Jacker from visiting the Mount of Gold on the same night with information and supplies, and now the boy was cheerfully unconscious of the black eye that still ornamented his broad visage. There were two well-worn shovels and a miner's pick in the drive. Jacker seized the pick.

'Might as well put in a bit of work,' he said.

'Hold hard,' replied Dick, 'Smoke-ho, old man. What's goin' on on top?'

'Whips! They had a meetin' about youse last night—Jo, an' Rogers, an' my dad, an' ole Tinribs, an' the rest. They're all after you. You're fairly in fer it.'

Dick's face became radiant with magnificent ideas.

'What! You don't mean they're goin' t' form a band t' capture us?'

'Well, they sorter agreed about somethin' like that.'

'My word, that's into our hands, ain't it? Lemme see, we must be a band of bushrangers what's robbed the gold escort an' the mounted p'lice're huntin' us in the ranges. I'll be—yes, I'll be Morgan. An' Ted—! What'll we make Ted? I know—I know. He'll be my faithful black boy, what'll rather die than leave me. You fellers bring a cork tomorrow, an' we'll pretty quick make a faithful black boy of Twitter.'

All eyes were turned upon Ted, who did not seem in the least impressed by the magnificent prospect. Indeed, the faithful native was palpably out of sorts; he took no part in the enthusiasm of his mates, his face was pale, and funk was legible in the diffident eye he turned upon the company. Dick noted this and put in an artful touch or two.

'Jacky-Jacky, the faithful black boy,' he said; 'brave as a lion, an' the best shot in the world—better'n me!

The ruse was not successful. Ted failed to respond.

'Twitter don't seem to want to be no black boy,' said Phil.

'I'll be Jacky-Jacky,' volunteered Peterson eagerly.

Peterson was a stolid youth with a face like a wooden doll; absolutely reliable since he was as stubborn under adult rule as a whole team of unbroken bullocks, and quite reckless of consequences for the reason that he never anticipated them. Peterson would have made a most successful Jacky-Jacky, but his suggestion was overlooked in the general concern inspired by Ted's conduct.

Feeling the eyes of the party upon him, Ted grew more uneasy, the corners of his mouth drew down, one finger went up slowly, and Twitter began to snivel.

'I—I—w—wa—want to go home,' he said.

The mates looked at each other in amazement. Ted was little, but his pluck had been tried on many occasions, and this was a great surprise.

'Well, he's on'y a kiddy,' said Phil pityingly, and with the superiority two years may confer.

Dick found the three were looking to him for an explanation.

'Ted's real scared,' he said. 'We made a discovery this afternoon—in there.'

'In the big drive?' asked Jacker. The others looked startled.

Dick nodded, and took up the candle. 'Come an' see,' he said.

Dick led the way along the opposite drive, and his mates followed, not too eagerly, Ted bringing up the rear. The drive was about eighty feet in extent. Having reached the end, Dick held the candle low, and made visible to his wondering mates a black cavity about eighteen inches in diameter in one corner near the floor.

'We were workin' in here a bit for a change this afternoon after Peetree hunted us, an' I broke through.'

'What's in there?' asked Jacker in an awed voice.

'Look,' said Dick.

Jacker backed away; the other three kept a respectful distance and stared silently.

'It's on'y another drive,' Dick explained. 'It must come from the Red Hand, I think.'

Dick was quite undisturbed, but the others were afraid, and even when they had returned to their own drive cast many doubting glances back into the darkness. In the mine as they had known it before everything was definite, and there was nothing of which a boy of spirit need be afraid. The shaft was choked with dirt a few feet below their landing-planks, and there was no spot in which a mystery might lurk; but it was very different now with that black hole leading Heaven knew into what awesome depths, harbouring goodness knew what horrors. Ted's defection had suddenly become the sentiment of the majority. At that moment Dick could have counted on Peterson alone had need arisen.

'We'll go down there an' explore them workin's,' said Dick, having lit a piece of dry root and composed himself for a smoke.

'In the daytime, Morgan,' said Jacker hastily and with diffidence.

'All right; but it don't make no difference down here, you know.'

Jacker thought it did, for although it was always night in the drives, the consciousness that the earth above was flooded with sunlight was a great heartener.

'Don't you think you'd best give this up for once—this bushranger game?' ventured Jacker.

'Why?' Dick's eyes were round with surprise.

'Oh, well, Twitter's jack of it, an' I don't think it's much fun.' Jacker had assumed a careless air. 'See here, Dick,' he continued smartly, 'the Cow Flat chaps made a raid last night, an' took Butts an' three others—mine among 'em.'

This was an important matter. Butts was Dick's big grey billygoat, the best goat in harness the boys had ever known or ever heard of; and the 'Cow Flat chaps' were the boys of a small centre about two miles and a half further down the creek, between whom and the boys of Waddy there existed an interminable feud that led them to fight on sight, and steal such of each other's possessions as could be easily and expeditiously removed. Dick's excitement soon evaporated; evidently root smoking was conducive to a philosophical frame of mind.

'We'll get them back all right—after,' he said.

'They'll work Butts to a shadder,' Jacker remarked insinuatingly.

'Then we'll go down some night, an' strip Amson's garden.' Amson was a prominent resident of Cow Flat, and had nothing whatever to do with the goat raid, but the boyish sense of justice does not stoop to find distinctions.

Jacker Mack had another string to his bow. 'They say Harry Hardy's comin' home this week,' he said.

'No!' cried Dick, much moved. 'Who says?'

'Gable says.'

'Pooh! Gable's a kid.'

'No matter, it's true. Mrs. Hardy had a letter, 'n Harry's coming down with cattle.'

'Gosh! he'll make it hot for Tinribs, I bet.'

Waddy had been waiting for Harry Hardy to come home, confident that he would do something of an exciting character to the disadvantage of those persons who had been instrumental in sending his brother Frank to gaol. Harry was much the younger of the two brothers; for some years he had been away droving, and the news of his brother's misfortune was bringing him home from a Queensland station. The township thought, too, there would be a score to wipe out on his mother's account, and the return was looked for as an important public event.

Dick pondered over the situation for a moment. It would never do to miss any entertainment that might result from Harry's return, and yet there was Joel Ham still to be reckoned with.

'I think we'd better wait,' he said. 'You fellows can let on as soon's he arrives.'

Ted's face fell again, and Jacker moved uneasily. He was anxious to be out of the mine and away from the uncanny possibilities of that dark chasm, and yet it was absolutely necessary that he should show no sign of funk, leave no opening for the tongue of derision. Some day, perhaps, when the full strength of the company was available and candles were numerous, he would follow Dick's lead in the work of exploration, but for the present his whole desire was to get to the surface. Now recollection came, and with it hope. Diving into his breast pocket, he drew and crumpled envelope, and handed it to Dick.

A letter,' he said, 'from your mother.'

Dick was surprised; as he took the note Jacker discovered an accusation in his eye.

'The oath don't say nothin' agin' letters,' said McKnight sullenly.

'No,' answered his mate, 'but really miners ain't supposed to have mothers runnin' after 'em, like if they were kids.'

'Well,' said the other, on the defensive, 'your mother comes to me at dinner time, an' she says: 'I s'pose 'taint likely you'll see my Dick, Jacker.' I said,' No, Missus Haddon, 'taint, s'elp me.' Then she says, 'Well, if he should come to see you, will you give him this?' So I took it, an' there you are.'

Dick read the letter slowly; it was a very artful letter, most pathetic, and sprinkled with drops which might have been tears. The writer spoke despondingly of her loneliness and her desolation, and the fears she endured when by herself in the house at night, knowing there was a camp of blacks in the corner paddock, and so many rough cattlemen about. She was entirely helpless since her only protector had deserted her, and she supposed that it only remained for her to be resigned to her fate. She signed her self, 'Your forsaken and sorrow-stricken mother.'

When Dick had finished reading he started to put on his clothes.

'What's up, Morgan?' asked Phil.

'Knock off!' was the brief reply.

'But what yer goin' to do?'

'I'm goin' home.'

'Home!' cried Peterson. 'Why?'

'Because!'

Dick had the instincts of a leader; he demanded reasons for everything, but gave none.

Before the lads parted that night young Haddon proffered Ted McKnight excellent advice.

'Your dad's night shift, ain't he?' he said. 'Well, don't you go in till near twelve. He'll be gone to work then, an' when he comes off in the mornin' he'll be too tired to lick you much.' This, from an orphan with practically no experience of paternal rule, argued a fine intuition.

CHAPTER V.

DICK HADDON did not enter his home immediately after parting with his mates. Mrs. Haddon's little cottage, four roomed, with a queer skillion front, was surrounded by a tumbled mass of tangled vegetation miscalled a garden, and Dick loitered in the shadow of the back fence to consider what manner of entrance would be most politic. He was shrewdly aware that his mother might be tempted to make an attack on the impulse of the moment, her most pathetic letter notwithstanding, and it was a point of honour with him to offer no resistance and make no evasion when Mrs. Haddon felt called upon to administer corporal punishment. To be sure the maternal beatings occasioned very little physical inconvenience; but they gave rise to much unpleasantness, and were to be avoided when possible.

As it happened, Dick was not put to the necessity of making a choice tonight. In the midst of his cogitations he felt himself seized from behind in a pair of long, strong arms. With the quick instinct of a wrongdoer he suspected evil, and kicked sharply back ward at the shins of the enemy.

'Le' go! You le' me go, see!' gasped the boy, struggling and fighting fiercely.

Resistance was quite useless. Dick was dragged through the gate, and up to the house. The door was opened, and he was bundled unceremoniously into the kitchen. Then Ephraim Shine—for it was the superintendent who had fallen upon Dick in the darkness—thrust his sparsely-whiskered, leathery face into the well-lighted room, and said shortly:

'Your boy, ma'am!'

Shine withdrew instantly, closing the door noiselessly after him, and left Dick flushed and furious.

'He didn't take me,' he cried. 'I was comin' home, an' he grabbed me just outside there—the beast!

Dick stopped short, suddenly conscious of the presence of visitors. Mrs. Hardy was sitting opposite his mother by the wide fireplace—the tall, white-haired gentlewoman in whose society he always felt himself transformed suddenly into a sort of saintly fellowship with the remarkably gentlemanly little boys whose acquaintance he made in the books provided by the chapel library. At the table sat Gable, the grey, chubby-faced third-class scholar whom Joel Ham had forgiven because of his extreme youth. The old man had a circular slab of bread and jam in his left hand, and was grinning fraternally at Dick. There was a third visitor, a stranger, a brown-haired, brown-skinned, bony young man, dressed after the manner of a drover. He had a small moustache, and a grave, taking face. He looked like a bushranger, Dick thought admiringly.

'This is Richard, Henry,' said Mrs. Hardy.

'You don't know me, eh, Coppertop?' said the young man, taking the boy's hand.

'Harry Hardy,' said Dick at random.

'Well, that's a good enough guess, young fellow

Dick fell back quietly. It was, he felt, a moment when an air of sadness and a retiring disposition would be likely to be most becoming in him—and most effective. He declined his mother's invitation to supper with such meekness that the little woman found it difficult to hide her concern. Could she have peeped into the drive of the Mount of Gold, where was scrap-food enough to victual a small regiment, not to mention pillage from Wilson's orchard, she might have been more at her ease—or have found fresh occasion for uneasiness. Dick had none of his mother's apple-like roundness—the widow, who was not yet thirty-five, always suggested apples and roses—he had inherited his father's flame-coloured hair, and a pale complexion that was very effective in turning away maternal wrath when allied with an appearance of pensive melancholy and a fictitious pain in the chest.

The conversation, which had been interrupted by Dick's entrance, was presently resumed. The women were recounting the story of Frank Hardy's arrest and trial for Harry's information. The subject was one of profound interest to Dick, and from his retreat at the far end of the table, where he sat disregarded, his crimes tacitly ignored for the time being, he listened eagerly. When Gable kicked him to attract his attention, and gleefully exhibited a handful of loaf sugar that he had slyly abstracted from the basin, the small boy frowned the old man down with a diabolical scowl.

Gable was Mrs. Hardy's brother, and although over sixty years of age, his mind had remained the mind of a child; mentally, he never grew beyond his eighth year. He was a child in all his ways and wishes, was happiest in the society of children, and was regarded by them, without question and without surprise, as one of themselves. He was sent to school because it pleased him to go, and it kept him out of mischief, and every day he learned over again the lessons he had learned the day before and forgotten within an hour. His admiration for Dick Haddon was profound, the respect and appreciation the boy of eight has for the big brother who is twelve and smokes.

Abashed by Dick's frown, the old man devoted himself humbly to his 'piece,' and the boy gave his whole attention to the conversation. He was eager to get an inkling of Harry's line of action. For his own part he had thought of a desperate band, with Harry at its head and himself in a conspicuous position, raiding the gaol at Yarraman under a hail of bullets, and bearing off the prisoner in triumph; but experience had taught him that the expedients of grown-up people were apt to be disgustingly common place and ludicrously ineffective.

'If he'd an enemy,' said Harry, 'there'd be something to go on. Was there nobody, no one at all, that he'd had any row with— nobody who hated him?'

Mrs. Haddon shook her head.

'Nobody,' she said. 'But he declared the real thieves had done it, either to shift suspicion or to be rid of him. He thought it a disgrace that all the men at the Stream should be marked as probable thieves because of one or two rogues; an' he was always eager to spot the real robbers. It was known gold-stealin' had been goin' on for some time. That's why they put on the searcher.'

'Shine. Mightn't he have had a finger in it?'

'No, no. It doesn't seem likely. Why should he?'

'I can't say. God knows! But there is somebody. If I only knew the man—if I only had him under my hand!

Harry's face became grey through the tan; he sat forward in his chair, with a sinewy arm thrust down between his knees, and his hand closed as if upon a throat. His mother touched his shoulder.

'Violence can only work mischief, my boy. Use what intelligence you have—only that can help. If we can save poor Frank and clear his name, we may leave vengeance to the law.'

'Yes, mother, you are right, but I am no saint. I hate my enemies, an' it is maddening not to know who you hate—who to hit at.'

'That may be so, Henry, but passion will only blind you. If you are not cool you will fail. Remember, the true culprits may be near you while you are seeking; do nothing to set them on their guard. You may learn much from the men. They are all Frank's friends, even those who believe him guilty.'

'Believe him guilty!

'O, my boy, my boy! You would want to fight them all. It is folly. The evidence did not leave room for a doubt as to his guilt, and these men have their own ideas as to the morality of such crimes. Many of them think none the worse of a man who helps himself to a nugget that he may find on his shovel.'

'An' you are the mother of a thief, I am a thief's brother; Frank is a convict, an' we must grin an' gammon we like it.'

'We must be discreet, we must be cunning, if we wish to prove we are no thieves and no kin to thieves.'

'Right you are, mother—always right.' The young man spread his rough, brown hand caressingly upon the small hand upon his knee. 'My fist always moves before my head, but I know your way is best, an' I don't mean to forget it.'

'Ephraim Shine seemed to be tryin' to do his best for Frank at the trial,' said Mrs. Haddon. 'I think he's a well-meanin' man, if he is a bit near an' peculiar in his ways. He always says it was his duty he did, an' that's true. We know Frank's not guilty, because—because we're fond of him'—here the little widow wiped her eyes, and her voice trembled—' an' know him better than others, but the case was black against him. Frank came straight up from below and into the searcher's shed, an' Shine found the gold in his crib bag, which was rolled up, an' forced under the handle of his billy.'

'Where it'd been for half the shift, the billy hanging in a dark drive where any man below might 'a 'got at it.'

'They found gold in a little box-place made in the heel of one of his workin' boots.'

'A boot that was always left in the boiler-house when he was off work.

'He had sold coarse water-worn gold to a Jew at Yarraman.'

'Yes, I know, I know. Got, he said, fossicking down the creek where nobody had ever won anything but fine gold before. Whoever put that gold in his crib bag an' faked his boot-heel salted Frank's puddling-tub. It was easy done. He on'y worked there now'n again when on night or afternoon shift, an' it was open to anyone. It was salted with Silver Stream gold by some double-damned cunning scoundrel.'

'We know it, Harry, and we have to prove it. To do that we must have all our wits about us.'

'Yes, mother, we must; but if that man ever is found I hope I may have the handling of him. Dick!' said the young man, turning suddenly.

Dick came forward somewhat diffidently, like a detected criminal.

'You know all about this business, eh?'

The boy nodded his head solemnly.

'Who do you think worked that dirty trick on my brother?' asked Harry gravely.

Dick had not thought of the matter in that light, but he answered, without hesitation:

'Ole Tinribs, I expect.'

'Dickie!' cried Mrs. Haddon, reprovingly.

'Why, why, Dick?' queried the young man.

Oh, I dunno; on'y he seems that sort, don't he?' Dick had been subjected to a grave indignity at the hands of the superintendent, and was not in a frame of mind to form a just estimate of the character of that good man. He spoke with the cheerful irresponsibility of youth.

'I'm afraid you won't be much good to us, Copper-top, old man, if you rush at conclusions in that desperate way,' said Harry.

Mrs. Hardy shook an impressive forefinger at the boy.

'You will say nothing to anybody of our intentions, Richard.'

'No,' said Dick simply; but that word given to Mrs. Hardy was a sacred oath, steel-bound and clamped.

CHAPTER VI.

THE school-ground next morning at nine o'clock showed little of its usual activity. Most of the boys were gathered near Sam Brierly's Gothic portico, now in unpicturesque ruins and hanging limply to the school front like an excrescence. Here Richard Haddon and Edward McKnight were standing in attitudes of extreme unconcern, heroes and objects of respectful admiration, but nevertheless inwardly ill at ease and possessed with sore misgivings. Some of their mates were offering sage advice on a matter that concerned them most nearly: how to take cuts from a cane so as to receive the least possible amount of hurt. Peterson was full of valuable information.

'See, you stan' so,' he said, giving rather a good imitation of an unhappy scholar in the act of receiving condign punishment, 'holdin' yer hand like this, you know, keepin' yer eye on Jo; an' jes' when his nibs comes down you shoves yer hand forwards, that sort, an' it don't hurt fer sour apples.'

'Don't cut no more'n nothin' at all,' added the boy 'who was called Moonlight, in cheerful corroboration.

Ted, who was very pale, and had a hunted look in his eyes, nodded his head hopefully, and rehearsed the act with pathetic gravity.

The little girls, who should have been at the other end of the ground, clustered at the corner and peeped round the portico, some giggling, others fully seized of the gravity of the situation. Dick in spite of his fine air of sang froid was well aware that there was one little girl there, a pretty little girl of about ten, with brown hair and dark serious eyes, who was suffering keenest apprehensions on his behalf, and who would weep with quite shameless abandonment when it came to his turn to endure the torments Mr. Joel Ham knew so well how to inflict. Dick was rather superior to little girls; his tender sentiment was usually lavished on ladies ten or twelve years his senior; but he could not hide from himself the fact that Kitty Grey's affection, however hopeless it might be, was at times most gratifying. Once he had resented its manifestations with bitterness, imagining that they were likely to bring him into contempt and undermine his authority; and when she interfered in his memorable fight with Bill Cole and fiercely attacked his opponent with a picket, cutting his head and incapacitating him for fighting for the rest of the day, he felt that he could never forgive her. She had violated the rule of battle and outraged the noble principle of fair play; and, worse and worse, had disgraced him in the eyes of the world by making him appear as a weakling seeking protection behind a despised petticoat. He reviled Kitty for that action in such overwhelming language that the poor girl fled in tears, and next day it was only with the greatest difficulty that she persuaded him to accept two pears and a blood-alley as a peace offering.

Dolf Belman came later with a little comfort.

'Gotter junk o' rosum,' he said, fumbling in his school-bag.

'Hoo! have you though?' said Parrot Cann. 'Rosum's great. Put some on my hand oust when I went to ole Pepper's school at Yarraman, an' near died laughin' when he gave me twenty cuts fer copy-in' me sums.'

The boys clustered about Dolf, who produced a piece of resin about the size of a hen's egg, and waved it triumphantly.

'You pound it up wif a rock,' said he confidently, 'an' rub it on yer hands.'

The pounding process was begun at once, amidst a babel of opinions. It was a fond illusion amongst the boys that resin so applied deadened the effects of the cane. It had been tried scores of times without in the least mitigating the agony of Ham's cuts, but the faith of youth is not easily shaken; so Ted's spirits revived wonderfully, and Dick developed a keen interest in the pounding. Dolf pulverised the 'rosum,' declaring that it should be powdered in one particular way which was a great secret known only to a happy few. If it were powdered in any other way, the resin lost its efficacy as a protection, and might even aggravate the pain. Several boys volunteered testimony in support of Dolf's claim, telling of the strange immunity they had enjoyed on various occasions after applying the resin, and Peter Queen distinctly remembered 'a feller up to Clunes' who, by a judicious use of the powder, was enabled to defy all authority and preserve an attitude of hilarious derision under the most awful tortures.

'This here cove he useter have hisself rubbed all over wif rosum every mornin', then he'd go to school an' kick up ole boots. What'd he care? My word, he was a terror!'

Dolf took up the theme, and enlarged upon the virtues of resin, particularly that resin of his, which was the very best kind of resin for the purpose and had been specially commended by an old swaggie with one eye, who gave it to him for a four-bladed knife and a clay pipe. So great was the effect of these representations that before Dick and Ted had transferred the powder to their pockets they had become objects of envy rather than commiseration, and one or two of their mates would gladly have changed places with them on the spot.

'Wouldn't care if I was in fer it, 'stead o' you, Dick,' said Peterson. 'Mus' be an awful lark to have Hamlet layin' it on, an' you not feelin' it all the time.'

'My oath I' said Jacker Mack feelingly.

'Good morning, boys.'

Joel Ham, B.A., had stolen in amongst them, and stood there in an odd crow-like attitude, his mottled face screwed into an expression of quizzical amiability, and his daily bottle sticking obtrusively from the inside lining of his old coat. The lads scattered sheepishly.

'Peterson,' he said, blinking his pale lashes a dozen times in rapid succession, 'the boy who thinks he can outwit his dear master is an egotist, and egotism, Peterson, is the thing which keeps us from profiting by the experiences of other fools.'

'I dunno what yer talkin' about,' answered Peterson, with heavy resentment.

Mr. Ham blinked again for nearly half a minute.

'Of course not,' he said, 'of course not, my boy.' Then he turned to Dick and Ted with quiet courtesy. 'Good morning, Richard. Good morning, Edward.'

Ted, who was painfully conscious of the large ink-splashes on the master's white trousers, kicked awkwardly at a buried stone, but Dick replied cheerily enough.

The attitude of the master throughout that morning was quite inexplicable to the scholars; he made no allusion whatever to the crimes of which Dick and Ted had been guilty, and gave no hint that he harboured any intentions that were not entirely generous and friendly. The two culprits, working with quite astounding assiduity, were beset with conflicting emotions. Dick, who had a vague sort of insight into the master's character, was prepared for the worst, and yet not blind to the possibility of a free pardon. Ted, after the first hour, was joyous and over-confident.

Mr. Peterson called during the morning and conferred with Joel for a few minutes. The gaping school knew what that meant, and awaited the out come with the most anxious interest. Mr. Peterson, a six-foot Dane, an engine-driver at the Stream, and Billy's father, was volunteering for service in case Mr. Ham should need assistance in dealing with the two culprits; but Joel sent him away, and the boys breathed freely again. Their confidence in Dolf's 'rosum' did not leave them quite blind to the advantages of an amicable settlement of their little difference with Mr. Ham.

It was not until the boys were marching out for the dinner hour, satisfied at last all was well, that Joel seemed suddenly to recollect, and he called after Ted, blighting the poor youth's new-born happiness and filling his small soul with a great apprehension.

'Teddy,' he called, 'you will remain, my boy. I have private business with you—private and confidential, Teddy.'

So Ted fell out and stood by the wall, a very monument of dejection.

When school met again the scholars noted that the ink-stains had been carefully washed and scraped from the wall and the floor, and they found Ted McKnight sprawling in his place, his head buried in his arms, dumb and unapproachable. If a mate came too close, moved by curiosity or a desire to offer sympathy, Ted lashed out at him with his heels. For the time being he was a small but cankered misanthrope full of vengeful schemes, and only one person in the whole school envied him. That person was Richard Haddon, whose turn was yet to come.

An hour passed and Dick had received no hint of the trouble in store. Then Joel Ham, prowling along the desks, inspecting a task, stopped before the boy and stood eyeing him with the curiosity with which an entomologist might regard a rare grub, clawing his thin whiskers the while. The interest he felt was apparently of the most friendly description.

'Ah, Ginger,' he said, 'I had almost forgotten that I am still your debtor. This way, Ginger, please.'

He stood Dick on his high stool, carefully tied the boy's ankles with a strap, and gave him a large slate, on which his faults were emblazoned in chalk, to hold up for the inspection of the classes; and so he left him for the remainder of the afternoon, every now and again pausing in his vicinity to deliver some incomprehensible sentiment or a sarcastic homily. This performance affected all the scholars, but it excited Gable so much that the little old man could do nothing but sit and stare at Dick with round eyes and open mouth, and mutter 'Oh, crickie!' in a frightened way. The little dark-eyed girl in the Third Class bore the ordeal badly, too, and every speech of the master's started a large tear rolling down her dimpled brown cheek.

When the rest of the youngsters marched out, Dick Haddon remained on his high perch. Kitty Grey, who brought up the tail of the procession, turned at the door and walked back to the master timorously and with downcast eyes; and Dick felt that a plea was to be made on his behalf, but could not hear what followed.

'Please, sir, if you won't cane him very much I'll give you this,' said Kitty.

The bribe was a small brooch that had originally contained the letters of the little girl's first name. It was a very cheap brooch when new, and now some of the letters were gone and the gilt was worn off, but it was still a priceless treasure in Kitty's eyes. Joel Ham examined the gift, and then looked down upon the petitioner, his face pulled sideways into its familiar withered grin.

Do you know this is bribery, little Miss Grey,' he said, 'bribery and corruption?'

Ye-es, please, sir,' said Kitty.

'And do you know that that fellow up there is a monster of infamy, a rebel and a riotous blackguard, who must be repressed in the interests of peace and good government?'

'Yes, please, sir; but—but he's only a little fellow.' The master's tremendous words seemed to call for this reminder.

Joel screwed his grin down another wrinkle or two.

'Yet you intercede for the ruffian try to buy him off, and at a valuation, too, that proves you to be deaf to the voice of reason and utterly improvident.'

'Oh, Mr. Ham, he didn't mean it—really, he didn't mean it!

Joel screwed out another wrinkle. His mirth always increased wrinkle by wrinkle, until at times it appeared as if he were actually going to screw his own neck by sheer force of repressed hilarity.

'I am incorruptible, Miss Grey,' he said. 'Take back your precious jewel; but I promise you this, my dear, our friend Dick shall not get as much as he deserves. Boys are like some metals, Miss Kitty, their temper is improved by hammering.'

Kitty left the master, entirely in the dark as to the effect of her intercession; but evidently it was not of much advantage to Dick. When the boy came from the school about half an hour later, he carried his chin high, his lips were compressed tightly, and he stared straight ahead. Three faithful friends who had waited to know the worst joined him, but no words were spoken. They followed at his heels, showing by their silence due respect for a profound emotion. Dick did not make for home; he turned off to the right and led the way down into one of the large quarries on the flat, and there turned a flushed face and a pair of flashing eyes upon his mates.

'I'm going to have it out of Ham,' he said. 'I don't care! He's a dog, and he ain't goin' to do as he likes with me.'

'How many, Dick?' asked Ted eagerly.

'Dunno,' said Dick, exposing his hands; 'he jus' cut away till he was tired, chi-ikin' me all the time. But I'll get even, you see!'

Dick's palms were very puffy; there were a couple of blue blisters on his fingers, and across each wrist an angry-looking white wheal. The boys were sufficiently impressed, and, in spite of his wrath against Joel Ham, Dicky could not resist a certain gratification on that account. Boys take much pride in the sufferings they have borne, and their scars are always exhibited with a grave conceit. Ted displayed his hands, still betraying evidence of the morning's caning, and Jacker Mack spoke feelingly of stripes and bruises remaining since Tuesday. Peterson was the only one quite free from mark or brand of the master's, and he recollected many thrashings with extreme bitterness, and was quite in sympathy with the party.

'What say if we give him a scare?' said Dick. 'Are you on?'

Jacker and Ted were dubious. It was too sudden; their recent experiences had made them unusually respectful of the master. Dick marked the hesitation, and said scornfully:

'Oh, you fellows needn't be afraid. You won't be let in for it. I know a trick that's quite safe—bin thinkin' about it all the afternoon.'

If Dick were quite sure it was safe, and if there were not the smallest possible chance of their complicity being disclosed, Jacker and Ted were quite agreeable. Peterson was always agreeable for adventure, however absurd. Dick explained:

'Hamlet's gone down to the pub. He's sure to get screwed tonight. There's a fool feller there from McInnes, knockin' down a cheque an' shoutin' mad. Hamlet'll get his share in spite of all, an' he'll be as tight as a brick by ten o'clock. You know my joey 'possum? Well, I'll fix him up into the awfullest kind of a blue devil, with feathers an' things. We'll push him into Jo's room, and when Jo comes home an' strikes a light he'll spot him, an' think he's got delirious trimmens again. That'll give him a shakin'.'

'My oath, won't it!' ejaculated Peterson.

Jacker was elated, and grinned far and wide.

'P'raps he'll go nippin' round, thinkin' he's chased by 'em like he did las' Christmas holidays,' suggested the elder McKnight gleefully.

This villainous scheme was the result of the boys' extraordinary familiarity with many phases of drunkenness. Waddy was a pastoral as well as a mining centre, and strange ribald men came out of the bush at intervals to 'melt' their savings at the Drovers' Arms. The Yarraman sale-yards for cattle and sheep were near Waddy too, and brought dusty drovers and droughty stockmen in crowds to the town ship every Tuesday. These men were indiscreet and indiscriminate drinkers, and often a vagrant was left behind to finish a spree that surrounded him with unheard-of reptiles and strange kaleidoscopic animals unknown to the zoologist. It must be admitted, too, that Joel Ham, B.A., was in a measure responsible for the boys' unlawful knowledge. Twice at holiday times, when he was not restricted at the Drovers' Arms, he had continued his libations until it was necessary for his own good and the peace of the place to tie him down in his bunk and set a guard over him; and on one of these occasions he had created much excitement by rushing through the township at midnight, scantily clad, under the impression that he was being pursued by a tall dark gentleman in a red cloak and possessed of both horns and hoofs.

It was nearly nine o'clock that night when the four conspirators met to carry out their nefarious project. Dick was carrying a bag—in which was the joey—a bull's-eye lantern, various coloured feathers, and other small necessaries, and the party hastened in the direction of Mr. Ham's humble residence. Ham was 'a hatter'—he lived alone in a secluded place on the other side of the quarries. The house was large for Waddy, and had once been a boarding-house, but was now little better than a ruin. The schoolmaster had reclaimed one room, furnished it much like a miner's but, with the addition of a long shelf of tattered books, and here he 'batched,' perfectly contented with his lot for all that Waddy could ever discover to the contrary. There was no other house within a quarter of a mile of the ruin, which was hemmed in with four rows of wattles, and surrounded by a wilderness of dead fruit-trees—victims to the ravages of the goats of the township—and a tangled scrub of Cape broom. The boys approached the house with quite unnecessary caution, keeping along the string of dry quarry-holes, and creeping towards the back door through the thick growth as warily as so many Indians on the trail. Dick Haddon cared nothing for an enterprise that had no flavour of mystery, and was wont to invest his most commonplace undertakings with a romantic significance. For the time being he was a wronged aboriginal king, leading the remnants of his tribe to wreak a deadly vengeance on the white usurper. A short conference was held in the garden.

'We'll go into one o' the old rooms, an' fix the joey up there. Then we can wait till Hamlet comes, if yonse fellows 're game,' said Dick softly.

'I'm on,' whispered Peterson.

'He won't be long, I bet. McKnight, 'r Belman, 'r some o' the others is sure to roust him out when he's properly tight. Foller me.'

Dick led the way up to the door, pushed it open, and entered. The others were about to follow, but to their horror they saw a large figure start forward from the pitch darkness beyond, heard an oath and the sound of a blow, and saw Dick fall face downwards upon the floor. Then the door was slammed from within, and the three terrorstricken boys turned and fled as fast as their legs would carry them.

Dick lay upon the floor with outthrown arms, and the figure stood over him in a listening attitude.

'Good God! 'ye you killed him?' cried someone in the far corner of the room.

'Sh-h, you cursed fool!' hissed the big man.

'Who is it?' asked the other tremulously.

The big man seized Dick, and dragged him to where the grey moonlight shone through a shattered window.

'Young Haddon,' he said. 'Blast the boy! a man never knows where he will poke his nose next.'

'The others 'ye gone?'

'Yes. They were on'y boys.'

'Didn't I tell you it wouldn't do to be meetin' in places like this? No more of it for me. They've been listenin', an' we're done men. We'll be nabbed!'

'Shut up your infernal cackle! The boys hadn't any notion we was here. They had some lark on. They couldn't have seen us— we're all right.'

'If they saw us together it'd be enough.'

'But they couldn't, I tell you. Here, clear out, the boy's comin' round. Go the front way, an' make for the paddocks. I'll go up the gully. Look slippy!'

A few seconds after the men had left the house Dick scrambled to his feet, and stood for a moment in a confused condition of mind, rubbing his injured head. Then he took up his hat and lantern, and stumbled from the room. As yet he had only a vague idea of what had happened, and his head felt very large and full of fly-wheels, as he expressed it later; but a few moments in the open air served to revive him. Along by the big quarry he met his mates returning. After talking the matter over they had come to the conclusion that the schoolmaster had got a hint of their intention, and had lain in wait. They gathered about Dick, whose forehead was most picturesquely bedabbled with blood.

'Crikey! Dick,' cried the wondering Jacker, 'did he hammer you much?'

'Feel,' said Dick, guiding one hand after another to a lump on his head that increased his height by quite an inch.

'Great Gosh!' murmured Peterson; ''ain't he a one-er? The beggar must 'a' tried to murder you.'

Dick nodded.

'Yes,' he said; 'but 'twasn't Hamlet.'

'Go on!' The boys looked back apprehensively.

'No, 'twasn't. 'Twas a big feller. I dunno who; but he must 'a' bin a bushranger, 'r a feller what's escaped from gaol, 'r someone. Did you coves see which way he went?'

'No,' said Ted fearfully; and a simultaneous move was made towards the township. The boys were not cowards, but they had plenty of discretion.

'Look here,' Dick continued impressively; 'no matter who 'twas, we've gotter keep dark, see. If we don't it'll be found out what we was all up to, an' we'll get more whack-o.'

The party was unanimous on this point; and when Dick returned home he shocked his mother with a lively account of how he slipped in the quarry and fell a great depth, striking his head on a rock, and being saved from death only by the merest chance imaginable.

CHAPTER VII.

The small, wooden Wesleyan chapel at Waddy was perched on an eminence at the end of the township furthest from the Drovers' Arms. The chapel, according to the view of the zealous brethren who conducted it, represented all that counted for righteousness in the township, and the Drovers' Arms the head centre of the powers of evil. For verbal convenience in prayer and praise the hotel was known as 'The Sink of Iniquity,' and the chapel as 'This Little Corner of the Vineyard,' and through the front windows of the latter, one sabbath morn after another for many years, lusty Cornishmen, moved by the spirit, had hurled down upon McMahon and his house strident and terrible denunciations.

Materially the chapel had nothing in common with a vineyard; it was built upon arid land as bare and barren as a rock; not even a blade of grass grew within a hundred yards of its doors. The grim plainness of the old drab building was relieved only by a rickety bell-tower so stuffed with sparrows' nests that the bell within gave forth only a dull and muffled note. The chapel was surrounded with the framework of a fence only, so the chapel ground was the chief rendezvous of all the goats of Waddy—and they were many and various. They gathered in its shade in the summer and sought its shelter from the biting blast in winter, not always content with an outside stand; for the goats of Waddy were conscious of their importance, and of a familiar and impudent breed. Sometimes a matronly nanny would climb the steps, and march soberly up the aisle in the midst of one of Brother Tregaskis's lengthy prayers; or a haughty billy, imposing as the he-goat of the Scriptures, would take his stand within the door and bay a deep, guttural response to Brother Spence; or two or three kids would come tumbling over the forms and jumping and bucking in the open space by the wheezy and venerable organ, spirits of thoughtless frivolity in the sacred place.

It was Sunday morning and the school was in. The classes were arranged in their accustomed order, the girls on the right, the boys on the left, against the walls; down the middle of the chapel the forms were empty; nearest to the platform on either hand of Brother Ephraim Shine, the superintendent, were the Sixth Class little boys and girls, the latter painfully starched and still, with hair tortured by many devices into damp links or wispy spirals that passed by courtesy for curls. Very silent and submissive were little girls of Class VI., impressed by the long, lank superintendent in his Sunday black, and believing in many wonders secreted above the dusty rafters or in the wide yellow cupboards. The first classes were nearest the door. The young ladies, if we make reasonable allowance for an occasional natural preoccupation induced by their consciousness of the proximity of the young men, were devoted students of the gospel a interpreted by Brother Tresize, and sufficiently saintly always, presuming that no disturbing element such as a new hat or an unfamiliar dress was introduced to awaken the critical spirit. The young men, looking in their Sunday clothes like awkward and tawdry imitations of their workaday selves, were instructed by Brother Spence; and Brother Bowden, being the kindliest, gentlest, most incapable man of the band of brothers, was given the charge of the boys' Second Class, a class of youthful heathen, rampageous, fightable, and flippant, who made the good man's life a misery to him, and were at war with all authority. Peterson, Jacker Mack, Dolf Belman, Fred Cann, Phil Doon, and Dick Haddon, and a few kindred spirits composed this class; and it was sheer lust of life, the wildness of bush-bred boys, that inspired them with their irreverent impishness, although the brethren professed to discover evidence of the direct influence of a personal devil.

The superintendent arose from his stool of office and shuffled to the edge of the small platform, rattling his hymn-book for order. Ephraim never raised his head even in chapel, but his cold, dull eyes, under their scrub of overhanging brow, missed nothing that was going on, as the younger boys often discovered to their cost.

'Dearly beloved brethren, we will open this morn-in's service with that beautiful hymn—'

Brother Shine stopped short. A powerful diversion had been created by the entrance of a young man. The new-corner was dressed like a drover, wearing a black coat over his loose blue shirt, and he carried in his right hand a coiled stockwhip. His face had the grey tinge of wrath, and his lips were set firm on a grim determination. He walked to a form well up in front, and seated himself, placing his big felt hat on the floor, but retaining his grip on the whip hanging between his knees.

Jacker Mack kicked Dick excitedly. 'Harry Hardy!' he said.

Dick nodded but did not speak; he was staring with all his eyes, as was every man, woman, and child in the congregation. Harry Hardy had not fulfilled expectations; he had been home five days, and had done nothing to avenge his brother. He moved about amongst the men, but was reserved and grew every day more sullen. He had heard much and had answered nothing; and now here he was at chapel and evidently bent on mischief, for the stockwhip was ominous. Ephraim Shine had noticed it and retreated a step or two, and stood for quite a minute, turning his boot this way and that, but with his eyes on Harry all the time. Now he cleared his throat, and called the number of the hymn. He read the first verse and the chorus with his customary unction, and, all having risen, started the singing in a raspy, high-pitched voice.

Harry Hardy stood with the rest, a solitary figure in the centre of the chapel, still holding the long whip firmly grasped in his right hand. Attention was riveted on him, and the singing of the hymn was a dismal failure. The young man stared straight before him, seeing only one figure, that of Ephraim Shine, until he felt a light touch on his arm. Someone was standing at his side, offering him the half of her hymn-book. Harry raised his hand to the leaves mechanically, and noticed that the hand on the other side was white and shapely, the wrist softly rounded and blue-veined. The voice that sounded by his side was low and musical.

'Oh! Harry, what are you going to do?' His neighbour had ceased singing, and was whispering tremulously under cover of the voices of the congregation.

Harry's face hardened, and he set it resolutely towards the platform.

'Don't you know me, Harry? I am Christina Shine. You remember Chris? We were school mates.'

His daughter! The young man let his left hand fall to his side.

'Please don't. You have come to quarrel with father, but you won't do it, Harry? You saved my life once, when we were boy and girl. You will promise me this?'

Harry Hardy answered nothing, and the pleading voice continued:

'For the sake of the days when we were friends, Harry, say you won't do it—you won't do it here, in—in God's house.'

'It was here, in God's house, he slandered my mother.' The man's voice sounded relentless.

'No, no, not that! He prayed for her. He did not mean it ill.'

'I have heard of his praying—how under the cover of his cant about saving souls he scatters his old-womanish scandals an' abuses his betters.'

'He means well. Indeed, indeed, he means well.'

'An' he prays for my mother—him! Says she's bred up thieves because she did not come here to learn better. Says she's an atheist because she does not believe in Ephraim Shine. He's said that, an' I'm here to make him eat his words.'

Harry's whispering was almost shrill in the heat of his passion, and the singing of the hymn became faint and thin, so eager were the singers to catch a word of that most significant conversation. Dick had not taken his eyes off the pair, and already had woven a very pretty romance about Chris and the young man. Christina Shine had only recently been raised to the pedestal in his fond heart formerly occupied by an idol who had betrayed his youthful affections, disappointed his hopes, and outraged his sense of poetical fitness. He espoused her cause with his whole soul, whatever it might be.

The young woman in the stress of her fears had clasped Harry's arm, as if to restrain him, and he felt the soft agitation of her gentle bosom with a new emotion that weakened his tense thews, and stirred the first doubt; but he fought it down. His revenge had become almost a necessity within the last three days. Nothing he had heard offered the faintest hope for his brother's cause; he was baffled and infuriated by the general unquestioning belief in Frank's guilt, and a dozen times had been compelled to sit biting on his bitterness, when every instinct impelled him to square up and teach the fools better with all the force of his pugilistic knowledge.

Of late years he had been schooled in a class that accepted 'a ready left' as the most convincing argument, and, being beyond the immediate province of law and order, repaired immediately with all its grievances to a twenty-four-foot 'ring' and an experienced referee. But whilst there was a little diffidence amongst the men in expressing their opinions about Frank, there was no reserve when they came to tell of Ephraim Shine's method of improving the occasion with prayer and preachment; and for a considerable time Harry had collected bitterness till it threatened to choke him and bade him defy all his mother's cautious principles.

Ephraim had given out the third verse, and the singing went on.

'Are you thinking?' whispered the girl. 'Do, do think! Think of the disgrace of it.'

'Disgrace! There's the disgrace whining on the platform, the brute that insults a woman in her sorrow, thinking there's no one handy to take it out of the coward hide of him!'

'It was wrong, Harry. I know it was wrong and cruel. I told him that, and he has promised me never to do it again. He has promised me that, really, truly.'

The word that slid through Harry's teeth was ferocious but inaudible.

'Say you won't do it!

The singing ceased suddenly, and the superintendent, who all the time had kept a lowering and anxious eye on the young couple, gave out the third verse again.

'Harry, you will not. Please say it!

The hand holding the stockwhip stirred threateningly, and the hymn was almost lost in the agitation of the worshippers. Chris remained silent, and Harry, who had taken the book again, had shifted his stern eyes to the slim white thumb beside his broad brown one. A stifled sob at his side startled him, and he turned a swift glance upon the face of his companion. That one glance, the first, left his brave resolution shaken and his spirit awed.

Harry remembered Chris as a schoolgirl, tall and stag-like, always running, her rebellious knees tossing up scant petticoats, her long hair rarely leaving more than one eye visible through its smother of tangled silk. She was very brown then and very bony, and so ridiculously soft of heart that her tenderness was regarded by her schoolmates as an unfortunate infirmity. She was tall still, taller than himself, with large limbs and a sort of manly squareness of the shoulders and erectness of the figure, but neatly gowned, with little feminine touches of flower and ribbon that belied the savour of unwomanliness in her size and her bearing. Her complexion was clear and fair, her abundant hair the colour of new wheat, her features were large, the nose a trifle aquiline, the chin square and, finely chiselled; the feminine grace was due to her eyes, large, grey, and almost infantile in expression. The people of Waddy called her handsome, and no more tender term would suit; but they knew that this fair girl-woman, who seemed created to dominate and might have been expected to carry things with a high hand everywhere, was in reality the simplest, gentlest, and most emotional of her sex. She looked strong and was strong; her only weakness was of the heart, and that was a prey to the sorrows of every human being within whose influence she came in the rounds of her daily life.

Hardy was amazed; almost unconsciously he had pictured the grown-up Chris an angular creature, lean, like her father, and resembling him greatly; and to find this tall girl, with the face and figure of a battle queen, tearfully beseeching where in the natural course of events she should have been commanding haughtily and receiving humble obedience, filled him with a nervousness he had never known before. Only pride kept him now.

'Say you will go! Say it!'

Harry lowered his head, and remained silent.

'Go now. Your action would pain your mother more than my father's words have done—I am sure of that.'

The hymn was finished, but Shine read out the last verse once more. His concern was now obvious, and the congregation was wrought to an unprecedented pitch. Never had a hymn been so badly sung in that chapel. It was taken up again without spirit, a few quavering voices carrying it on regardless of time and tune. Chris had noted Harry's indecision.

'Do not stay and shame yourself. Go, and you will be glad you did not do this wicked thing. You are going. You will! You will!'

He had stooped and seized his hat. He turned without a word or a glance, and strode from the chapel. The congregation breathed a great sigh, and as he passed out the chorus swelled into an imposing burst of song—a paean of triumph, Harry thought.

Through the chapel windows the congregation could see Harry Hardy striding away in the direction of the line of bush.

Christina, from her place amongst her girls, watched him till he disappeared in the quarries; and so did Ephraim Shine, but with very different feelings. Many of the congregation were disappointed. They had expected a sensational climax. Class II was inconsolable, and made not the slightest effort to conceal its disgust, which lasted throughout the remainder of the morning and was a source of great tribulation to poor Brother Bowden.

CHAPTER VIII.

HARRY HARDY sought the seclusion of the bush, and there spent a very miserable morning. He was forced to the conclusion that he had made a fool of himself, and the thought that possibly that girl of Shine's was now laughing with the rest rankled like a burn and impelled many of the strange oaths that slipped between his clenched teeth. The more he thought of his escapade the more ridiculous and theatrical it seemed. It was born of an impulse, and would have been well enough had he carried out his intention; but, oh the ignominy of that retreat from the side of the grey-eyed, low-voiced girl under the gaze of the whole congregation! It would not bear thinking of, so he thought of it for hours, and swung his whip-lash against the log on which he sat, and quite convinced himself that he was hating Shine's handsome daughter with all the vehemence the occasion demanded.

In many respects Harry was a very ordinary young man; bush life is a wonderful leveller, and he had known no other. His father had been a man of education and talent, drawn from a profession in his earlier manhood to the goldfields, who remained a miner and a poor man to the day of his death. His wife was not able to induce their sons to aspire to anything above the occupations of the class with which they had always associated, so they were miners and stockmen with the rest. But the young men, even as boys, noticed in their mother a refinement and a clearness of intellect that were not characteristic of the women of Waddy; and out of the love and veneration they bore her grew a sort of family pride—a respect for their name that was quite a touch of old-worldly conceit in this new land of devil-may-care, and gave them a certain distinction. It was this that served largely to make the branding of Frank Hardy as a thief a consuming shame to his brother. Harry thought of it less as a wrong to Frank than as an outrage to his mother. It was this, too, that made the young man burn to take the Sunday School superintendent by the throat and lash him till he howled himself dumb in his own chapel.

Harry returned to his log in Wilson's back paddock again in the afternoon to wrestle with his difficulties, and, with the gluttonous rosellas swinging on the gum-boughs above, set himself to reconsider all that he had heard of Frank's case and all the possibilities that had since occurred to him. Here Dick Haddon discovered him at about four o'clock. Dick was leading a select party at the time, with the intention of reconnoitring old Jock Summers's orchard in view of a possible invasion at an early date; but when he saw Harry in the distance he immediately abandoned the business in hand. An infamous act of desertion like this would have brought down contempt upon the head of another, and have earned him some measure of personal chastisement; but Dick was a law unto himself.

'So long, you fellows,' he said.

'Why, where yer goin'?' grunted Jacker Mack.

"Cross to Harry Hardy. He's down by that ole white gum.'

'Gosh! so he is. I say, we'll all go.'

'No, you won't. Youse go an' see 'bout them cherries. Harry Hardy don't want a crowd round.'

'How d'yer know he wants you?'

'Find out. Me 'n him's mates.'

'Yo-ow?' This in derision.

"Sides, I got somethin' privit to say to him—somethin' privit 'n important, see.'

This was more convincing, but it excited curiosity.

"'Bout Tin ribs?' queried Peterson.

'Likely I'd tell you. Clear out, go on. You can be captain of the band if you like, Jacker; 'n mind you don't give it away.'

Dick gained his point, as usual, and prepared for a quite casual descent upon Harry, who had not yet seen the boys. The plan brought Dicky, 'shanghai' in hand, under the tree where Hardy sat. The boy was apparently oblivious of everything but the parrots up aloft, and it was not till after he had had his shot that he returned the young man's salutation. Then he took a seat astride the log and offered some commonplace information about a nest of joeys in a neighboring tree and a tame magpie that had escaped, and was teaching all the other magpies in Wilson's paddocks to whistle a jig and curse like a drover. But he got down to his point rather suddenly after all.

'Say, Harry, was you goin' to lambaste Tinribs?'

Tinribs?

'Yes, old Shine—this mornin', you know.'

Harry looked into the boy's eye and lied, but Dick was not deceived.

''Twould a-served him good,' he said thoughtfully; 'but you oughter get on to him when Miss Shine ain't about. She's terrible good an' all that—better 'n Miss Keeley, don't you think?'

Miss Keeley was a golden-haired, high-complexioned, and frivolous young lady who had enjoyed a brief but brilliant career as barmaid at the Drovers' Arms. Harry had never seen her, but expressed an opinion entirely in favour of Christina Shine.

'But her father,' continued Dick, with an eloquent grimace, 'he's dicky!

'What've you got against him?'

'I do' know. Look here, 'tain't the clean pertater, is it, for a superintendent t' lay into a chap at Sunday School for things what he done outside? S'pose I float Tinribs's puddlin' tub down the creek by accident, with Doon's baby in it when I ain't thinkin', is it square fer him to nab me in Sunday School, an' whack me fer it, pretendin' all the time it's 'cause I stuck a mouse in the harmonium?'

Dick's contempt for the man who could so misuse his high office was very fine indeed.

'That's the sorter thing Tinribs does,' said the boy. 'If I yell after him on a Saturdee, he gammons t' catch me doin' somethin' in school on Sundee, an' comes down on me with the corner of his bible, 'r screws me ear.'

Harry considered such conduct despicable, and thought the man who would take such unfair advantage of a poor boy might be capable of any infamy; and Dick, encouraged, crept a little nearer.

'I say,' he whispered insinuatingly. 'You could get him any day on the flat, when he comes over after searchin' the day shift.'

Harry shook his head, and slowly plucked at the dry bark.

'I don't mean to touch him,' he said.

Dick was amazed, and a little hurt, perhaps. His confidence had been violated in some measure. He thought the matter over for almost a minute.

'Ain't you goin' to go fer him 'cause of her, eh?' he asked.

'Her? Who d'you mean?'

'Miss Chris.'

'It's nothin' to do with her.'

Dick deliberated again.

'Look here, she was cryin' after you went this mornin'. Saw her hidin' her face by the harmonium, an' wipin' her eyes.'

Harry had not heard evidently; he was, it would appear, devoting his whole attention to the antics of a blue grub. Dick approached still closer, and assumed the tone of an arch-conspirator.

'Heard anything 'bout Mr. Frank?'

'Not a thing, Dick.'

'What yer goin' to do?'

'I can't say, my boy.'

'Well, I'll tell you. Know what Sagacious done?'

'Sagacious? Who is he?'

'Sam Sagacious—Sleuth-hound Sam.'

Harry looked puzzled.

'What, don't you know Sleuth-hound Sam? He's a great feller in a book, what tracks down criminals. Listen here. One time a chap what was a mate of his got put in gaol for stealin' money from a bank where he worked, when it wasn't him at all. Sam, he went an' got a job at the same bank, and that's how he found out the coves 'at done it.'

The young man turned upon Dick, and sat for a moment following up the inference. Then he gripped the latter's hand.

'By thunder!' he cried excitedly, 'that's a better idea than I could hit on in a week.'

Dick did not doubt it; he had but a poor opinion of the resourcefulness of his elders when not figuring in the pages of romantic literature, but he was gratified by Harry's ready recognition of his talent, and proceeded to enlarge upon the peculiar qualities of Sleuth-hound Sam, give instances of his methods, and relate some of his many successes.

At tea that evening Harry broached the subject of his visit to the chapel. He knew his mother would hear of it, and thought it best she should have the melancholy story from his lips.

'Do you see much of Shine's daughter, mother?' he asked.

'I do not see her often, but she has grown into a tall, handsome girl; very different from the wild little thing you rescued from the cattle on the common eight years ago.'

'Yes; I've seen her—saw her in the chapel this morning.'

'In the chapel,' said Mrs. Hardy, turning upon him with surprise; 'were you in the chapel, Henry?'

Harry nodded rather shamefacedly.

'Yes, mother,' he said, 'I went to chapel, an' took my whip with me. I meant to scruff Shine before the lot o' them, an' lash him black an' blue.'

'That was shameful—shameful!

'Anyhow, I didn't do it. She came an' put me off, an' I sneaked out as if I'd been licked myself. I couldn't have hammered the brute before her eyes, but—but—'

'But you meant to; is that it? Henry, you almost make me despair. Have you no more respect for yourself? Have you none for me?'

'I couldn't stand it. You've heard. It made me mad!'

'I have heard all, and I think Mr. Shine is a well intentioned man whose faith, such as it is, is honest; but he is ignorant, coarse-fibred, and narrow-minded. He is doing right according to his own poor, dim light, and could not be convinced otherwise by any word or act of ours; but his preachings can do me no injury. They do not irritate me in the least—indeed, I am not sure that they do not amuse me.'

'Ah, mother, that's like you; you philosophise your way through a difficulty, and I always want to fight my way out. It's so much easier.'

'Yes, dear; but do you get out? Do you know that Ephraim Shine is the most litigious man in the township? He runs to the law with every little trouble, whilst inviting his neighbours to carry all theirs to the Lord. Had you beaten him he would have proceeded against you, and—Oh! my boy, my boy! are you going to make my troubles greater? And I had such hopes.'

'Hush, mother. 'Pon my soul, I won't! I'm going to hold myself down tight after this. An', look here, I've got an idea. I'm going to Pete Holden tomorrow to ask him to put me on at the Stream, same shift as poor Frank was on, if possible.'

'Put on the brother of the man who—'

'Yes, mother, the brother of the thief. But Holden is a good fellow; he spoke up for Frank like a brick. Besides, d'you know what the men are saying? That the gold-stealing is still going on. I'll tell Holden as much, an' promise to watch, an' watch, like a cat, if he'll only send me below.'

'Yes, yes; we can persuade him. I wonder we did not think of this before.'

''Twas young Dick Haddon put me up to it, with some yarn of his about a detective.'

'Bless the boy! he is unique—the worst and the best I have ever known. Johnnie, how dare you?'

The last remark was addressed to Gable, who had been eating industriously for the last quarter of an hour. The old man, finding himself ignored, had smartly conveyed a large spoonful of jam from the pot to his mouth. He choked over it now, and wriggled and blushed like a child taken red-handed.

''Twas only a nut,' he said sulkily.

'You naughty boy! Will you never learn how to behave at table? Come here, sir. Ah, I see; as I suspected. You did not shave this morning. Go straight to bed after you have finished your tea. How dare you disobey me, you wicked boy!'

Gable knuckled his eyes with vigour, and began to snivel. He hated to have a beard on his chin, but would put off shaving longer than Mrs. Hardy thought consistent with perfect neatness. The ability to shave himself was the one manly accomplishment Gable had learned in a long life.

This ludicrous incident had not served to draw Harry's thoughts from his project. All his life he had seen his Uncle Jonnie treated as a child, and there was nothing incongruous in the situation, even 'when the grey-haired boy was rated for neglecting to shave or sent supperless to bed for similar sins of omission or commission. To Mrs. Hardy also it was a simple serious business of domestic government. Ever since she was ten years old Uncle John, who was many years her senior, had been her baby brother and her charge, and although gifted with a good sense of humour, the necessity of admonishing him did not interfere with the gravity of mind she had brought to bear on the former conversation.

'Mr. Holden was an old friend of your father's, Henry,' she said.

'I know,' Harry replied. 'They were mates at Buninyong and Bendigo. I'll remind him of that.'

Harry Hardy found Manager Holden in his office at the Silver Stream when he called on the following morning.

'Couldn't do it, my lad,' said the old miner; 'but I'll put in a word for you with Hennessey at the White Crow.'

'I want a job here on the Stream—want it for a purpose,' said Harry.

'There'd be a row. The people at Yarraman would kick up, after the other affair. I'd be glad to, Harry; but you'd best try somewhere else.'

'Mr. Holden,' said the young man, 'do you believe my brother guilty?'

The manager met his eager eyes steadily.

''Tisn't a fair question, lad,' he answered. 'I always found Frank straight, an' he looked like an honest man; but that evidence would have damned a saint.'

'Do you think the gold-stealing has stopped?'

The manager looked up sharply.

'Do you know anything?'

'I know what the men hint at; nothing more. If they could speak straight they wouldn't do it.'

'Well, to tell you God's truth, Hardy, I believe we are still losing gold.'

'Send me below, then, an' by Heaven I'll spot the true thieves if they're not more cunning than the devil himself. You think Frank guilty, so do most people; it's what we ought to expect, I s'pose.' Harry's hands were clenched hard—it was a sore subject. 'We don't, Mr. Holden; we believe his story, every word of it. Give me half a chance to prove it. You were our father's mate; stand by us now. Put me on with the same shift as Frank worked with.'

'Done!' said the manager, starting up. 'Come on at four. Go trucking; it'll give you a better chance of moving round; and good luck, my boy! But take a hint that's well meant: if the real thief is down there, see he plays no tricks on you.'

'I've thought of that—trust me.'

Harry Hardy's appearance below with the afternoon shift at the Stream occasioned a good deal of talk amongst the miners; but he heard none of it. Shine was in the searching-shed when he came up at midnight, on his knees amongst the men's discarded clothes, pawing them over with his claw-like fingers.

The searcher rarely spoke to the men, never looked at them, and performed his duties as if unconscious of their presence. Custom had made him exceedingly cautious, for it was the delight of the men to play tricks upon him, usually of an exceedingly painful nature. The searcher is no man's friend. When putting on his dry clothes, Harry heard Joe Rogers, the foreman, saying:

'D'yer know them's Harry Hardy's togs yer pawin', Brother Tinribs?'

Shine's mud-coloured eyes floated uneasily from one form to another, but were raised no higher than the knees of the men, seemingly.

'Yes, search 'em carefully, Brother. I s'pose you'd like ter jug the whole family. 'Taint agin yer Christian principles, is it, Mr. Superintendent, to send innocent men to gaol? Quod's good fer morals, ain't it? A gran' place to cultivate the spirit o' brotherly love, ain't it—eh, what? Blast you fer a snivellin' hippercrit, Shine! If yer look sidelong at me I'll belt you over—'

Rogers made an ugly movement towards the searcher; but Peterson and another interposed, and he returned to the form, spitting venomous oaths like an angry cat. Shine, kneeling on the floor, had gone on with his work in his covert way, as if quite unconscious of the foreman's burst of passion.

CHAPTER IX.

JACKER MACK'S report having been entirely favourable, the invasion of Summers' orchard was under taken at dinner-time on the Tuesday following. The party, which consisted of Dick Haddon, Jacker McKnight, Ted, Billy Peterson, and Gable, started for the paddocks immediately school was out, intending to make Jock Summers compensate them for the loss of a meal. It was not thought desirable to take Gable, but he insisted, and Gable was exceedingly pig-headed and immovable when in a stubborn mood. Dick tried to drive him back, but failed; when the others attempted to run away from him the old man trotted after them, bellowing so lustily that the safety of the expedition was endangered; so he was allowed to stand in.

'He'll do to keep nit,' said Dick.

Gable could not run in the event of a surprise and a pursuit, but that mattered little, as it was long since known to be hopeless to attempt to extract evidence from him, and his complicity in matters of this kind was generously overlooked by the people of Waddy.

The expedition was not a success. Dick planned it and captained it well; but the best laid plans of youth are not less fallible than those of mice and men, and one always runs a great risk in looting an orchard in broad daylight—although it will be admitted, by those readers who were once young enough and human enough to rob orchards, that stealing cherries in the dark is as aggravating and unsatisfactory an undertaking as eating soup with a two-pronged fork.

Dick stationed Gable in a convenient tree, with strict orders to cry 'nit' should anybody come in sight from the black clump of fir-trees surrounding the squatter's house. Then he led his party over the fence and along thick lines of currant bushes, creeping under their cover to where the beautiful white-heart cherries hung ripening in the sun. Dick was very busy indeed in the finest of the trees when the note of warning came from Ted McKnight.

'Nit! nit! NIT! Here comes Jock with a dog.'

Dick was last in the rush. He saw the two McKnights safe away, and was following Peterson, full of hope, when there came a rush of feet behind and he was sent sprawling by a heavy body striking him between the shoulders. When he was quite able to grasp the situation he found himself on the broad of his back, with a big mastiff lying on his chest, one paw on either side of his head, and a long, warm tongue lolling in his face with affectionate familiarity. The expression in the dog's eye, he noticed, was decidedly genial, but its attitude was firm. The amiable eye reassured him; he was not going to be eaten, but at the same time he was given to understand that that dog would do his duty though the heavens fell.

A minute later the mastiff was whistled off; Dick was taken by the ear and gently assisted to his feet, and stood defiantly under the stern eye of a rugged, spare-boned, iron-grey Scotchman, six feet high, and framed like an iron cage. Jock retained his hold on the boy's ear.

'Eh, eh, what is it, laddie?' he said, 'enterin' an' stealin', enterin' an' stealin'. A monstrous crime. Come wi' me.'

Dick followed reluctantly, but the grip on his ear lobe was emphatic, and in his one short struggle for freedom he felt as if he were grappling with the great poppet-legs at the Silver Stream. Summers paused for a moment.

'Laddie,' he said, 'd'ye mind my wee bit dog?'

The dog capered like a frivolous cow, flopped his ears, and exhibited himself in a cheerful, well-meaning way.

'If ye'd rather, laddie, the dog will bring ye home,' continued the man.

'Skite!' said Dick, with sullen scorn; but he went quietly after that.

At the house they were met by Christina Shine, and Dick blushed furiously under her gaze of mild surprise. Christina had been a member of the Summers household for over five years, ever since the death of her mother, and had won herself a position there, something like that of a beloved poor relation with light duties and many liberties.

'Dickie, Dickie, what have you been doing this time?' asked Miss Chris.

'Robbin' my fruit-trees, my dear. What might we do with him, d'ye think?'

Miss Chris thought for a minute with one finger pressed on her lip.

'We might let him go,' she said, with the air of one making rather a clever suggestion.

'Na, na, na; we canna permit such crimes to go unpunished.'

'Poor boy, perhaps he's very fond of cherries,' said Chris in extenuation.

Summers regarded the young woman dryly for a moment.

'Eh, eh, girl,' he said, 'ye'd begin to pity the very De'il himself if ye thought maybe he'd burnt his finger.'

Dick was greatly comforted. As a general thing he writhed under sympathy, but, strangely enough, he found it very sweet to hear her speaking words of pity on his behalf, and to feel her soft eyes bent upon him with gentle concern. Probably no young woman quite understands the deep devotion she has inspired in the bosom of a small boy even when she realises—which is rare indeed—that she is regarded with unusual affection by Tommy or Billy or Jim. Jim is probably very young; his hair as a rule appears to have been tousled in a whirlwind, his plain face is never without traces of black jam in which vagrant dust finds rest, and in the society of the adored one he is shy and awkward. The adored one may think him a good deal of a nuisance, but deep down in the dark secret chamber of his heart she is enshrined a goddess, and worshipped with zealous devotion. Men may call her an angel lightly enough; Jim knows her to be an angel, and says never a word. His romance is true, and pure, and beautiful while it lasts—the only true, pure, and beautiful romance many women ever inspire, and alas! they never know of it, and would not prize it if they did.

That was the feeling Dick had for Christina Shine. There had been others—Richard Haddon was not bigoted in his constancy—but now it was Miss Chris, and to him she was both angel and princess; a princess stolen from her royal cradle by the impostor Shine under moving and mysterious circumstances, and at the instigation of a disreputable uncle. It only remained for Dick to slaughter the latter in fair fight, under the eyes of an admiring multitude, in order to restore Chris to all her royal dignities and privileges.

Jock Summers had not relaxed his grip on the boy's ear. He led him to a small dairy sunk in the side of the hill and roofed with stone.

'Ye may bide in there, laddie,' he said, 'till I can make up my mind. I think I might just skin ye, an' I think maybe I might get ye ten years to Yarraman Goal, but I'm no sure.'

Dick had to go down several steps to the floor of the dairy, and when the door was shut his face was on a level with the grating that let air into the place. He passed the first few minutes of his imprisonment making offers of friendship to the dog that sprawled out side, opening its capacious mouth at him and curling its long tongue as if anxious to amuse. The boy had no fears as to his fate; he felt he could safely leave that to Miss Chris; and, meanwhile, the dog was entertaining. The animal was new to Dick: had he known of its existence, his descent upon the orchard would have been differently ordered. In time Maori came to be intimately known to every boy in Waddy as the most kindly and affable dog in the world, but afflicted with a singularly morbid devotion to duty. If sent to capture a predatory youth he never failed to secure the marauder, and always did it as if he loved him. His formidable teeth were not called into service; he either knocked the youngster down and held him with soft but irresistible paws, or he gambolled with him, jumped on him, frisked over him, made escape impossible, and all the time seemed to imply: 'I have a duty to perform, but you can't blame me, you know. There's no reason in the world why we shouldn't be the best of friends.' And they were the best of friends in due course, for Maori bore no malice; there came a time when youngsters invaded Jock's garden for the pleasure of being captured by his wonderful dog.

Ere Dick had been in his prison ten minutes Chris came to him with tea and cake and scones, and when he had finished these she showered cherries in upon him. This time she whispered through the grating:

'You haven't got a cold, have you, Dick?'

'No, miss; I never have colds.'

'Oh, dear, that's a pity! I thought if you could catch a cold I might be able to get you out.'

'Oh!' Dick thought for a moment, and then coughed slightly. 'It will have to be a very bad cold, I think.'

Dick's cough became violent at once, and when Chris led Summers into the vicinity of the dairy a few minutes later the cold had developed alarmingly. Summers heard, and a quizzical and suspicious eye followed Christina.

'He—he doesn't appear to be a very strong boy, Mr. Summers,' said the young woman with obvious artfulness.

'Strong as a bullock,' said Summers.

'He looked very pale, I thought, and that place is damp—damp and dangerous.'

Summers dangled the keys.

'Let the rascal go,' he said. 'Justice will never be done wi'in range o' those bright eyes. Let the young villain loose.'

Chris liberated the boy, and filled his pockets with fruit before sending him away.

'My word, you are a brick,' murmured Dick, quite overcome, and then Chris, being hidden from the house by the shrubbery, did an astounding thing; she put her arm about the boy's neck and kissed him, and Dick's face flamed red, and a delicious confusion possessed him. If he were her worshipper before he was her slave now—her unquestioning, faithful slave.

'You know,' she said, 'I must be your friend, because if it had not been for you my father might have died out there.'

Dick had recalled the incident several times lately, but always, it must be regretfully admitted, with a pang of angry compunction. There were occasions when he felt that it would have been wise to have left the superintendent to his fate. He wondered now, casually, why the daughter should entertain sentiments of gratitude that never seemed to find a place in the arid bosom of her sire.

'Oh, that ain't nothin',' he said awkwardly, digging his heel into the turf, all aglow with novel emotions. Never had he felt quite so grand before.

'Dick, will you take a message from me to—to—' The young woman was toying with his sleeve, her cheeks were ruddy, and the girlish timidity she displayed was in quaint contrast with her fine face and commanding figure.

'To Harry Hardy?' said Dick, with ready conjecture.

'Yes,' said Chris. 'However could you have guessed that? Tell him I am very thankful to him—'

'Fer clearin' out Sunday. Yes, I'll tell him. I say, Miss Chris, do you know I think he's awful fond o' you—awful.'

'No, Dick, he is not. He hates us—father and I.'

'No fear, he don't. He was at our place Sunday night, lookin' at that photo of you in our albium. He looked at it more'n he looked at all the rest put together, an' kep' sneakin' peeps, an' that don't show hate, if you ask me.'

Dick was half an hour late for school that afternoon, but he never faced Joel ham with a lighter heart or more careless mien. The master pretended to be absorbed in a patch on the roof till Dick had almost reached his seat; then he beckoned the boy, took him on the point of his cane, like a piece of toast, and backed him against the wall, where he held him transfixed for a few moments, blinking humorously.

'Ginger, my boy, I regret to have to say it, but you are late again.'

'Never said I wasn't,' said Dick, accepting the inevitable.

'True, Ginger, perfectly true. Any explanation? But let me warn you anything you may say will be taken down as evidence against you.'

'I was visitin'—visitin' Mr. John Summers up at The House' (Summers' residence was always 'The Rouse '), 'an'—an' he detained me.'

Joel's face suddenly fell into wrinkles, and his disengaged fingers clawed his sparse whiskers.

'And you used to be quite a clever liar, Ginger,' he said with philosophical regret.

'Arsk Jock Summers yerseif if you don't believe me,' growled the boy.

'No, no,' said the master shaking his head sadly, 'you are lying very badly today, Ginger. You have the heart to do it, but not the art. Hold up!'

Dick's hand went out unfalteringly.

'One,' said the master. 'Two! Hurt, eh? Well, be consoled with the reflection that all knowledge is simply pain codified. Three! Four—no, I will owe you the fourth.'

Jacker Mack, and Ted, and Peterson were prey to the wildest curiosity. Peterson risked cuts with criminal recklessness in his efforts to communicate with Dick when the latter took his seat, and Jacker, who sat next, edged up close to Dick and whispered excitedly:

'What happened? What'd he do? Where yer been?'

'Been,' said Dick, 'oh, just havin' dinner up at The House.'

'Wha-at—with ole Jock?'

'With Mr. and Mrs. Summers, J.P.'

'Gerrout! yer can't stuff me.'

'Oh, all right, Jacker, don't excite yerseif. Perhaps they didn't give me a load o' cherries to bring away, an' strawberries—thumpin' ripe strawberries, hid somewhere what I know of. Oh, I think not. An' maybe I wasn't told to come up to The House Sundays an' help myself. Very likely not.' All this in an airy whisper.

'Halves!' hissed Jacker.

'Quarters!' murmured Peterson from his hiding place behind the desk.

'P'raps I don't know somethin' too,' continued Jacker mysteriously.

Dick Haddon cocked his eye.

'Pompey, the woodjammer, tol' me he see that bandy whimboy what you fought at the picnic ridin' your billy down to Cow Flat, an' Butts seemed to like it.'

This was serious. The idea of Butts becoming attached to another master gave Dick a real pang. Already he had suffered many twinges of conscience in consequence of his neglect of the goat in captivity.

'Wait till r get hold o' that cove,' he said bitterly. 'I'll murder him.'

'Ain't we never goin' after them goats?' asked Jacker.

Dick nodded emphatically.

'My oath, I'll fix it.'

'An' you'll shell out wif the strawb'ries?'

Dick nodded again; Jacker went peacefully to his work and Peterson crawled back to his seat. Confidence was restored.

CHAPTER X.

HARRY HARDY'S first few shifts below only served to convince him of the difficulties of the task he had set himself. The Silver Stream was a big alluvial mine working two levels, and there were close upon a hundred hands below on each shift. All these he could not watch; but he was working in the same drive and with the set of men Frank had worked with, and was always alert for hint or sign that would give him a clue, whilst at the same time being careful not to set the thieves on their guard. He must watch closely without letting it be seen that he was watching at all. Keen as he was in the pursuit of his object, he found, with some self-resentment, that his mind frequently reverted to another subject altogether; and that subject was Miss Christina Shine. When he caught himself absorbed in a reverie in which Miss Chris was the centre of interest, he metaphorically took himself by the neck and shook himself up, and during the next few minutes reviewed with quite extravagant ferocity the excellent reasons he had for hating Chris for her father's sake. It was a melancholy pleasure to him to see the searcher pawing his clothes about, digging into his pockets and his billy, and examining his boots. His old instinct would have prompted him to attack Ephraim on the floor of the shed, but now, with lamentable unreason and injustice, he nursed the insult as good and sufficient cause for contemning the daughter. He had seen Chris once since Sunday, and then only from the recesses of a clump of scrub into which he had retreated on seeing her approach; but he felt, without admitting the knowledge even to himself, that he would need all the excuses he could find, just or unjust, reasonable or otherwise, to battle with something that was rising up within him to drive him on his knees to the feet of this grey-eyed girl, a humble and abject penitent.

For an hour or two each day Harry was fossicking in the creek on the spot where Frank had been working, with the idea of satisfying himself whether or not such gold as Frank had sold was obtainable there; and here the searcher's daughter came upon him one morning shortly after the incident of the Sunday School. Harry had his cradle pitched near the crossing, and to ignore the young woman would be an avowal of enmity. Here was his opportunity. Harry set his face over the hopper and cradled industriously. He thought he was displaying proper firmness, but his hand trembled, his heart beat like a plunger, and he was the victim of an ignoble bashfulness. Chris approached with some timidity; but Maori bounded up to the young man, making elephantine overtures of friendliness, which were resented by Harry's cattle-dog Cop, who walked round and round the mastiff in narrowing circles, bristling like a cat and snarling hoarsely. Maori treated the challenge with a lordly indulgence. Cop went further, he snapped and brought blood. There were some things Maori could not stand: this was one. Out of a small storm of pebbles, chips, leaves, and dust, the two dogs presently came into view again, Cop on his back, pawing wildly at the unresisting air, and Maori at his throat, pinning him with a vice-like grip.

Harry rushed to the rescue, tore his dog free, and held back the furious animal up-reared and exposing vicious fangs. Chris laid a trembling hand on the collar of the penitent Maori, and in this way the young people faced each other. Their eyes met for a moment, Harry's frowning blackly, hers anxious and beseeching.

'I'm sorry,' she said. 'Is he hurt?'

'No,' replied Harry sulkily. 'No thanks to that brute of yours, though.'

'Oh!' This very reproachfully.

Harry looked up and encountered her eyes again, and they shattered him, as they had done in chapel, giving him a sense of having exerted his strength to hurt something sweet and tender as a flower; and yet the girl seemed to tower above him. Nature, in putting the fresh sympathetic soul of a child into the grand body of a Minerva, had set a problem that was too deep for Harry Hardy.

'Beg pardon,' he said, humbly; ''twas my dog started it. Down, Cop! To heel—!'

He checked himself suddenly on a 'stock term.' There were tones of his master's that Cop never dared to disobey; he went down at full length and lay panting, regarding Maori fixedly with a sidelong and malevolent eye. Harry returned to his cradle, and Chris approached the stepping-stones and paused there.

'Did Dickie Haddon give you my message?' she asked in a low voice.

Harry nodded.

'It's all right,' he said.

There was another pause, broken at length by Chris.

'You ought not to be angry with me. It isn't fair.'

She was thinking of the day years ago when she was carried, all tattered and torn, from the midst of that mob of sportive cattle. She was a very little girl then, but the incident had remained fresh and vivid in her mind, and ever since Harry Hardy had been a hero in her eyes. He only remembered the affair casually and without interest.

'I am really very grateful to you for—for going away, because I know you had good cause for your anger.'

Oh, that's all right,' said Harry again, inaptly.

'But you ought not to be angry with me. It pained me very much—the trial and your mother's sorrow, and all the rest. It hurt me because it seemed to set me on the side that was against Mrs. Hardy, and I—I always admired her. I knew she was a good woman, and it was easy to see the trouble cut into her heart although she bore it so proudly.'

'Oh, that's all right.' Harry was fumbling with the gravel in the hopper. He was conscious that his replies were foolish and trivial, but for the life of him he could do no better.

She waited a few moments, then bade him good morning and went across the creek and away amongst the trees beyond; and Harry, resting upon the handle of his cradle, watched her, absorbed, a prey to a set of new emotions that bewildered him hopelessly. He was still in this position when Chris looked back from the hill, and half an hour later Dick Haddon found him day-dreaming amongst the tailings.

Day-dreams were not possible in the vicinity of Richard Haddon. The boy was an ardent fossicker, and loved to be burrowing amongst old tailings, or groping in the sludge of an auriferous creek after little patches. He was soon peering into the ripples of Harry's cradle.

'Poor,' he commented, with the confidence of an expert.

'Not up to much, Dick,' said Harry. 'I've just been prospectin' a bit round here.'

'Frank was tryin' that bank. 'Tain't no good. Say, I can lay you onter somethin' better not far from here.'

'Yes—where is it?'

'Tellin's. What'll you give us?

'Depends. What's it worth?'

'Got half a pennyweight prospect there onst. Look here, you lend me yer dog t'-night, an' I'll show where.'

'What do you want with Cop?'

'You won't split? Well, some coves down to Cow Flat come up an' stole my goat, Butts, an' a lot of others, an' me an' some other fellers is goin' after 'em t'-night, late. A good sheep-dog what's a quiet worker 'd be spiffin. Cop's all right. He'd work fer me.'

Harry had not forgotten the time when a lordly billy was the pride and joy of his own heart, and his sympathies were with Dick; so Cop accompanied the band of youthful raiders that assembled with much mystery in the vicinity of the schoolhouse late that night. The desperadoes had stolen from their beds while their parents slept, and were ripe for adventure. Dick, who had Cop in charge, put himself at the head of the rising with his customary assurance, and gave his orders in a low, stern voice. According to his authorities, a low, stern voice was proper to the command of all such midnight enterprises.

But before starting for Cow Flat it was necessary to forage for ammunition. Two or three of the boys were provided with bags. It was proposed to fill these with such vegetables as would serve to allure the coy but gluttonous goat, and a silent, systematic descent was made upon several kitchen gardens of Waddy.

Go fer carrots an' cabbages, specially carrots,' whispered the commandant, whose experience of goats was large and varied, and taught him that the average nanny or billy would desert home and kindred and go through fire and water in pursuit of a succulent young carrot not larger than a clothes-peg.

When the boys turned their backs on Waddy the expedition carried with it vegetables enough to bribe all the goats in the province. The garden of Michael Devoy was a waste place, desolation brooded over the carrot beds of the Canns and the Sloans, and Mrs. Ben Steven's cabbage-patch lay in ruins.

For this night only Dick had assumed the role of Moonlighter Ryan, a notorious Queensland cattle duffer, recently hanged for his part in a disputation with a member of the mounted police. The dispute ended with the death of the policeman, who succumbed to injuries received. As Moonlighter Dick was characteristically remorseless, his courage and cunning were understood to verge upon the inhuman, and his band was composed of the most utterly abandoned ruffians the history of the country afforded; only two of them had not been hanged, and these two justified their inclusion by having richly deserved hanging several times over.

Across the flat and past the toll-bar, where the light sleep of Dan, the tollman, was not disturbed by the creeping band, Moonlighter led his outlaws warily, then struck the long bush road between two lines of straggling fence running with all sorts of lists and bends, going on and on endlessly, according to the belief of the boys of Waddy. The road was overhung by tall gums and nourished many clumps of fresh green saplings, about which the tortuous cart-track wound in deep yellow ruts, baked hard in summer, washed into treacherous bog in winter. Here caution was not necessary, and there were divers fierce hand-to-hand attacks on clumps of scrub representing a vindictive and merciless police, out of which Moonlighter and his men issued crowned with victory and covered with glory. A scarecrow in a wayside orchard was charged with desperate valour, and only saved from instant destruction as a particularly hateful police spy by the sudden intervention of the leader.

'Back, men!' he cried imperiously. 'Moon lighter never makes war on women!'

He pointed to the protecting skirt in which the scarecrow was clad, and his bold bad men drew off and retired abashed.

For the next half-mile Moonlighter led his men in stealthy retreat from an overwhelming force of troopers armed to the teeth. Tracks had to be covered and diversions created, and there was much hiding behind logs and in clumps of scrub; indeed, the police were only foiled at length by the exertion of that subtle strategy for which Moonlighter was notorious.

It was after one o'clock in the morning when Cow Flat was reached. The little township slept, steeped in darkness, beside its sluggish strip of creeping 'slurry' miscalled a creek. Beyond, on the rise, a big mine clattered and groaned, and puffed its glowing clouds of steam against the sky; but Cow Flat had settled down into silence after the midnight change of shifts, and a mining township sleeps well. For all that it was a stealthy and cautious band Moonlighter led down to the old battered engine-house by the edge of the common, where the goats of Cow Flat were known to herd in large numbers. Sure enough here were goats of both sexes, and all sorts and sizes— sleeping huddled in the ruined engine-house, on the sides of the grass-grown tip, in the old bob-pit, and upon the remains of the fallen stack. Carefully and quietly the animals were awakened; slyly they were drawn forth, with gentle whispered calls of 'Nan, nan, nan!' and insidious and soothing words, but more especially with the aid of scraps of carrot, sparingly but judiciously distributed. An occasional low, querulous bleat from a youthful nanny awakened from dreams of clover-fields, or a hoarse, imperious inquiry in a deep baritone 'baa' from a patriarchal he-goat, was the only noise that followed the invasion. Then, when the animals within the ruin were fully alive to the situation and awake to the knowledge that it all meant carrots, and that outside carrots innumerable awaited the gathering, they streamed forth: they fought in the doorways, they battered a passage through the broken wall; faint plaintive queries went up from scores of throats, answered by gluttonous mumblings from goats that had been fortunate enough to snatch a morsel of the delectable vegetable. Down from the tips and up from the bob-pit they came, singly and in sets, undemonstrative matrons with weak-kneed twins at their heels, skittish kids and bearded veterans, and joined the anxious, eager, hungry mob.

'Away with them, my boys,' ordered Moonlighter. 'Head 'em fer the common. We'll have every blessed goat in the place.'

He sent away three bands in three different directions, fully provisioned, and commissioned to collect goats from all quarters.

'Bring 'em up to the main mob on the common, an' the man what makes a row I'll hang in his shirt to the nearest tree. Don't leave the beggars any kind of a goat at all.'

Dick had undertaken a big contract. Cow Flat was simply infested with goats; every family owned its small flock, and the milk-supply of the township depended entirely upon the droves of nannies that grubbed for sustenance on the stony ridges or the bare, burnt stretch of common land. Probably Cow Flat was so called because nobody had ever seen anything remotely resembling a cow anywhere in the vicinity; consequently goats were hold in high esteem, for ten goats can live and prosper where one cow would die of hunger and melancholy in a month.

Jacker Mack, Peterson, and Parrot Cann had recognised their billies in the heard, but Butts was still missing. On an open space near the road by which Moonlighter's gang had come, and at a safe distance from the township, a few of the raiders held the main body of the goats. Parrot Cann, with a bag of cabbages on his shoulder, was the centre of attraction, and the dropping of an occasional leaf kept the goats pushing about him, some uprearing and straining toward the tantalising bag, others baa-ing in his face a piteous appeal. Suddenly, however, an astute billy with a flowing beard came to the rescue. He drove at Cann from the rear with masterly strategy and uncommon force, and brought him down; then in a flash boy and bag were hidden under a climbing, butting, burrowing army of goats, from the centre of which came the muffled yells of poor Parrot clipped in a hundred places by the sharp hoofs of the hungry animals.

Moonlighter promptly led a desperate charge to the rescue, and after a hard struggle Cann was dragged out, tattered and bleeding; but the bag was abandoned to the enemy.

In about twenty minutes Jacker Mack and a couple of subordinates brought up a herd gathered from the hill on the left bank of the creek; Peterson came soon after with a good mob from the right, and Dolf Belman and another followed with a score or so from about the houses. But still Butts had not been captured.

'You fellers take 'em on slowly,' said Moonlighter. 'Me an' Gardiner'll go back an' have a try after Butts.' Ted McKnight represented Gardiner in this enterprise.

The hunt for Butts had to be conducted with great circumspection. The boys crept from place to place; Dick called the goat's name softly at all outhouses and enclosures, and won a response after a search of over a quarter of an hour, Butts's familiar 'baa' answering from the interior of a stable in a back yard. Ted was stationed to keep 'nit,' and Dick stole into the yard, broke his way into the stable, and was leading the huge billy out of captivity when the savage barking of a dog broke the silence; and then an adjacent window was thrown up and a woman's voice called 'Thieves!' and 'Fire!

Dick had given Butts the taste of a carrot and now fled, dangling the inviting vegetable, Butts following at his heels.

'Go for it, Ted!' he yelled, and the two rushed over the flat ground, up the hill, and across the thinly-timbered bush to the road. A good run brought them up to the main flock, Butts still ambling gaily in the rear, making hungry bites at the carrot hitched under Dick's belt at the back.

'Rush 'em along!' cried the panting Moonlighter. 'We've waked the blessed town. Heel 'em, Cop, heel 'em!

Peterson and Jacker went ahead dangling cabbages; the dog entered into the spirit of the thing with enthusiasm and worked the flock in his very best style; and so the boys of Waddy, hot, excited, very frightened of probable pursuers, but wondrously elated, swept the great drove of goats up the road in the light of the waning moon. The pace was warm for a mile, but then, the dread of pursuit having evaporated, the marauders slowed down, and for the rest of the journey they were experienced drovers bringing down the largest lot of stock that had ever been handled by man, full of technical phrases and big talk of runs, and plains, and flooded rivers, and long, waterless spells. It was Jacker Mack who sounded the first note of dismay.

'Jee-rusalem! How 'bout the toll?'

Nobody had thought of the toll-bar, and there were the big, white gates already in sight, stretching across the road, threatening to bring dismal failure upon the expedition when complete success seemed imminent.

'Down with the fence!' ordered the implacable Moonlighter.

In two minutes the boys had found a weak set of rails in the fence, and shortly after the goats were being driven across Wilson's paddock, cutting off a great corner, and heading for the farmer's gates that opened out on to the open country on which Waddy was built. Through these gates the flock was driven with a racket and hullaballoo that set Wilson's half-dozen dogs yapping insanely, and started every rooster on the farm crowing in shrill protestation. Then helter-skelter over the flat the goats were swept in on the township and left to their own devices, whilst a dozen weary, dusty, triumphant small boys stole back to bed through unlatched windows and doors carefully left open for a stealthy return.

CHAPTER XI.

THERE was great wonder in Waddy next morning, and much argument. Neighbours discussed the sensation with avidity. Mrs. Sloan, uncombed and in early morning deshabille, with an apron thrown over her head, carried the news to Mrs. Justin's back fence, and Mrs. Justin ran with it to the back fence of Mrs. McKnight, and Mrs. McKnight spread the tidings as far as the house of Steven; so the wonder grew, and families were called up at an unusually early hour, and sage opinions were thrown from side windows and handed over garden gates. An invasion of goats had happened at Waddy, a downpour of goats, an eruption of goats: goats were all over the place, and nobody knew whence they came or when they arrived. Waddy's own goats were many and various, but the invasion had quadrupled them, and goats were everywhere—bold, hungry, predatory goats—browsing, sleeping, battling, thieving, and filling the air with incessant pleadings. They invaded gardens and broke their way into kitchens and larders; they assaulted children and in some cases offered fight to the mothers who went to eject them; and here and there the billies of Waddy fought with the bearded usurpers long unsatisfactory contests, rearing and butting for hours, and doing each other no morsel of injury that anybody could discover. A few of the women were out with buckets, making the most of the opportunity, milking all the nannies who would submit; and Devoy, with characteristic impetuosity, was already on the warpath, seeking vengeance on the person or persons whose act had led to the pillage of his vegetable beds.

During all this the innocence of the boys of Waddy, particularly those boys who had composed Moonlighter's gang, was quite convincing. They had kept their secret well, and for some time no act of vandalism was suspected. In school during the morning they were most attentive, and particularly assiduous in the pursuit of knowledge; and when the echoes of a disturbance in the township penetrated the school walls, Richard Haddon and his friends may have exchanged significant winks, but nothing in their general demeanour would have betrayed them to the ordinary intelligence. However, Joel Ham's intelligence was not of the ordinary kind, and after looking up two or three times and catching the master's little leaden eye fixed upon him with a glance of amused speculation, Dick began to feel decidedly uncomfortable.

The first hint of the truth was brought to Waddy by an infuriated female from Cow Flat. She drove up in an old-fashioned waggon drawn by a lively and energetic but very ancient and haggard bay horse, with flattened hoofs and a mere stump of a tail. She was tall and stout, with great muscular arms bare to the shoulder, and her face was pink with righteous indignation. This woman drove slowly up the one road of Waddy, and standing erect in her vehicle roundly abused the township from end to end. Crying her cause in a big strident voice, she insulted the inhabitants individually and in the mass, and wherever several people were assembled she pulled up and poured out upon them the vials of her wrath in a fine flow of vituperation; and after every few sentences she interpolated an almost pathetic plea to somebody, she did not care whom, to step forward and resent her criticism that she might have an opportunity of hammering decency and religion into the benighted inhabitants of an unregenerate place.

'Who stole the goats?' she screamed, and, receiving no answer, screamed the question from house to house.

'Waddy's a township of thieves an' hussies!' she cried, 'thieves an' hussies! Gimme me goats or I'll have the law on you all—you low, mean stealers an' robbers, ye! Who stole the goats? Who came by night an' robbed a decent widdy woman of her beautiful goats? Who? Who? Who? Say you didn't, someone! Gi' me the lie, you lot o' gaol-birds an' assassinators!'

All Waddy turned out to hear, and many followed the woman up the road. The school children heard the noisy procession go by with amazement and regret, and the visitor grew shriller and fiercer as her search progressed. At length she discovered what she declared to be one of her goats in the possession of Mrs. Hogan, and she left her waggon and charged the latter, who fled in terror, bolting all her doors and throwing up a barricade in the passage.

But the stranger was not to be foiled: she sat down on the doorstep and proclaimed the house under siege, announcing her intention to remain until she had wreaked her vengeance on Mrs. Hogan, and offering meanwhile to fight any four women of Waddy for mere diversion.

It was not till the tired miners off the night shift had secured all the goats she pointed out as hers, tied their legs and packed them on her waggon, that the woman could be induced to leave; and as she drove away she heaped further insult on the township, and from the distant toll-bar signalled a final gesture of contempt and loathing.

This woman took back to Cow Flat her own explanation of the mystery of the lost goats, and in due time deputations from the rival township began to reach Waddy, so that the Great Goat Riot developed rapidly. It was long since friendly feeling had existed between Waddy and Cow Flat. There was a standing quarrel about sludge and the pollution of the waters of the creek; there were political differences, too, and a fierce sporting rivalry. By the majority of the people of Cow Flat the purloining of their goats was accepted as further evidence of the moral depravity and low origin of the people of Waddy, and the feeling between the townships was suddenly strained to a dangerous tension.

The first few skirmishing parties from Cow Flat were composed of women and boys, and an undisciplined and rash pursuit of goats followed each visit. The nannies and billies, under stress of the new excitement, ran suddenly wild and developed a fleetness of foot, an expertness in climbing, and powers of endurance hitherto all unsuspected by their owners; so very few animals were recovered by the visitors.

The hunt was continued throughout the next day. Goats were rushing wildly about the place from morning till midnight pursued by their wrathful owners, to the detriment of the peace of Waddy and the undoing of the tractable local milkers; and at last a great resentment took possession of the matrons of the township— there were counter-attacks among the houses, rescue parties beset the women carrying off prizes, and a few skirmishes happened on the flat. Now the men were induced to take a hand, and there was talk of battle and pillage and sudden death.

Devoy, pugnacious and vengeful, provoked the first serious struggle. Discovering a man of Cow Flat who claimed a small family of aggressive brown goats which he had marked out as the vandals that had wrought ruin amongst his well-kept beds, Devoy bearded the stranger and spoke of damages and broken heads, and his small son, Danny, a young Australian with a piquant brogue and a born love of ructions, moved round and incited him to bloodshed.

'Go fer him, daddy. Sure, ye can lick him wid one hand, dear,' pleaded Danny.

'Yer dir-rty goats have ate me gar-rden, sor. D'ye moind me now? It's ruined me gar-rden is on me,' said Devoy aggressively.

'Hit him, daddy,' screamed Danny.

Devoy accepted the advice and struck the first blow. The man from Cow Flat was very willing, and they fought a long, destructive battle; and through it all Danny danced about the ring, bristling with excitement and crying fierce and persistent encouragement to his sire.

'Let him have it, daddy!' 'Now ye have him!' 'Good on you, daddy!' 'Sure, you'll do him!' 'One round more, daddy, an' ye have him beat!' These phrases, and shrill inarticulate cries of applause and astonishment and joy, Danny reiterated breathlessly until his father was pronounced the victor; then he took the battered hero fondly by the hand and led him away to be bathed and plastered and bandaged by a devoted wife and mother.

The downfall of Devoy's opponent brought other champions from Cow Flat; there were open fights in Wilson's paddocks by day and assaults and sallies by night, and the bitterness deepened into hatred. Waddy now resisted every attempt to carry off the stolen goats, and parties coming from Cow Flat by night were content with any animals they could lay their hands on; so for nearly a week the township was beset with alarums and excursions, and Jo Rogers, as its admitted champion, had more engagements on his hands than he could reasonably be expected to fulfil in a month.

Dickie and his accomplices were amazed at the developments, and watched the trouble grow with the greatest concern. The contests on the open ground beyond the quarries were frequent and free, and then there came a lull; but from Cow Flat came rumours of a grand coup meditated by the leaders on that side. Preparations were being made for an attack by a large body, and the forcible abduction of all the goats, irrespective of individual rights. The excitement had now reached fever heat, and there were few men in Waddy who were not ready, even anxious, to strike a blow for the preservation of the flocks and herds and the credit of the township.

On the side of approach from Cow Flat Waddy was protected for the greater part of the distance by the string of quarries; under the command of Big Peterson, who as an ex-soldier had some military reputation, logs were dragged from the bush, and the space between the end of the quarries and the fence of Summers' south paddock was smartly barricaded. The defenders were armed with light sticks, and it was understood that these were to be used only if the enemy refused to abide by Nature's weapons.

All the mines in the vicinity of Waddy worked short-handed on the day of the Great Goat Riot; the men, under the command of Captain Peterson, were sitting in bands, hidden from view in the quarries, smoking, discussing the situation, and patiently awaiting the attack. They did not wait in vain. At about eleven o'clock a scout came in with the intelligence that a large body was advancing in irregular order through Wilson's paddock, and a quarter of an hour later the men of Cow Flat swarmed out of the bush and over the fence and charged Waddy at a trot.

'Toe the scratch, men!' yelled Peterson; and the defenders of Waddy climbed out of the holes and presently turned a solid front to the enemy. The Cow Flat commander, who had expected to take the place by surprise, wavered at the sight of organised opposition and called a halt at the other edge of the quarries; and invaders and besieged faced each other across the broken ground while the Cow Flat leaders held a council of war. On the level behind the entrenched army the women of Waddy and their families were picknicking gaily on the grass, for it was accepted as a great gala day in the township, and flags of all shapes and colours, devised from all kinds of discarded garments, fluttered from tree-tops, chimneys, posts, clothes-props, and any other eminence to which a streamer could be fastened.

Perceiving their opponents reluctant to charge, Peterson's command presently developed a fine flow of sarcasm.

'Won't ye stip over, ye mud-gropers?' cried Devoy. 'It's a nice little riciption we've arranged for yez.

'Who stole the goats?' retorted the enemy.

'Sure, is it the bits of goats, then? Ye might come an' take them if ye won't be stayin' all day there dishcussin' polemics.' Devoy was understood to be a man of learning and unequalled in argument.

'Kidnappers an' goat-stealers!' yelled the foe.

Devoy posed on a rock in an oratorical attitude.

'Ye came suspectin' t' have a foine aisy time the mornin',' he said. 'Yez contimplated playin' the divil wid a big shtick among the weemin an' the childther. Tom Moran, ye thunderin' great ilephant av a man, d'ye think ye cud fight a sick hen on a fince?'

Moran replied with uproarious profanity and frantic pantomime, and the abuse became general and vociferous. Devoy mounted a larger rock and commenced a scathing harangue; but a sod thrown by an invader took him in the mouth and toppled him over backwards, so that he arose gasping and spitting and clawing dirt out of his beard, and made a rush for his enemy, mad for battle; friends grappled with him and held him back, and he could only shriek defiance and rash challenges as the two parties moved along the quarries towards the log barricade. Here the men of Cow Flat halted again and their leaders conferred, but the rank-and-file were rapidly losing temper and restraint under the black insults heaped upon them by the besieged. They scattered along the row of logs into a long thin line and the men of Waddy followed, till the two parties were almost man to man, facing each other, exchanging jibes and gestures of contempt.

'Moran, ye scut! don't be skirmishin' an' in thriguin' t' get forninat a shmall man. My meat ye are, an' come on, ye—ye creepin' infor-r-mer, ye!

It was the last insult. Moran led the charge, roaring like a goaded bullock, the two parties clashed over the logs, and in an instant comparative silence fell upon the men. The yelling, the derisive voices, and scoffing laughter ceased, and nothing was heard but the sharp rattle of the strokes. The fight was fierce, earnest, and bloody; all thoughts of the absurdity of the cause of contention had long since been forgotten, and the battle was as remorseless as if it were waged for an empire.

The women had never expected anything serious to happen, and now they were dreadfully afraid. A valiant few took arms and joined in the fray by the sides of their husbands; but the rest, finding after a few minutes that the fight raged furiously, gave way to bitter tears, and wailed protests from a safe distance, while the children followed their example with all the vigour of young lungs.

In time Peterson and Devoy and Rogers found voice and yelled encouragement to their men, and sticks and fists worked grievous mischief. The Cow Flat men were at an enormous disadvantage in having to scale the logs to make headway; whenever a hero did succeed in gaining the top, Big Peterson, who moved swiftly and tirelessly up and down the line, was there to cope with him, and he was hurled down, bruised and broken. The besiegers struggled valiantly, but it dawned on them in the course of ten minutes that they were waging a vain and foolish fight. A rally and a rescue of Moran, who was on the point of being captured by the enemy, gave them an excuse to draw off, dragging their defeated leader beyond harm's reach. A few moments later, in the midst of excited cheering and jeering, a number of the men became aware of a small, bare-headed, red-haired, white-faced boy standing on the logs between the foes, where he had stood whilst the fight was still waging, whirling his hat, and crying something at the top of his voice:

'The troopers! The troopers! The troopers!

It was Dick Haddon, very frightened apparently, and ablaze with excitement.

'Don't fight, don't fight!' he cried. ''Twas me took the goats, an' the troopers're comin'! Look, the troopers!

Sure enough, far off across the level country leading down to Yarraman, a small body of mounted police could be seen riding at a canter towards Waddy, their swords and cap-peaks glittering in the sun. The men stared in the direction pointed by Dick in silence, wondering what this development might mean. Devoy was the first to move. Gripping Dick, he lifted him from the logs.

'Run, run, ye bla'gard!' he said. 'Fetch yer school football.'

Then as Dick hastened away Devoy took a commanding position on the barricade.

'Hear me, all of yez,' he cried. 'Down wid yer sticks, every divil of yez! You Cow Flat min, too, down wid 'em! Look it here—the troopers is comin'. Shine have infor-rmed on us in Yarraman. Moind, now, this is jist a bit of divarsion we've been havin'.'

The Waddy men had dropped their weapons, so also had most of their foes, and all gathered closer about Devoy.

'T'row away thim shticks,' he yelled. 'D'ye want tin years fer riot, an' murther, an' dish turbin' the peace? Look peaceable, an' frindly, an' lovin', if it's in yez so to do. Moran, ye sulky haythen, wud ye be hangin' the lot av us? Shmile 'r I'll black the other oye of ye! Shmile, ye hi-potomus!

At this instant the line of troopers rode in between the parties, with a clattering of scabbard and chain. The sergeant drew his foaming bay up sharp and confronted Devoy.

'What is the meaning of this, my man?' he demanded.

'Meanin' which, sor?' Devoy cocked a black and swollen eye at the officer, and smiled innocently over a lacerated chin.

'Meaning this.' The trooper waved a white glove over the congregation.

'Sure, it's a bit of a game only—a bit of a friendly game o' football, as ye may see wid the own eyes of ye.'

Dick's football had just bounced in between the opposing bodies. The officer ran an eye over the crowd, noting the bloodstains.

'You play football in a funny way at Waddy,' he said.

'We play it wid enthusiasm.'

'Enthusiasm! I should say you played it with shillelahs. Do you always get cracked skulls and black eyes when you play football?'

'It's our pleasant way, sor.'

'Is it? Well, how the devil do you play football? What is the meaning of this pile of logs?'

'Meaning the fines, sergeant? It's this way: we of Waddy stands on this side, an' thim of Cow Flat forninst us on the other side, an' we kicks it over t' thim, an' they kicks it back to ourselves, an', sure, the side what kicks it over the most frequent wins. Would you like t' see, sergeant?'

The miners grinned, the troopers giggled, and the sergeant began to feel huffy.

'"Tention!' he cried. 'Who won this precious game?'

Devoy pinched hi chin tenderly and grimaced. It was hard to abandon the glory of a well-won battle, but there was no option.

'It was a dthraw,' he said manfully.

'And what were you playing for?'

'Playin' for? Oh, fer natural love an' affection, nothin' more, barrin' a few goats.'

'Goats, eh? Now look here, my fine fellow, we were told there was to be riot and fighting here over those goats. I don't believe a word of your cock-and-bull story about football, and for two pins

I'd clap a few of you where you wouldn't play again for some time to come. Now you'd all better settle this goat business while my men are here, and take my advice and drop football if you want to keep on the comfort able and airy side of a gaol. Now then, you fellows from the Flat, round up your goats and look slippy in getting out of this.'

Devoy was the picture of outraged innocence.

'Tut, tut, tut!' he said mournfully, 'an' see how they take off the characther of dacent, paceable, lovin' min. 'Twas a tinder an' frindly game we was playin', sergeant, but if ye will break it up, sure I'm a law-abidin' man. We did intund t' axe the min av Cow Flat t' have the bite an' sup wid us at the banquit this night, but we rispict the law, an' we say nothin' agin it. But, sor, if ever yer men would be likun' a game of football, we—'

'Get down, you ruffian!' said the sergeant, grinning, and rode his horse at Devoy.

So the Great Goat Riot was settled, and under the eye of the sergeant and his troopers the goats of Cow Flat were drafted from those of Waddy. It was a difficult task, and was not accomplished without trouble and argument and minor hostilities: but the judgment of the sergeant, who seemed to be aware of the whole merits of the case, was final, so that in due time the men of Cow Flat departed driving their goats before them, and comparative peace fell upon Waddy once more.

CHAPTER XII.

ALL through the next day Waddy was very calm; it was repenting recent rash actions and calculating laboriously. At the Drovers' Arms that evening several members of the School Committee compared conclusions and resolved that something must be done. It was evident that the youth of the township, under the leadership of 'the boy Haddon,' had dragged Waddy into a nasty squabble, some of the results of which were unpleasantly conspicuous on the faces and heads of prominent committeemen. Then the ravaged gardens had to be taken into consideration. Calmer judgment had convinced the residents that the destruction wrought was not all due to goats, and there was a general desire to visit the responsibility on the true culprits, whose identity was shrewdly suspected.

Friday was rather an eventful day at the school. The boys had heard of the meeting and expected serious developments. Mrs. Ben Steven called in the morning. She was a tall heavily-framed woman, short-tempered, and astonishingly voluble in her wrath. She had selected Richard Haddon as the vandal who had despoiled her cabbage-patch, and was seeking a just revenge. Already she had called upon Mrs. Haddon and delivered a long, loud, and fierce public lecture to the startled little widow on the moral responsibilities of parents, and the need they have of faithfully and regularly thrashing their sons as a duty they owe to their neighbors. Now it was her intention to incite Joel Ham to administer an adequate caning to the boy, or to do herself the bare justice of soundly spanking the culprit. She bounced into the school, angry, bare-armed, and eager for the fray, and all the children sat up and wondered.

'I've come about that boy Haddon,' said Mrs. Ben.

Joel Ham blinked his pale lashes and regarded her thoughtfully, in peaceful and good-humoured contrast with her own haste and heat.

'Have you, indeed, ma'am?' he said softly.

'Have I, indeed! 'cried the woman, bridling again at a hint of sarcasm; 'can't you see I have?'

'Madam, you are very obvious.'

'Am I, then! Well, look here, you; you've got to cane the hide off that boy.'

'You surprise me, Mrs. Steven. For what?'

'For breakin' into my garden an' robbin' me. Nice way you're teachin' these boys, ain't you? Makin' thieves an' stealers of 'em. Now, tell me, do you mean to thrash him?'

Joel considered the matter calmly, pinching his under lip and blinking at Mrs. Ben in a pensive, studious way.

'No, ma'am, I do not.'

'For why?' cried the woman.

'I am not the public hangman, Mrs. Steven.'

Mrs. Steven could not see the relevance of the excuse, and her anger rose again.

'Then, sir, I'll thrash him myself, now an' here.'

The master sighed heavily and clambered on to his high stool, took his black bottle from his desk, and deliberately refreshed himself, oblivious apparently to the lady's threat and forgetting her presence.

'Do you hear me, Joel Ham?' Mrs. Ben Steven beat heavily on the desk with the palm of her large hand. 'I'll whack him myself.'

'Certainly, ma'am, certainly—if you can catch him.'

Dick accepted this as a kindly hint and dived under a couple of desks as Mrs. Steven rushed his place. The chase was obviously useless from the first; the woman had not a possible chance of catching Dick amongst the forms, but she tried while her breath lasted, rushing in and out amongst the classes, knocking a child over here and there, boxing the ears of others when they got in her way, and creating confusion and unbounded delight everywhere. The children were overjoyed, but Gable was much concerned for Dick, and stood up in his place ejaculating 'Crickey!'in a loud voice and following the hunt with frightened eyes.

Meanwhile Joel Ham, B.A., sat at his desk, contemplating the roof with profound interest, and taking a casual mechanical pull at his bottle. Joel was in a peculiar position: he was selected by the people of Waddy and paid by them, and had to defer to their wishes to some extent; and, besides, Mrs. Ben Steven was a large, powerful, indignant woman, and he a small, slim man.

Mrs. Steven stood in front of the classes until she had recovered sufficient breath to start a fierce tirade; then, one hand on her hip and the other out-thrown, she thundered abuse at Richard Haddon and all his belongings. The master bore this for two or three minutes; then he slid from his stool, seized his longest cane, and thrashing the desk—his usual demand for order—he faced Mrs. Ben and, pointing to the door, cried:

'Out!'

The woman backed away a step and regarded him with some amazement. He was not a bit like the everyday Joel Ham, but quite imperious and fierce.

'Out!' he said, and the long cane whistled threateningly around and over her.

She backed away a few steps more; Joel followed her up, cutting all around her with the lightning play of an expert swordsman, just missing by the fraction of an inch, and showing a face that quite subdued the virago. Mrs. Steven backed to the door.

'Out!' thundered Ham, and she fled, banging the door between her and the dangerous cane.

'Oh crickey!' cried Gable in a high squeak that set the whole school laughing boisterously.

Mrs. Ben Steven reappeared at one of the windows, and threatened terrible things for Ham when her Ben returned; but Joel was consoling himself with his bottle again and was not in the least disturbed, and a minute later the school was plunged in a studious silence.

Peterson and Cann called late in the afternoon, as representatives of the School Committee.

'We've come fer your permission to ask some questions of the boy Haddon, Mr. Ham, sir,' said Peterson.

Joel received a great show of respect from most of the men of Waddy in consideration of his position and scholarship.

Dick was called out and faced the men, firm-lipped and with unconquerable resolution in the set of his face and the gleam of his eye.

''Bout this job o' goat-stealin'?' said Cann, with a grave judicial air.

'They stole my billy. I went to fetch him back, an' all the other goats come too,' Dick answered.

'Who helped?'

'Just a dog—a sheep an' cattle dog.'

'What boys?'

'Dunno !'

The examination might as well have ended there. It is a point of honour amongst all schoolboys never to 'split' on mates. The boy who tells is everywhere regarded as a sneak—at Waddy he speedily became a pariah—and Dick was a stickler for points of honour. To be caned was bad, but nothing to the gnawing shame of long weeks following upon a cowardly breach of faith. To all the questions Cann or Peterson could put with the object of eliciting the names of the participators in the big raid, Dick returned only a distressing and wofully stupid 'Dunno!

Peterson scratched his head helplessly, and turned an eye of appeal upon the master.

'Very well,' said Cann, 'we'll just have to guess at the other boys, an' their fathers'll be prevailed on to deal with 'em; but this boy what's been the ring leader ain't got no father, an' it don't seem fair to the others to leave his punishment to a weak woman, does it?'

Peterson's eye appealed to the master again. 'Not fair an' square to the other boys,' he added philosophically.

Joel Ham shook his head.

'I teach your children,' he said. 'I neither hang nor flagellate your criminals.'

'No, no, a-course not,' said Peterson.

'Might you be able to spare us this boy fer the rest o' the afternoon, in the name o' the committee?' asked Cann. 'We'll go an' argue with his mother to leave the lickin' of him to the committee.'

'As a question o' public interest,' said Peterson.

The master consented to this, and Dick was led away between the two men. The interview with Mrs. Haddon took place in the widow's garden. Mrs. Haddon quite understood what it meant when Peterson entered with Dick in custody.

'Good day, Mrs. Haddon,' said the big man gingerly. 'O' course you know all 'bout the trouble o' those goats.'

'Made by you stupid men, mostly,' said Mrs. Haddon.

Peterson stammered and appealed to Cann—he had not expected argument.

'What we men did, ma'am,' said Cann, 'was to protect our property. If the goats hadn't bin brought here there wouldn't 'a' bin any need fer that. Not to mention garden robbin' before, an' broken fences an' such.'

'The School Committee, ma'am,' said Peterson, 'has drawed up a list of suspects, an' the fathers of the boys named will lambaste 'em all thorough. Now it occurred to the committee that your boy, bein' the worst o' the pack, an' havin' confessed, oughter get a fair share o' the hammerin'.'

'An' you've come to offer to do it?'

'That's just it, ma'am, if you'll be so kind.'

Mrs. Haddon had a proper sense of her public duties, a due appreciation of the extent of Dick's wickedness, and a full knowledge of her own inefficiency as a scourger. She looked down and debated anxiously with herself, carefully avoiding Dick's eye, and Dick watched her all the time, but did not speak a word or make a single plea.

'Can't I beat my own boy?' she asked angrily.

'To be certain sure, ma'am, but you're a small bit of a woman, an' it don't seem altogether square dealin' fer the others to get a proper hidin' an' him not. 'Sides, 'twould satisfy public feelin' better if one of us was to lam him. Sound, ma'am, but judicious,' said Cairn.

'Au' 'twould save you further trouble,' added Peterson. ''Twould ease the mind o' Mrs. Ben Steven.' This latter was a weighty argument. Mrs. Haddon's terror of the big woman with the terrible tongue was very real.

'Well, well, well,' she said pitifully. 'You—you won't beat him roughly?'

'I'm a father, as you know, ma'am,' said Peterson, 'an' know what's a fair thing by a boy.'

Cann was unbuckling his belt, and the widow stood trembling, clasping and unclasping her hands. It was a severe ordeal, but public spirit prevailed. Mrs. Haddon turned and fled into the house, and shutting herself in her bedroom buried her head in the pillows and wept.

Ten minutes later she was called out, and Dick was delivered into her hands.

'Better lock him up fer the night,' said Peterson, looking in a puzzled way at Dick.

The boy bad not shed a tear nor uttered a cry. He stood stock still under the flailing, and the heart went out of Peterson. Had Dick fought or struggled, it would have been all right and natural; but this was such a cold-blooded business, and a strange but strongly-felt superiority of spirit in the boy awed and confused the big man, and the beating was but gingerly done after all.

'Come, Dickie, dear,' said Mrs. Haddon, in a penitent tone and with much humility.

She led the boy into his room, and there addressed a diffident and halting speech to him. There were times when Mrs. Haddon had a sense of being younger and weaker than her son, and this was one of them. She felt it her duty to tell Dick of the sinfulness of his conduct, and to try to justify the punishment, but her words fell ineptly from her lips,—she knew them to be vain against the power that held Dick silent and tearless, and yet without a trace of boyish stubbornness. She was not a very wise little woman, or her son's force of character might have been turned early to good works and profitable courses.

In truth the thrashing had had an extraordinary effect on Richard Haddon. For a boy to be kicked, or clouted, or tweaked by strange men is the fortune of war—it is a mere everyday incident, the natural and accepted fate of all boys, and is swiftly resented with a jibe or a missile and forgotten on the spot; but to be taken in cold blood by one strange man, not a schoolmaster or in any way privileged, and deliberately and systematically larruped with a belt under the eyes of another, is burning shame. It tortured all Dick's senses into revolt, and awakened in him a hatred of what he looked upon as the injustice and cowardliness of the outrage that was too deep and too bitter for trivial complaints.

Dick's temperament was poignantly romantic, and the natural tendency had been fed and nourished by indiscriminate reading. The Waddy Public Library, in point of fact, was largely responsible for many of the minor worries and big troubles Dick had been instrumental in visiting on the township. The 'lib'ry' was in the hands of a few men whose literary tastes were decidedly crude, with a strong leaning towards piracy on the high seas, brigandage, buccaneering, and sudden death. Dick read all print that came in his way. Once he started a book he felt in honour bound to finish it, however difficult the task. To set it aside would be a confession of mental weakness. For this reason he had once, during a week of humiliation, fought his way stubbornly through Tupper's 'Proverbial Philosophy.' But it was the rampant fiction that influenced him most directly. He took his romance very seriously; his vivid sympathies were always with the poor persecuted pirate driven to lawless courses by systematic oppression at school, or by a cold proud father's failure to appreciate the humour of his youthful villainies. The bushranger, too, urged from milder courses of crime by the persecutions of the police, found in Dick a devoted friend. It never occurred to the boy that the excuses given were anything but adequate and satisfactory justification for pillage and arson and homicide.

On leaving Dick's room, Mrs. Haddon locked the door very carefully and quietly. She suspected that he was planning mischief that would lead to further trouble, and hoped that by next morning he would be in a frame of mind to be won over by a little motherly strategy. But she went about her work with a heavy heart. Later she took the impenitent young 'duffer' a tea cunningly designed to appeal to his rebellious heart, and spread it neatly on the big dimity-covered box in his bedroom; but Dick was implacable.

In the evening the widow had a visitor in whom she could confide without reservation. Christina Shine had called about her new dress for the Sunday School anniversary, and the weakest and most indulgent of mothers could not have wished for a more sympathetic confidant than big Miss Chris, who saved all her tears for other people's troubles.

'You know, dear,' murmured Mrs. Haddon. 'I can't change Dickie's nature. He's wild, an' he thinks he's all kinds of ridiculous people, an' they lead him into mischief.'

'Poor Dick! I shouldn't have let them beat him,' said Chris, flushing with indignation.

'An' he just as eager for good, you know,' continued the widow, 'but then nobody makes any fuss over him when he does something really creditable.'

Chris nodded her head reproachfully. 'Even father forgets,' she said.

Miss Chris had enormous faith in her father and a great affection for him, and his want of consideration for the boy who she believed had saved him from much suffering, if not a slow and terrible death, was a trait in his character that gave her a good deal of concern.

'Dickie thinks a lot of you, Christina,' said Mrs. Haddon. 'P'r'aps if you went an' spoke a few words with him he might be persuaded to overlook what's past.'

'Yes, yes,' said Chris brightly.

'Tell him how much trouble he is givin' his poor mother, who'd be alone but for him. You might dwell on that, my dear, will you?

'I will, of course; and it's true, too.'

'It always seems to soften him. If it doesn't, you can hint I'm not very well tonight.'

Miss Chris, who stood head and shoulders above her friend, laid an affectionate hand upon the plump and rosy widow.

'When he's unmanageable other ways I take ill for a little while, you know,' said the widow mournfully. 'Come in,' she cried in answer to a sharp knock at the door.

The caller was Harry Hardy. He stopped short in confusion on beholding Christina Shine, and Chris blushed warmly in answering his curt 'Good evening.'

'I called to see Dick 'bout that tin dish,' he said, beating his leg with his hat in an obvious effort to appear at his ease.

Mrs. Haddon glanced sharply from Harry to Chris and conceived a new interest.

'I will go to Dickie,' said Chris, taking the key from the widow.

Mrs. Haddon explained to Harry when they were alone, and added insinuatingly:

'That's a dear good girl.'

'Shine's daughter?' said Harry with emphasis.

'Yes, Shine's daughter, an' she's as good as he pretends to be.'

Harry contrived to look quite vindictive and gave no answer, and a minute later Chris returned. Dick had barred his door on the other side and would give her no reply.

'The window!' cried Mrs. Haddon.

Harry hastened out and around the house. Finding the window of Dick's room unlatched he threw it up and climbed into the room. The door was barred with a chair; this he removed, and

Mrs. Haddon entered with a candle. There was no sign of the boy, but pinned on the wall was a large strip of paper on which was written in bold letters:

'Goodbye for ever. I've run away to be a bushranger.—DICK HADDON. P.S.—Pursuit is useless.'

The widow sank upon the edge of the bed and mopped her tears with a snow-white apron.

'That means that I sha'n't see him for two days at least,' she said, 'unless I'm either taken very ill or attacked by a burglar. Why, why can't a poor woman be allowed to bring up her own children in her own way?'

Chris was soothing and Harry reassuring.

'He knows how to take care of himself. He'll be all right,' cried the young man heartily.

'If you could get some o' the boys to let him know I wasn't safe from a sundowner, or a drunken drover, or someone, I'd be much obliged,' said Mrs. Haddon.

'Very well,' replied Harry, laughing. 'I'll manage that.'

Mrs. Haddon smiled through her tears, much comforted, and turned her mind to other things. Within the space of about two minutes she had satisfied herself that no woman in all the world would make Harry Hardy a better wife than Christina Shine, and, being convinced, it was manifestly her duty to help the good cause.

'Won't you stay awhile an' keep me company, Christina?' she asked. 'Harry'll see you home.'

Miss Chris would stay with pleasure, but she couldn't think of troubling Mr. Hardy, and she said so with a girl's shyness. Mr. Hardy stammered a little and tried to say that it would be no trouble at all, but the effort was not a brilliant success considered as a compliment. He longed to stay, and yet hated and feared to stay. This anomalous frame of mind was new; it confused and staggered him. He seemed to be swayed by an external impulse, and resented it with miserable self-deceit. But he stayed.

Harry did not greatly enrich the conversation during the hour spent in Mrs. Haddon's kitchen, but he found his eyes drawn to the handsome profile of Christina Shine, standing out in its soft fairness against the dark wall like a wonderfully carven cameo. Her hair, turned back in beautifully flowing lines, helped the queenly suggestion. Harry looked resolutely away; then he heard her voice, sweet and low, and recollected that beside himself no man, woman, or child in Waddy was mean enough to cherish a hard thought of Miss Chris. Beside himself? He turned fiercely, as if for refuge, to his dislike for her father. His failure to find the smallest clue to justify his opinion and that of his mother as to the real merits of the crime at the Silver Stream left him more bitter towards the searcher, the one man whose words and actions had convicted Frank. He would not admit his hatred to be unfair or unreasonable, and his moroseness deepened as time showed him how heavily the disgrace and sorrow lay upon his mother, although her words were always cheerful and her faith unconquerable.

The walk home that night was not a pleasant one to Chris. She was piteously anxious to have him think kindly of her, and this made itself felt through Harry's roughest mood; then he had an absurd impulse to throw out his arms and offer her protection and tenderness. Absurd because, turning towards her, he was compelled to look upwards into her eyes, and the tall, strong figure at his side, walking erect, with firm square shoulders, dwarfed his conceit till he felt himself morally and physically a pigmy.

Their conversation drifted to dangerous ground.

'Have you found nothing to help poor Frank?' she asked.

'Nothing,' he said sharply and suspiciously.

'I am sorry. Oh! how I wish I could aid you!'

'There's one man that might do that, but he won't.'

'One man? One? You said that strangely. One man? Who would be so brutal?'

His silence stung her. She turned sharply.

'Oh, you don't mean—surely, surely you don't mean father?'

Again he did not answer.

'It is not right,' she cried out. 'You can have no reason to think that. You say it to hurt me.'

'I didn't say it.'

'You meant it—you mean it still.'

She quickened her pace and they exchanged no more words until the walk was ended, then she gave him her hand over the gate.

'Goodnight,' she said. 'You were more generous as a boy, Harry.'

He took her hand. It was ungloved, and felt small and tender in his hard palm. The touch awoke a sudden passion in him. Both of his hands held hers, his head bent over it, and he blurted something in apology. 'Don't mind me! I didn't mean it! Please, please—' He did not know what he was saying, and the words were too low and confused to reach her ears; but she went up the garden path with an elate bird in her heart singing such a song of gladness that the world was filled with its music, and the girl knew its meaning and yet wondered at it.

Harry stood nervously gripping the pickets of the gate and gazed after her, and continued gazing for many minutes when she had gone. Then he swung off into the bush, walking rapidly, and was glad in a stern rebellious way—glad in spite of his mission, in spite of his brother, in spite of and defiance of every thing.

CHAPTER XIII.

MEANWHILE matters of interest were progressing below at the Mount of Gold mine. The juvenile shareholders of the Company had done a fair amount of work in the soft reef of the new drive at odd times during the last fortnight; and the drive, which diminished in circumference as it progressed, and threatened presently to terminate in a sharp point, had been driven in quite fifteen feet. But tonight the young prospectors were not interested in mining operations. On top Dick Haddon's big billy-goat was feeding greedily on the lush herbage of the Gaol Quarry; below, Dick and his boon companions were preparing for a tremendous adventure.

After escaping from his room Dick had hunted up Jacker Mack, Phil Doon, and Billy Peterson. He came upon the two former at a propitious time, when both were slowly recovering from the physical effects of an 'awful doing' administered by their respective fathers at the instigation of the School Committee; when they were still filled with bitterness towards all mankind, and satisfied that life was hollow and vain, and there was no happiness or peace for a well meaning small boy on this side of the grave. Peterson had succeeded in avoiding the head of his house so far, but was filled with anxiety. Dick easily persuaded all three to accompany him to the mine, there to discuss the situation and plot a fitting revenge.

His proposal was that they should all turn bushrangers on the spot, form a band to ravage and lay waste the country, and visit upon society the just consequences of its rashness and folly in tyrannising over its boys, misunderstanding them, and misconstruing their highest and noblest intentions.

'When anyone shakes our goats, ain't we a right to demand 'em back at the point o' the sword?' asked Dick indignantly.

The boys were unanimous. They had such a right—nay, it was a bounden duty.

'Very well, then, what'd they wanter lick us fer?' continued Dick. 'Won't they be sorry when they hear about us turnin' bushrangers, that's all!

'D'ye really think they will, though?' asked Jacker McKnight dubiously. He had found his parents very unromantic people, who took a severely commonplace view of things, and retained unquestioning faith in the strap as a means of elevating the youthful idea.

'Why, o' course!' cried Dick. 'When our mothers read in the papers 'bout the lives we're leadin', it'll make 'em cry all night 'cause o' the way we've been treated; an' you coves' fathers'll hear tell o' yer great adventures, an' they'll know what sort o' chaps they knocked about an' abused, an' they'll respect you an' wish you was back home so's they could make up for the fatal past.'

Jacker looked doubtful still; he could not imagine his parents in that character; but Peterson was delighted with the prospect, and Phil Doon, whose mother was a large, stout woman, who spent half her day in bed reading sentimental stories, was quite impressed, and enlisted on the spot.

'You'll be my lieutenant, you know, Jacker,' said Dick; 'an' we'll call you Fork Lightnin'.'

'Hoo! Will you, though?' cried Jacker.

Dick nodded and made an affirmative noise between his closed lips.

'Fork Lightnin',' said Jacker, trying the name. 'Sounds well, don't it? What sorter feller will I be? Brave, eh?'

'Frightened o' neither man nor devil, but awful cruel, 'cause you was crossed in love.'

Jacker was delighted. He was naturally a combative youth, with a fine contempt for rules that would deny him the advantages to be derived from his ability as a swift and vigorous kicker; so a bloodthirsty and rebellious character was quite to his taste.

'Not crossed in love, though,' he complained. 'That seems measley, don't it? S'pose I shot a man once, an' the p'lice won't let me have no peace.'

'Good enough!' said Dick.

'Then I'm in. When do we start?'

'To-morrer night. We want one more. Twitter will come. That'll be five. Five is a fine gang; sides, we don't want fellers what ain't got billies. Bushrangers ain't no account on foot. My men must be all mounted. So I propose we meet on the toll-bar road just when it's gettin' dark, all riding our billy-goats an' armed to the teeth; an' we'll stick up all the Cow Flat people goin' home from Yarraman.'

'My word!' cried Phil ecstatically. 'We owe it to that lot.'

'Couldn't we start now?' said Peterson, who had been sitting with wide eyes and open mouth, and was consumed with impatience.

'Oh, no,' said Dick; 'we gotter prepare our arms an' ammunition an' things. An' Saturdee night's best, 'cause the Cow Flats what have been to Yarraman buyin' things come up to the Drovers' Arms on the coach, an' walk home from there.'

It was agreed that Peterson should stay with Dick in the mine that night. The boys had no longer any fear of the black hole discovered at the end of the main drive. An exploring party had made its way through the opening and into the workings beyond, and had found itself in a drive communicating with the Red Hand shaft. Dick, who once in an emergency had served as tool-boy in the Silver Stream for a fortnight, knew that at a lower level there was another and a much longer Red Hand drive by which access to the Silver Stream No. 1 workings was possible; but he kept this knowledge to himself.

Shortly after midnight Dick and Billy ventured to return to Waddy, with the idea of securing Billy's goat, Hector, a sturdy black brute much admired as the most inveterate 'rusher' in the country. With the boys of Waddy a goat that butted or 'rushed' was highly prized as an animal of spirit. Peterson caught his goat, and then Dick, with unnecessary wariness and great waste of stratagem, 'stuck up' his own home, and secured a parcel of food carefully left for him on the table near the unlatched window by a thoughtful mother.

On Saturday the other boys turned up at the appointed time. There were rules commanding the utmost caution in entering the mine by daylight. Every care had to be taken to satisfy the shareholders that no stranger was in sight, and the last boy was compelled to keep a vigilant look-out while the others were descending, and then to make his way to the opening by a roundabout route, exercising a vigilance that would have puzzled an army of black-trackers.

Dick, who before leaving home had rifled his small savings bank, had provided Jacker Mack with money for supplies, and Jacker brought with him a pound of candles, some black material for masks, and half a dozen packets of Chinese crackers. The Chinese crackers represented cartridges for the pistols of Red Hand's gang. Dick had decided to be known as Red Hand. The pistols were made by fashioning a piece of soft wood in the shape of a stock, and securing to this a scrap of hollow bone for a barrel. Into the barrel a cracker was thrust, the wick was ignited at a piece of smouldering 'punk '—which could be carried in the pocket in a tin matchbox—and it only needed the exercise of a little imagination to satisfy oneself that the resulting explosion spread death and desolation in the ranks of the enemy.

All preliminaries were arranged during the afternoon: in the evening, just before night fell, Dick and Peterson, hidden with their trusty steeds amongst the saplings about three hundred yards beyond the toll-bar, awaited the coming of their companions in crime. They had not long to wait; in a few minutes Jacker Mack, Ted, and Phil Doon came riding up the dusty track on their brave billies. They were accompanied by a pedestrian, an interloper, who lurked behind and evidently did not anticipate a friendly reception. It was Gable.

'He saw us comin' an' he would foller,' explained Jacker.

'Yah!' cried Dick in disgust; 'why didn't you boot him?'

'So I did. Fat lot o' good that done. He otl'y bellered like a bullock, an' kep' on follerin'. We pretended we wasn't goin' nowhere, but he just hung round an' couldn't be fooled.'

Dick approached the old man threateningly.

'Clear out!' he said.

Gable put up a defensive elbow and backed away, knuckling his eye piteously the while.

'Are you goin'?' cried Dick, and kicked Gable just as he would have kicked any inconvenient and mutinous youngster in the same case.

'You look out whatcher doin',' muttered the old man, skipping about to avoid the second kick. I'll get someone what'll show you,' he added darkly.

Dick ran at him with a big stick, but Gable only retreated a few yards. He threw stones, knocking up the dust about the old man's feet, and Gable hopped and skipped with the agility of a kid;

but after each attack he returned humbly to the heels of the party like a too faithful dog.

'Better let him come, I s'pose,' said Dick at last. 'Come on, nuisance!

Gamble jigged up, radiant, and grinning all over his face.

Red Hand selected a suitable clump of saplings about half a mile from the toll-bar, and the gang secreted themselves and made preparation for the first attack. They carried their 'cartridges' loose in small bags hung from their belts, in which were thrust three or four of the bone-barrelled pistols. Black masks were donned, Fork Lightning was stationed on a stump near by to give warning of the approach of a victim, and the others took up suitable positions, while Dick fitted Gable with a mask so that his appearance might not discredit the gang.

'There,' said Dick. 'you're a bushranger now, re member.'

'Crickey!' cried the old man, delighted.

'An'; you'll be hanged if you're caught.'

'Oh, crickey!' Gable was more delighted still, and danced up and down, clapping his hands.

Suddenly there was a warning whistle from Fork Lightning, and that black scoundrel crept stealthily in amongst his mates.

'Someone's comin',' he said.

'To horse!' cried Red Hand. 'When I give the word, gallop into the road an' cut off their retreat. Don't fire till I give orders, an', mind, spare the women an' children.'

Sounds of horses' hoofs were heard approaching. The gang, masked, and mounted on bridled and saddled goats, anxiously awaited the word of command.

'Back, men, back for your lives!' cried Dick. 'It's the p'lice, fifteen thousan' strong, an' they're hot on our track; but Red Hand's gang will never be taken alive.'

The bushrangers cowered back into the shadow as a party of three young men riding tired horses ambled slowly by, singing dolorously and brandishing bottles. Red Hand was discreet if valiant. However, another warning came not a minute later. This time it was a solitary man in a farmer's cart; his old horse was shuffling wearily through the dust at a jog-trot, and the boys could just discern the tall gaunt figure of the driver.

'Surround him, my lads!' yelled Red Hand. 'Bail up!' he cried riding forward on Butts and presenting what passed very well for a pistol in the dusk. 'Your money or your life!

The driver snatched a stick out of the cart and, uttering a great yell, began to belabour his poor horse mercilessly.

'Fire!' shrieked the implacable Red Hand; and a few seconds later six crackers exploded about the unhappy farmer, who instantly fell upon his knees and, still pounding at his horse, was whirled away amongst the trees by the startled brute. For some time the bush-rangers could hear him still hammering his old horse, and catch the sound of his voice encouraging the poor animal to more reckless speed, and the crashing of saplings as the dray pounded its way through the undergrowth. The boys were delighted; this was noble sport; the lust of victory was upon them. Gable was waving his arms and ejaculating 'Oh, crickey!' and the others capered about on their goats, and felt themselves to be very large and terrible persons indeed.

'Bushrangin's easy ez snuff,' said Peterson.

'Course it is,' said Phil. 'Wisher few p'lice'd come along and let's have a go at 'em.'

'That was splendidly done, men,' said Red Hand with superior coolness. 'Back to your places. Someone's comin'.'

The next corner was a man on a grey horse.

'Bail up!' cried Red Hand from the cover of the saplings. 'Stir a foot an' you're a dead man.'

The rider waited for no more, but threw himself forward on his horse's neck, dug in his spurs, and galloped furiously away in the direction of Cow Flat, hearing the reports of the boys' crackers only when he was far out of range. The next victim was a small boy on a pony, who, as soon as he heard the terrible command, fell plump on to the road and then jumped up and fled in terror after his bolting horse. The gang had now spread consternation and dismay along quite two miles of the highway, and were jubilant in consequence and primed for any adventure however desperate.

Dick entertained his men with talk of the glory they had earned by their actions that night, and predicted a reputation for them beside which the reputation of every other gang of bushrangers Australia had known would fade into insignificance.

The boys listened soberly, very elated and perfectly happy.

'But we mustn't let the nex' one go so easy,' said the leader.

'Here is someone,' whispered Fork Lightning.

Sure enough, a pedestrian could be dimly discerned approaching from the direction of the toll-gate.

'To yer horses! commanded Red Hand.

'Why, it's a woman,' said Peterson.

'Who cares?'

'Thought bushrangers never did nothin' to the women?'

'Oh,' said Dick, 'that's on'y when they're young an' pretty. If this one's young an' pretty I'll 'polo gise, an' it'll be all right. There ain't no reason not to bail 'em up when they're big an' strong an' able to take care o' themselves.'

This seemed quite reasonable to the gang, and they saw as the lady approached that her size did not give her any claim upon their gallantry. She was very tall and stout. In point of fact she was the woman who had driven through Waddy on the day after the goat raid, calling down infamy on the township.

'Bail up!' cried Red Hand.

Phil, Ted, and Peterson rode up in front, barring the way. Red Hand and Fork Lightning approached from either side, and all presented pistols. The woman backed away a few paces, staring at the goat-mounted, masked apparitions that seemed to have started out of the ground under her very nose, but the bushrangers followed her up.

'Be not afraid, madam,' said Dick in his best literary style; 'I am Red Hand, an' if you obey no injury'll be done you.'

The woman threw up her hands in amazement.

'Well I never,' she muttered. Without the least warning she darted at Ted, seized him, pulled him from the back of his billy, and in spite of his wild struggles promptly bent him over her knee; then, with a hand like that of a navvy, backed by a great muscular arm, began to spank the terrible outlaw.

'You look out! You le' me alone!' gasped Ted, struggling and writhing with all his power; but the flailing went on, bat—bat—bat—with blows that might have disturbed an elephant. Ted's feelings became too strong for words; he started to howl, and the night re-echoed with the cries of the outraged bushranger. The rest of the gang stood mute, staring at this shocking scene, amazed and deeply offended. It was all so incongruous, so utterly opposed to rule and precedent; they could scarcely believe their senses. Dick was the first to recover.

'Fire!' commanded Red Hand.

Cracker-wicks were ignited and four explosions followed, but when the smoke was gone the gang still beheld the terrible woman beating away at their unhappy comrade, too absorbed in a congenial occupation to care a solitary button for the fire of the outlaws. This was too much for Jacker. The brothers were always ready to fight each other's battles, let the odds be what they might, and the elder rushed to the rescue. The onslaught did not seem to make the least difference, however; the woman simply dropped Ted and grasped his brother. Jacker Mack was a strong boy and a fierce one, but strength and tricks availed him nothing against those powerful arms; in ten seconds he was in Ted's place, and the massive hand was dealing with him, heavily and with startling rapidity.

'Charge!' shrieked Red Hand.

But the gang was demoralized. Peterson and Doon moved back from the danger, and only one member obeyed the order— Peterson's formidable goat, Hector. Goodness knows what inspired the animal; possibly a grateful instinct, probably the sight of means to do an ill deed. Anyhow, he charged. He rushed the woman from a commanding position, with force and judgment, and a second later Jacker, woman, and goat were rolling and struggling in the dust. Red Hand and the faithful Ted dragged Jacker from the hands of the enemy, and the gang fled to a safe distance, and watched the shadowy form of the woman as she gathered herself up and shook the dust out of her dress. Then for two minutes she stood and addressed them through the darkness in strident tones and language that would have shocked an old drover or a railway ganger.

'Bushrangin' ain't up to much,' whimpered Ted, rubbing himself with both hands.

'It's rot!' said Jacker fiercely.

Peterson and Doon muttered words of approval, and Dick felt that four pairs of reproachful eyes were turned upon him. Gable was still hopping about ecstatically murmuring 'Crickey! Oh, crickey!' as he had been doing all through the encounter.

'How'd I know?' said Dick in self-defence. 'You fellers oughter had better sense'n to let her get hold o' you.'

'You started it!' groaned Ted.

'Pretty lot o' bushrangers you are, anyway,' Dick sneered, 'howlin' 'cause a woman gave you a bit of a doin'.'

'How' d you like it?' asked Jacker sullenly.

Dick disdained to reply; indeed his attention was occupied with more important things. Out of the night came the sound of galloping hoofs and calling voices. The boys listened anxiously for a minute or so, and then realised their danger.

'They're after us!' exclaimed Dick. 'Scatter an' run for the scrub. Meet at the mine!'

The pursuers dashed up on their horses just as the boys swarmed over the fence into Wilson's paddock. It was the party of young men who first passed the bushrangers, and the man on the grey horse. They were armed with bottles, three parts drunk, and bent on making an heroic capture. Some of them sprang from their horses and pursued the flying bushrangers through the trees.

Dick and Peterson reached the Gaol Quarry safely, and sat in doleful silence waiting for their mates, and wondering if any had been taken. Ted and Jacker joined them a few minutes later, and Phil Doon came limping up in the course of a quarter of an hour. He had bad news.

'They've got Gable!' he cried from a distance.

'No. Go on!'

'S'help me. I fell gettin' over the fence an' sneaked into a hollow tree, an' saw 'em snavel him. 'Here's one of 'em' said one, an' they put him on a horse an' tied his legs under its belly, an' they've gone into Yarraman with him.'

'Gee-rusalem! An' what'd he say?' gasped Dick.

'Nothin' 'sept 'Oh, crickey!''

'Well, he won't split on us. He won't know a word about it in the mornin'. We're all right if none of us blabs. You fellers goin' to stay?'

'I ain't. I'm sick o' bein' a bushranger,' said Jacker, with a reflective and remorseful rub at his hurt place.

'So'm I,' said Ted.

Phil Doon, it appeared, had pressing reasons for returning home, but Peterson remembered that he had still an account to settle with his father, and resolved to share Dick's fortune.

'Right you are,' said Dick. 'You fellers bring some crib to-morrer, an' if you see Parrot Cann tell him to fetch some too—an', mind, no blabbin'.'

Reverses of this kind did not depress him; he had experienced many failures, but the wreck of one enterprise only implied the necessity of starting another.

'Say,' he said mysteriously, 'there's a big reason why we should keep things darker'n ever. Listen. We've struck the reef!

The others stared incredulously.

'You're havin' us,' said Jacker.

'Am I? Tell 'em, Billy.'

'No, he ain't,' said Peterson. 'It's true, strike me breath. We got a specimen this mornin' wif three colours in it.'

'So if anyone's told where we're hidin' they'll see the stone an' go an' jump the mine,' said Dick artfully.

CHAPTER XIV.

NEITHER of the McKnights nor Parrot came to the boys on the Sunday morning, and Dick and Billy, whose larder had run short, were compelled to make a raid on Wilson's garden—which yielded little in the way of fruit, but carrots and turnips were not despised. At about eleven o'clock, from an outlook amongst some scrub on the Red hand tip, Dick and his mate could see that something unusual was going on in Waddy. They saw a crowd gathering near the Drovers' Arms, and could catch the glitter of the accoutrements of a couple of troopers. A little later a mounted policeman actually came cantering into the paddock and forced them to creep stealthily to their safe retreat at the bottom of the mine. Here they sat and talked, prey to the most torturing curiosity. Dick's theories to explain the apparent sensation were fine and large, investing himself and his companion with profound dignity as the heroes of a thrilling adventure; but Billy's for a wonder were somewhat gloomy, reckoning with parental castigations and ten years in gaol. This unusual frame of mind was induced, no doubt, by a limited and strictly vegetarian diet. Dick took into account the possibility that Jacker, Ted, or Phil Doon might divulge the Company's great secret, although his faith in the loyalty of his mates was strong. If the worst came to the worst he meditated a retreat through the hole into the Red Hand drive, and flight from thence down the ladder-shaft and into the spacious workings of the Silver Stream.

To help pass the time the two worked a little in the drive, breaking down about a hundredweight of the quartz ridge that had cut in across the narrow face. The stone showed gold freely. At another time this would have occasioned the wildest jubilation, but now everything was secondary to the wonder inspired by what they had seen in Waddy, combined with their dread of the results of last night's work. It was well on in the afternoon when they were joyfully startled by the sound of a whistle in the shaft.

'Hello, below there!' cried a voice, and a few seconds later Parrot Cann, too excited to go through the usual formalities, rattled down and landed in a heap at Dick's feet.

'What's up?' asked Dick eagerly, as Parrot crept into the drive.

'Oh, I say,' gasped Parrot, 'youse fellers are in fer it!'

'How? Who split? What're the troopers doin'?'

'They're after youse.'

'After us!' Peterson's face paled at this corroboration of his worst suspicions.

'My oath! Gable's in gaol at Yarraman; Phil an' Jacker an' Ted's been took, an' now they're after you.'

Fer what?'

'Rob'ry under arms, the feller said, an' shooting with intent' r somethin'.

Dick whistled incredulously. Here was fame, here was glory. His favourite authors were justified, and yet there was the dark side; thought of his mother came with a sharp twinge.

'Who went an' split—Ted?'

'None o' the Company,' said Parrot. 'The troopers came to arrest Gable's mates, thinkin' they was men, an' Toll-bar Sam told who you was. He saw you all last night.'

'Did they take Ted, an' Jacker, an' Phil right away?'

'Um. Off to Yarraman. You don't know what a row's on. It's awful. Them fellers what captured Gable told a yarn about a gang o' bushrangers'n a terrible fight, an' swore Gable was the blood thirstiest of 'em all. The Yarraman Mercury printed a special paper this mornin', with all about the outbreak of a new gang o' bushrangers in great big type, an' every one's near mad about it, 'sept those what's laughin'.'

The boys gazed at each other for a few moments in silence. It took some time to grasp the astounding facts. They were real bushrangers, their escapades had been printed in the papers, they were actually being pursued by bona fide troopers on flesh-and-blood horses—what more could ambitious youth demand?

Dick's unconquerable romanticism upheld him; he had achieved distinction, and the prospect of deluding and outwitting the police after the manner of his most brilliant heroes filled him with delight; but Billy Peterson was awed and out of spirits.

'It's all right, Billy,' said Dick, 'they'll never find us here. We can defy 'em all fer weeks.'

'Yes,' said Billy bitterly, 'but I'm hungry!'

'You didn't bring no crib, Parrot.' Dick had made it a rule that the necessities of a shareholder temporarily in difficulties and hiding in the mine were to be attended to by the free members of the Company or others who, like Parrot Cann, were admitted to the Company's councils.

'Wasn't game,' answered Parrot; 'they'd 'a' watched me. Had to sneak away as it was.'

Dick puckered his face wisely. It was a very dirty face just now; his red hair, long neglected, hung in wisps over his forehead and about his ears, giving him an elfish look in the candlelight.

'Never mind,' he said, 'bring us some tonight, first chance you get; but be cunnin'. We'll shake some fruit soon ez it's dark, to keep us goin'.'

'What's the good o' fruit?' groaned Peterson. Fruit ain't grub.'

Dick looked anxiously at his mate. There was an immediate danger that the outlaws might be starved out.

'Parrot's goin' to fetch some,' he said brightly.

Parrot promised to do his best for them, but, although they waited till nearly nine o'clock in hungry anticipation, he did not return that night. The last carrot was eaten, and a cautious excursion to Summers' orchard produced nothing, Maori's warning bark driving the boys back to the Gaol Quarry, empty and disconsolate. Billy could hold out no longer, but he did not meditate an open desertion.

'I'll jes' sneak round our house till I get a chance to slip in an' shake a junk o' bread or somethin'; then I'll come right back an' we'll go halves,' he said.

'Sure you'll come back, are you?'

''S that wet? 'S that dry?'

Dick accepted the oath. He would have gone home himself with burglarious intentions, but feared that the official anxiety to catch the notorious head of the new gang must have concentrated police vigilance about his mother's house, and the risk was too great.

'Hurry back ez quick's you can,' he commanded. "'N you'll have to be slyer 'n a black snake 'r they'll nab you.'

Dick spent the first hour alone under the saplings in the quarry, and then, as Billy had not returned and the time hung heavily on his hands, he crept out and up the hill towards the Red Hand. He prowled about amongst the old tips for a time, then seated himself at the foot of a dead butt and gave himself up to thought. He began to fear that Peterson would prove unfaithful, or, worse still, that he had fallen into the hands of the enemy; and the idea made him very uneasy. He hesitated about returning to the drive.

Although he was singularly free from the superstitious fears that would make such a place a haunt of horrors to the average youngster, the notion of sleeping alone below there did not please him, and he had still some hope of hearing Billy's signal.

He was beginning to feel the pangs of hunger, too, and now that it was too late recollected that he might have found a ministering angel in Miss Chris. It would have been an easy matter to have met her when coming through the paddock from chapel at nine o'clock, and an easier matter to have appealed to her tender sympathies with a story of hunger and misfortune. The boy's thoughts lingered with Miss Chris; he found a melancholy satisfaction in the belief that she would pity him, and probably shed a few tears over the sorrows of a noble and generous youth driven to crime by persecution, and outlawed through the machinations of an unscrupulous constabulary. So real could he make these sentimental fancies that her keen sorrow for him filled him with acute emotions of self-pity, and a large tear actually rolled down his freckled nose.

Suddenly romance was swept out of his mind, and wonder and fear possessed him. Throwing himself forward, he crept noiselessly to a rotten trunk over grown with suckers that lay between him and the Red Hand shaft, and, raising himself on his hands, peered through the bushes. A belt of pale golden light, thrown by the rising moon between the converging tips, lay right across the mouth of the shaft; and up through the rusty bark of the door were thrust a thin long hand and a bony arm. As Dick gazed, trembling and amazed, a second hand appeared. He heard the rattle of a chain, the click of a lock; then the door was thrust upwards and let noiselessly back upon the timber. Now a man's head came into view, and up out of the shaft crawled a figure that Dick recognised in spite of the precautions taken. Reaching into the darkness of the shaft, the man, who remained on his knees in a crouching position, drew up a skin bag containing something of considerable weight apparently; then came another head, and a second man slid, snake-like, from the shaft. At the sight of the second, Dick, whose heart seemed to have swollen within him to an enormous size, gasped aloud; he heard a warning 'Hush!' from the shaft, and lay perfectly still. The door was closed, the lock clicked again, and when he ventured to look the two men were stealing away towards the quarry. The boy crept after them to the extent of the trunk behind which he was hidden, and when he looked again they had disappeared. Creeping silently in the shadows and amongst the scrub ferns, Dick followed until, resting a moment, he heard distinctly the words:

'Why did you hit him again? Good God! did you want to kill him?' The voice was Ephraim Shine's.

'No. That won't kill him. Don't be so blasted chicken-hearted I didn't want to be seen, you ass!' Dick knew the voice for that of Joe Rogers, whose face he had seen in the moonlight.

'The lick I gave him was enough; it must 'a' stunned him.' Shine spoke in a low voice.

'D'yer think he recognised you?' asked Rogers hoarsely.

'No, I was in the shadder. I d'know, though—I d'know.'

'Listen here, an' take a grip on that screamin' woman's tongue o' yours. It don't matter whether he saw you 'r didn't see you, 'cause he won't live t' tell it.'

'Oh, Heaven! Oh, Lord! Oh, Lord! I didn't mean that—I swear to Heaven, I on'y meant to stun him!'

'I know yer didn't. Pull yerself together, you quiverin' idiot. D'ye think I meant to do murder?'

'No, no, no; o' course not. P'raps he ain't hurt ez bad ez you think.'

'Tain't the hurt, it's this. I on'y thought of it comin' up the ladders. Did yer notice where he fell? He went back down the incline, fallin' with his head a few feet up from the pumps. Know what that means? Harry Hardy'll be found drowned!'

Dick heard Shine gasping for breath, and Rogers went on coolly:

'He was in the Sunday afternoon shift at the pumps. The water in the incline'll rise up over him before the first workin' shift goes down.'

'Let's go back, an' drag him out. Let's go back!'

'Sit still, damn you! Go back an' be trapped, or be recognised if his senses return? His candle was burnin'.'

'But it's murder—it's murder!'

'Is it? Listen here. I noticed a lump o' rock had fallen out o' the roof. It'll be thought he was stunned by it, an' drowned in the water as it rose.'

'Man, it's terrible. Two brothers! My sin is findin' me out, Joe Rogers!

'Shut up cant, d'you hear! It served him thunderin' well right. What'd he want to come pokin' into the mine at all fer? What the devil did the other one interfere in what didn't concern him fer? But we've got it in spite of 'em.' Rogers had plunged his hands into the skin bag.

'All, Rogers, all!' For the moment Shine's cupidity triumphed over his fears. 'Every blessed ounce. All the stuff I've been puddlin' away in the floor o' that drive fer weeks. An' the nugget, ain't it a beauty—ain't it a beauty? An' to think I've been shepherdin' that daisy fer ten shifts!

Dick crept closer and, peering through a slit in the great hollow trunk of the tree, saw that Rogers was handling the contents of the bag. On his knee lay a gleaming mass that the boy knew to be a beautiful nugget.

'What devil's luck brought that young fool to the 'T' drive?'

'He must 'a' heard you splashin'. You wasn't careful.'

'Ez careful ez I could be. I had to scoop the stuff outer holes in the wet floor o' the drive where I'd puddled it away in the mud.'

'Ain't there a chance fer him—not a single hope?'

'Oh, yes, but it's a bad un for us if he recognised you. There's the chance o' him recoverin', an' draggin' himself out o' the water. Hullo! what in hell's name's happenin' now? Quick, cut for the scrub; someone's comin'. I'll hide the bag here. Come back when they've passed.'

Dick heard Rogers throw the calfskin bag into the hollow of the tree and scrape the loose rubbish over it, and then both glided away in the shadow of the Red Hand tips. From beyond the tips came the beat of a horse's hoofs, and the sound of human voices. Dick's first thought was of his pursuers, the troopers; his second of his escape; his third sent the blood surging through his veins and his heart beating like a piston. A grand thought, a magnificent thought! He could have cried out with exultation as it swept into his mind. Creeping around the tree he silently unearthed the gold-stealers' bag and dragged it after him, retreating to the quarry. At the edge of the incline he let the bag slide, and it went to the bottom with the noise a cow might have made moving through the scrub. Dick followed, scrambling down the rocks. Having recovered the bag, he dragged it under the scrub to the opening in the wall, hastily concealing his tracks. There was some difficulty in getting the bag through the space in the rock but he managed well; then he swung it free of the ladder, so that it dropped into the shaft and on to the broken reef below. He clambered through on to the ladder, drew the loose scrub ferns into their places, and fitted into the crevice the wedge-shaped stone, kept as a last concealment of the retreat.

Standing on the ladder Dick waited, and presently heard sounds of men making their way into the Gaol Quarry. His suspicions were correct: the party was seeking him. Presently he heard a voice he recognised as that of Jim Peetree, saying:

'This is the spot, boss; I've seen him here scores o' times. If he ain't here I give it up.'

Dick heard the jingle of spurs, and an authoritative voice.

'Search all about amongst the scrub and the rocks. Keep my horse ready in case the boy makes a bolt for it.'

There were three or four men, Peterson and McKnight amongst them. They searched industriously, coming pretty close to Dick's hiding place more than once.

'We should have let the other lad go and have followed him,' said the authoritative voice. 'Fancy three troopers being kept a whole day and half the night dancing after a bit of a kid.'

Dick's heart thrilled at this.

'Well, he's not here, that's certain sure,' said Peterson. 'My boy said he left him in the paddock, an' I s'pose he can't be fur, but I tell you you won't get him, he's that cunnin'. He's fuller o' wickedness an' wisdom, an' good an' bad, than any boy you ever see, sergeant.'

'Ah, well, we'll move on and try the other spot; but I would like to have the dear boy for five minutes now, while I feel in the humour to knock some of the bad out of him.'

They started off again, and when the beat of hoofs was lost in the distance Dick crept from his hiding-place and climbed up out of the quarry. He now stole to a position from which he could command a view of the hollow tree, whilst remaining under thick shelter and leaving himself an excellent opening for retreat. His blood was full of the excitement of this new adventure, a true adventure dealing with theft and murder. He was afraid, terribly afraid, but it seemed to him that all his emotions were held in abeyance: he was conscious of their existence, but they no longer ruled him. One thing was paramount, his determination to know everything of the crime that had been perpetrated in the main drive of the Silver Stream. Fragments of thoughts seemed to flicker up like flames within him and die out again instantly, and he repeated constantly under his breath without knowing why:

'Her father! Her father! Her father!'

There was something to be done—much to be done, and one important thing, one thing that meant life or death; but these must come after. Now he was wild to know all that the thieves might tell.

Rogers was the first to come crawling back to the tree. He scattered the loose rubbish in the hollow trunk, and uttered a fierce oath.

'It's gone, gone, gone!' he almost shouted as Shine joined him.

'You lie, you lie! You want to rob me!' the long searcher had flown at his throat, and for a few seconds they struggled together, but Rogers threw the older man off fiercely and dragged him by the throat to the tree.

'Feel, search, look for yourself, you hound!' he cried. 'Could I eat it?'

Shine, going on his hands and knees, clawed amongst the rubbish; then, whining and muttering, went scratching about like a dog, seeking high and low, and Rogers followed him blaspheming with insensate fury.

'It's no good, I tell you, you snuffling, whimpering, white-livered cur!' he said. 'Those men have got away with it, curse them!'

But Ephraim continued his search, creeping under the scrub, scratching in the grass; and as he searched his whimper grew louder and louder, and he cried like an old woman at a wake.

'An' we killed a man, we killed a man!' he wailed again and again.

Rogers rushed at him viciously, and kicked him heavily in the ribs.

'Get up, you dog!' he cried hoarsely, with a string of oaths. He dragged Shine to his feet, and continued: 'Listen to me. Go home an' go to bed fer a while. Turn up at the mine all right at one, and in the mornin'. Keep your mouth shut, an' wait till you hear from me again, or—or—' He did not finish his threat. After a moment he continued, in a more composed tone: 'We're in no danger if we've not been seen. That was the trooper after the cub Haddon. He's got the gold all right. Bury the key. Get back to your house, an' lie down fer a while. Be careful—p'raps we're watched now.'

The two men moved off together. After they had passed the tips Dick quickly made his way into the quarry, and from thence to the drive of the Mount of Gold.

CHAPTER XV.

HER father did it! Her father! Her father! Dick continued to repeat these words as he procured candles and prepared himself for a journey into the deep mines. He was conscious of a double duty; he must rescue Harry Hardy from the rising waters and save the father of Christina Shine from a terrible crime, and yet he went about his task as if moved by an external impulse. The work had been mapped out for him by someone or something apart, and he undertook it without a thought of its dangers or a hint of revolt. In fact, he was feverishly anxious to face the black Red Hand shaft and the great, lone workings beyond. He lit one candle, put several pieces in his pocket with the matches, and started on his journey. He was oblivious to his surroundings, oblivious to everything but the object of his quest—Harry Hardy, lying far below in the dripping main drive of the Silver Stream. His large dark eyes, staring unblinkingly, seemed as if set on a vision of his friend prone on the muddy floor of the drive, with the treacherous waters stealing amongst his hair. The present mission had nothing in common with those fanciful adventures that had served to make the boy the wonder and despair of his native township. Richard Haddon was entirely forgotten for the time being, and this concentration of mind and energy served to carry the boy bravely over every obstacle.

Dick made his way through the opening he and Ted had fashioned, dropped into the Red Hand drive beneath, and then turned with familiar feet and hastened towards the shaft. A few centres had been knocked out and thrown across the pit as a staging, so that access to the ladder was possible, but not with out some risk. The boy paused at nothing, reached the iron rungs with a bound, and started down the perpendicular ladder. Down, down he went for many minutes, his candle feebly illuminating a blurred patch about his head. Above, through a bewildering space of darkness, the grated opening at the surface shone like a faint star in another sphere; below was solid blackness; about him the slime of the dripping timbers sparkled in the candle's rays. Down, down, down! The journey might have seemed interminable—a long pilgrimage into the earth's black distances—had the boy had a mind for it, but he thought nothing of the task; at length his feet struck the slabs over the well, and turning he flashed his light into the cavernous depth of a big drive.

He plunged into the drive without a pause, and now the way was familiar again. Voyages of discovery made during crib time when he officiated as tool boy in the Silver Stream had often brought him up the jump-up into the Red Hand drive. Down that jump-up he scrambled now, and stood in the first level of the Silver Stream where the rich gutter had dipped away. A short journey brought him to a balance shaft. Down this to the lower level he travelled without any difficulty, and his journey was almost completed. He was in the bottom drive hastening towards the face where Rogers and Shine had left their victim. He could hear the far-off throbbing of the plunger in the big Stream pumps as it drew the water into the lifts, and above it all the strange murmur of a great mine, like the voice of a distant sea.

Finding an empty truck the boy ran it before him on the rails. He was experienced miner enough to know that one can only travel quickly in this way in a wet drive full of ruts and pitfalls. Passing the 'S' drive, where the robbers had done their work, Dick found Harry Hardy just as Rogers had described him, on his back a few feet up the incline from the hand-pump that served to drain the low-lying part of the drive. His arms were thrown out, and his deadly pale face turned up, the chin pointing to the roof. Upon his forehead were stains of blood, and he lay like a corpse in the black water. The flood had risen above his ears, and the boy knew he had come only just in time.

Dick stuck his candle in the soft clay, ran to Harry's head, and lifted it from the water, and kneeling gazed intently into the cold white face. He thought his friend dead.

'Her father done it!' he murmured. 'Her father! Her father!

He looked and listened for signs of life; he called Harry's name again and again, and felt for the beating of his heart, having at the same time only a vague idea of the location of that organ. He tried to lift the young man away, but his strength was not equal to the task; and so, after collecting some pieces of reef to keep Harry's face above the water, he attempted to drag him out of the reach of the flood. By putting forth all his power he contrived to draw his inanimate friend a few feet up the incline; then, by lifting the shoulders an inch or two at a time, he succeeded in turning Hardy right round with his head farthest from the rising stream. The boy was now smothered from head to foot with yellow clay and his lustrous eyes shone from a face daubed with a puddled reef; and he crouched in the slurry of the drive holding Hardy's head upon his knee, gazing intently into his face, muttering ever, in a half-puzzled way the same words:

'Her father! Her father!

The sound of a lump of reef falling from the roof somewhere far down the drive brought Dick sharply to his feet. His work was not yet accomplished. The scheme that had come to him without volition was nevertheless clearly set forth in his mind. He started dragging at Hardy again, and gradually drew him to the ordinary level of the drive. Once the water attained this height it would flow away towards the shaft, and do the young man no harm. Dick feared Harry was dead; but he did not reason, he only obeyed the instinct that possessed him and that also bade him avoid the incoming shift. If the men found him there he would have to tell all, and her father had done it—her father! A swift panic seized Dick; he snatched up his candle and ran back the way he had come. It was hours, he imagined, since he lay listening to Rogers and Shine above the quarry, and he wondered that the night-shift men were not below long ere this. He reached the balance shaft without having seen a man, and climbed swiftly to the upper level. His race was continued along these workings to the jump-up. Once in the Red Hand drive he was safe from discovery, but the feverish activity still possessed him. How he climbed that fearful flight of ladders up the black wet shaft he never knew. He remembered nothing of the agony of the toil the day after, when all seemed like a dream.

He made his way into the Mount of Gold drive again. An impulse moved him to block the opening connecting the two drives with loose reef, and the same impulse led him to hide the skin bag containing the gold away under the dirt in the shaft of the Mount of Gold. The excitement that had driven him to the rescue of Harry Hardy sustained him till he had crawled out into the quarry; then his strength all went out of him, and left him sick and wretched. He was famished, all his limbs ached with a dull insistent pain after he had rested for a few minutes, and his weariness was so great that it was a terrible task to drag himself out of the quarry. But he succeeded in gaining the hillside at length, and hastened as quickly as he could through the trees in the direction of the Silver Stream, stumbling as he went, and sobbing quietly in utter collapse of strength and spirit.

When Dick reached the vicinity of the big mine he was surprised to find the brace deserted. He stole up and peered through the engine-house window at the driver's clock, and saw with dull amazement that it was not yet half-past twelve. It had taken him little over half an hour to reach Harry Hardy and return—it seemed to him that he had been toiling for many hours. He crept in between the long stacks of firewood, made a bed on the soft bark, and waited. The first night shift of the week did not start work till one o'clock on Monday morning, and the mine was silent save for the slow puffing of the pumping engine and the deliberate rumbling of the bob.

Lying on his stomach on the bark, the boy fixed his eyes upon the mine and suffered through the slow dragging minutes. He wept incessantly, and his teeth chattered, although the night was warm. A new fear had taken possession of him, a fear that Harry Hardy, if alive, would perhaps move and roll down the incline into the water again before the miners reached him. He waited in an agony of anxiety, and his eyes never moved from the cage at the surface.

The miners began to come in at length, with heavy footsteps, swinging their crib billies, calling to each other in gruff voices. Lamps were lit upon the brace, and in the boiler-house and changing shed, and Dick saw the first cageful of men drop out of sight, as the engine groaned and the mine took up its busy duties again.

One cage-load after another went down, and still Dick waited. At last there came a wild, unusual beat of the knocker. The boy knew the signal and started up on his knees. A man rushed past the end of the stacks to knock up Manager Holden. Others gathered excitedly about the mouth of the shaft, and the long flat ropes spinning over the pulleys travelled at top speed.

Soon Harry was brought to the surface, and placed upon a hurdle, and four men carried him away across the paddocks towards Waddy. Dick followed at a safe distance. Locky McRae, the boss of the shift, had run on ahead, probably to warn Mrs. Hardy.

The boy saw Harry carried to his mother's house, saw a man hurry by to call Mrs. Haddon, and waited for some time after she arrived, hidden in a gutter near at hand, listening for every word. After about a quarter of an hour Pete Holden drove his trap to the door, and Dick heard them talking of the hospital and Yarraman; then he knew that Harry was not dead, and dragged his worn, aching limbs to his own home, stupefied with suffering, hunger, and fatigue.

When Mrs. Haddon entered her kitchen an hour later, carrying a flaming match in her fingers, she was shocked to see a small, yellow-clad figure crouched in her own particular armchair near the chimney, and surmounting it a small white face in which burned two astonishing eyes. The little widow screamed and dropped the light and then screamed again, but a feeble voice reassured her.

'Richard Haddon, is that you?' she said severely. 'Oh! you wicked, bad, vicious boy! Where have you been? What've you been doing?'

She was busying herself preparing the lamp, and her tongue ran on.

'You're breakin' your poor mother's heart—breakin' my heart with your bushrangin' an' villainy, bringin' down the police, an' trouble, an' sorrow on me.'

The little woman's nerves had been sorely tried of late with her own troubles and her neighbours', and she broke down now and wept.

'An' you don't care,' she sobbed, 'you don't care a bit how I suffer!

Now the lamp was lit, and the widow turned her streaming eyes upon her incorrigible young son, and instantly her whole expression changed. She forgot to weep, she ceased to complain; she gazed at Dick and her bosom was charged with terror, pity, and remorse. Truly he was a pitiful and ghostly object, sitting there in his mud, looking very small and pinched, with unaccustomed hollows in his pale cheeks, and here and there a nasty bloodstain showing brightly against the yellow clay.

'Dick!' screamed Mrs. Haddon.

The next moment he lay in his mother's arms, clinging to her with tenacious fingers, crying hysterically, utterly unlike the Dick she thought she knew so well; and she kissed him, and wept over him, and murmured to him as if he were really a baby again. She ascribed all to terror aroused by the knowledge that the police were after him. He had covered himself with slurry in strange hiding-places, and had had a fall probably or a blow. He was fed, his clothes were put in water, and finally he fell asleep in his own bed with his mother sitting by his side, her hand clasped in his. If Dick had been told a week earlier that he would ever go to sleep clinging to his mother's hand, he would have scouted the idea with indignation and scorn; and he remembered the act later with a blush as something shamefully effeminate or infantile, betraying a weakness in his character hitherto quite unsuspected.

CHAPTER XVI.

DICK'S limbs were all stiff and sore when he awakened, but he was wolfishly hungry, and that fact satisfied his mother that he had suffered no particular physical injury. He was still much paler than usual and suspiciously reserved, but he ate a good breakfast, and would have given his mother even more gratifying evidence of the perfect state of his health Had not Miss Chris interrupted his meal by a sudden and disconcerting entrance. The young woman came into the room breathless, eager-eyed, and white to the lips. She drew herself up by the door, and made a poor pathetic effort to compose herself, to frame her plea in conventional words; but she was too agitated to remember customary greetings.

'Tell me! Tell me!' she said faintly.

Dick sat stock still, wondering what new thing had happened, asking himself how much Chris knew of his secret; but sympathetic little Mrs. Haddon started up in astonishment.

'Tell you what, my dear?' Then light came to her. 'About the accident?'

'Yes, oh, yes! Is it true? They say he is dying!'

'It isn't true. He is not very badly hurt. His mother went to the hospital with him, an' has come back. It's concussion, the doctors say, an' nothin' serious.'

Miss Chris was plucking nervously at the bosom of her dress with her left hand, steadying herself against the table with her right; now that she knew there was no occasion for her great alarm, woman-like she trembled on the verge of tears. Mrs. Haddon had resumed her seat, and for a moment the eyes of the two women met; then, much to the boy's astonishment, Miss Chris covered her face with her hands and darted forward and knelt by his mother's side, and there was a repetition of the incident in which he had figured a few hours earlier. Mrs. Haddon clasped Christina to her tender breast, and spoke little soothing speeches over the fair head, whilst Chris wept a little, and laughed a little, and clung tightly to her friend.

'Yes, yes, I know, my dear,' whispered Mrs. Haddon. 'I know, I know. But don't you fret. It'll all come out right.'

The women seemed thoroughly to understand each other, but to Dick this was quite inexplicable. He perceived, however, that Miss Chris was troubled in some way, and all his romantic chivalrous feelings were stirred, and his determination to spare her at all costs was strengthened again. Looking at the pair, and remembering the consolation he had derived from his mother's strong embrace, the boy wondered what peculiar virtue lay in that kindly bosom that seemed to make it the natural refuge of the afflicted; and, wondering, he stole out and left the two together.

When the women of Waddy had anything exceptional to talk about they talked amazingly, and on this particular Monday there was so much of interest to be discussed that even the most voluble could only do justice to the subjects by neglecting domestic duties and devoting themselves to back-gate arguments. Harry Hardy's accident was considered and debated from many points of view. Harry was twice reported dead during the morning—on the authority of Mrs. Ben Steven and Mrs. Sloan—but this was contradicted by Mrs. Justin, who declared that the young man still breathed, but was suffering from many and various injuries which she alone was able to minutely describe. Then Mrs. Hardy arrived home from Yarraman, and it became known that the injuries were not likely to prove mortal; so the subject lost interest and was abandoned in favour of Richard Haddon and his blood thirsty gang. 'The boy Haddon' had been captured after a desperate encounter, and would be called upon to stand his trial, along with the poor lads he had so grievously misled, at Yarrarnan next day. It was conceded that he was about to meet his deserts at last; but there was some slight difference of opinion as to the exact nature of Dick's deserts. Some of the ladies thought ten years' imprisonment with various floggings and other heavy penalties in the way of solitary confinement, leg-irons, and an unvarying diet of dry bread and water would be the severest punishment with which the youthful malefactor could reasonably be afflicted. Mrs. Ben Steven stood out resolutely for hanging, and, taking into account the thrilling report of his crimes supplied by the extraordinary issue of the Yarraman Mercury, many of the ladies were compelled to admit that this extreme view was probably the correct one; besides, it possessed the advantage of coinciding admirably with long-established popular opinion about Dick's end. They generously admitted, however, that they were sorry for his mother, poor lady.

The Mercury could not very well have made more of what it called 'The Outbreak of a New Gang' in its Sunday extraordinary. A whole page was filled with various accounts of the depredations of the gang, the terrifying appearance of its members, and certain moral reflections thrown in by the editor for the benefit of the Government and the police. There was 'Mr. Bilison's account,' 'Mr. Hogan's account,' and 'the account given by Master Mathieson.' Each of these persons had been stuck up by the gang, and had escaped most miraculously after displaying great daring in the face of a bloodthirsty fire. The Mercury exhausted all its resources in the way of large black capitals and display type to do justice to the biggest sensation that had come in its way for years, and the appearance of the paper created the most profound amazement throughout the town and district. Gable was described as a cunning scoundrel whose affectations of almost imbecile simplicity might easily have deceived intelligences less keen than those at the service of the Mercury, and neither Messrs. Billson and Hogan nor Master Mathieson hinted that their assailants were anything less than grown men of the largest size and most ferocious type.

Alas! in Monday morning's Mercury the editor was reluctantly compelled to repudiate the most enthralling portions of Sunday's story, but he still took a very serious view of the affair, and vehemently contended that recent facts did not in any way tend to relieve the Government of its responsibilities in the matter of increased police-protection for Yarraman and district. It had transpired that the perpetrators of the series of outrages on the Cow Flat road were boys, undisciplined and dangerous youths, fully armed and led by the man Gable, whose mental infirmities were of such a nature as to render him unfit to be at large in a civilised community. The Mercury was informed that all the young ruffians who had taken part in the sticking-up incidents were in custody, and would appear in the police court on the following morning.

Mrs. Haddon, who still believed Dick's strange reserve and lack of spirits to be due to his fear of the law and the dread prospect of having to appear in court, endeavoured indirectly (and very cleverly, as she imagined) to ease his mind. She did not wish him to think he had done no wrong, or that she did not regard his conduct as most reprehensible; but his mute misery appealed to her motherly heart, and she heaped derision on those 'fool men' who had been deluded by the silly pretence of a pack of boys, and who would be the laughing-stock of the whole countryside when the truth was made known in court and the magistrates abused them for cowards and simpletons. This was comforting to Dick; but in truth he thought little of the pending court case, and it gave him no concern even when he found himself in the troopers' hands. His secret weighed heavily upon him, and the sight of Mrs. Hardy, erect and brave and composed as ever, but with traces of suffering in her face that the boy could not fail to detect, brought home to him an aspect of the case that he had not considered up to now. Her son Frank was a prisoner suffering for a crime committed by Ephraim Shine: in protecting Shine for Christina's sake he must sacrifice Mrs. Hardy, Frank, and Harry.

The problem tried Dick sorely, but he had plenty of time to think it over and he determined to wait for Harry's story. He must be true to Chris in any case, and he knew her love and admiration for her father were deep and sincere. He could not understand it: he admitted to himself that affection for such a man as the searcher was quite absurd and uncalled for; but he knew full well that the blow would fall upon the girl with crushing force, and his heart fought for her, and every romantic impulse he cherished bade him be leal and bold in the cause of the queen of her sex. In the end he resolved that if Harry had not recognised his assailants he would warn Shine in some way, and when the searcher had made good his escape he would tell the whole truth. This, according to his boyish logic, was fair treatment to all parties, so the resolution brought him some peace of mind.

The appearance of the Waddy bushrangers in the police court excited extraordinary interest at Yarraman, and Tuesday morning witnessed something very like an exodus from Waddy. Every man and woman who could possibly get away made the journey to Yarraman, all as partisans of the prisoners. In Waddy Dick and his fellow imps could not be too severely condemned; but Waddy refused to recognise the right of outsiders to abuse them, and however vicious they may have been, it was felt to be the duty of the township to stand by its own as against the 'townies' and the witnesses from Cow Flat.

The court was packed, and most of the people of Waddy had to be content to stand with the crowd that filled the street. An attempt had been made at the last moment to alter the charge against the boys to insulting behaviour, or something equally trivial, and all in court looked for much amusement. In fact, the tremendous bushranging sensation had degenerated into something very like a farce.

The witnesses for the prosecution were the three young men from McIvor's run, who made the gallant attack upon the gang and captured Gable; Billson, the farmer who had been bailed up in his cart; Hogan, the horseman; the boy Mathieson, the tollman, and the woman, Cox by name.

The young men were now sober and subdued, and the evidence they gave differed materially from the story told to the police on Saturday night when they cantered into Yarramnan with their prisoner, drunk and vainglorious. They admitted now that the gang did not make a very strenuous resistance to their gallant charge, but insisted that the boys were armed with revolvers, and that Gable struggled like a demon; and the old man, standing amongst his fellow prisoners, evidently immensely delighted with the part he was playing, smiled brightly upon the court and ejaculated 'Oh, I say! Oh, crickey! 'a propos of nothing in particular.

Bilison testified to having been bailed up on the Cow Flat road by a gang of bushrangers, who demanded his money or his life and fired upon him. He described his hairbreadth escape with primitive eloquence, and was certain the gang meant to murder him. He was too agitated at the time to notice whether the bushrangers were men or boys. It was he who overtook the three young men, but they could not be induced to turn back till the boy Mathieson came up with them and declared the highwaymen to be a mob of boys.

Hogan was equally positive about the firearms, and thought he heard the bullets whistling past his ears, but could not swear to it. At this stage the defendants' lawyer, who had been harrowing the witnesses with many questions and heaping ridicule upon their devoted heads, called for the prisoners' arms to be produced, and the sight of the toy pistols with their mutton-boned barrels provoked yells of laughter in the court, which were presently echoed in the streets.

But it was not till brawny Mrs. Cox took her stand in the witness-box that the absurdity of the Meroury's story and the charge was exposed fully to a delighted audience. Mrs. Cox marched into the box in an aggressive way, saluted the book with an emphatic and explosive kiss, and then stood erect, square-shouldered and defiant, giving the court and all concerned to understand by her attitude that it must not be imagined any advantage could be taken of her. She told her story in a bluff dogmatic way. She was bailed up by the miscreants and scared out of her seven senses. They demanded her money or her life, and she believed that it was their intention to leave her 'welterin' in her gore'; and having said as much she squared round upon the lawyer, arms akimbo and head thrown back, inviting him to come on to his inevitable destruction.

'Come, come, madam,' said the barrister, 'you must not tell us you imagined for a moment you were ever in any serious danger from these terrible fellows.'

'Mustn't! mustn't!' cried Mrs. Cox. 'An', indeed, why not, sir? Who're you to tell me I musn't?'

Mrs. Cox stopped deliberately and carefully rolled up both sleeves of her dress. Then, unhampered and in customary trim, she smote the cedar in front of her and cried:

'Mustn't, indeed!

'No offence, ma'am,' said the small lawyer in a conciliatory tone; 'no offence in the world. Please explain what you did when attacked by the prisoners.'

'What' d I do? First I said a prayer for me soul.'

'And then?'

'And then I grabbed one o' the young imps, an'
I—,

Here Mrs. Cox's actions implied that she had a struggling bushranger in her grip. She drew him over her knee, and then, for the education and edification of the court, went through the task of enthusiastically spanking a purely imaginary small boy.

The pantomime was most convincing, and provoked roars of laughter that completely drowned the shrill pipe of the policeman fiercely demanding order; when the noise had subsided Gable, flushed with excitement and with dancing eyes and jigging limbs, cried out 'Oh, crickey!' with such gusto that the laughter broke loose again in defiance of all restraint, and was maintained until the chairman of the bench, himself almost apoplectic from his efforts to swallow his mirth, arose and talked of clearing the court; then the crowd, fearful of missing the fun to come, quietened in a few seconds and the case was resumed.

'You thrashed the young rip, Mrs. Cox,' said the lawyer. 'You did well. A pity you did not serve them all alike and save us the folly of this most ridiculous case.'

'I did grab another,' said the witness, 'an' I—' Mrs. Cox repeated her eloquent pantomime.

'Oh, crickey!' cried Gable. 'Oh, I say, here's a lark!'

'Silence in court,' squealed the asthmatical policeman.

'Excellent,' said the lawyer. 'And so, madam, you drove off this desperate and bloodthirsty gang by simply slapping them all round?'

'Yes, after I'd been assaulted with a goat,' cried the witness, flushing with a recollection of her wrongs and shaking a formidable fist at the prisoners. 'After I'd been assaulted with a goat sooled on by one o' the bla'guards.'

The lawyer spoke a few soothing words:

'You deserve the thanks of the community, Mrs. Cox, for the businesslike way in which you suppressed this diabolical gang. Your method is in pleasing contrast with the ridiculous effeminacy of the previous witnesses. I have no doubt you would treat an adult bushranger in exactly the same way.'

'Or a lawyer either,' said Mrs. Cox, detecting sarcasm.

The case was practically decided when Mrs. Cox stepped down. The bench desired to have some evidence as to Gable's character, and leading residents of Waddy described his infirmity, and spoke of him as unentirely harmless and innocent old man. The case was dismissed; but the chairman, in acquitting the prisoners, took occasion to remind their parents that if the excellent example set by Mrs. Cox were followed by them all, it would probably tend to the moral advantage of the boys and the benefit of society at large.

The return to Waddy was something in the nature of a triumphal march in which the late prisoners figured as heroes, but they lost importance immediately after reaching the township. A new topic of great interest had sprung up during the absence of the crowd; news had arrived of Harry Hardy's recovery, and it was known that his injuries were not the result of a fall of reef, but were inflicted by gold-stealers who had got into the mine in some mysterious way and had escaped again just as mysteriously. Already Waddy had decided upon the identity of the culprits who, it was confidently asserted, would be found amongst the small community of Chinamen whose huts were situated on the bank of the creek at a distance of about two miles from the township, and who made a precarious living by fossicking and growing vegetables. Waddy always settled matters of this kind out of hand, and the presence of those Chinamen saved it much mental trouble in accounting for thefts small or great.

Late that night Joe Rogers and the searcher sat together in a hidden place in the corner paddock discussing the turn events had taken. The last three days had told upon Shine, who was pallid, hollow-cheeked, and nervous; he fumbled always with his bent bony fingers bunched behind him, and when in the presence of others twisted and turned his curious feet continuously with a dull anxiety that irritated the men beyond bearing. Now, crouched amongst the scrub by the side of his mate, he whined about their danger.

'We should 'a' cleared. We oughter clear now. We'll be nabbed if we stay.'

'We'll be nabbed if we bolt,' replied Rogers. 'The man as cleared now would be spotted as the guilty party, an' half the p'lice in the country 'd be up an' after him. No, here we are, an' here we stick fer better or worse.'

'But if they've got the gold, why don't they do somethin'? There's no word of it. Rogers, if you're foolin' me over this—'

'Will you stop twiddlin' those cursed feet of yours an' listen to me? They haven't got the gold, but I think I've guessed who has. That young whelp Haddon.'

'Dickie Haddon? How, how? Where's it now?'

'How in thunder should I know? But I know the troopers didn't get it. They would have made some noise about it afore this. See here, they were huntin' that kid when they went into the quarry. He must 'a' hid somewhere about when he heard them comin';

p'raps in that very tree. Then he dragged the gold away before we got back, an' hid it. That's my idea.'

'An' d'ye think he saw us?'

'I don't. He'd 'a' split at once.'

'Well, well, an' what'll you do?'

'Collar young Haddon, an' frighten the truth out o' him or break every bone in his cursed skin.'

'But he'd know then, you fool.'

'Will he? I'll take all sorts o' care he doesn't know me, you can take your colonial oath on that.'

'An' if you get the gold back, no dirty tricks. It's halves, you know—fair halves!'

'Yes, an' haven't you always got your share all fair an' square? An' what' ye you ever done fer it but whimper an' cant an' snuffle, like the cur you are?'

'I was goin' to give it up after this,' whined Shine, disregarding Joe's outburst, 'an' get married again, an' live God-fearin' an' respectable.'

Rogers glared at him in the darkness, and laughed in an ugly way.

'Marry!' he sneered. 'Man, the little widow wouldn't have you. She's waitin' fer Frank Hardy; an', as fer yer God-fearin' life, you're such an all-fired hippercrit, Shine, that I believe you fool yourself that you're a holy man in spite o' everythin,' 'pon me soul I do!

'Ah, Joseph Rogers, the devil may triumph fer a while, but I'm naturally a child o' grace, an' if you'd on'y turn—'

Rogers uttered an oath, and drawing back struck the searcher in the face with his open hand.

'Enough o' that!' he cried. 'None o' your sick'nin' Sunday-school humbug fer me, Mr. Superintendent. We've talked o' that before.'

Shine arose, and moved back a few paces.

'I'd better be goin',' he said. "Taint fer us to quarrel, Joseph. Leave the usual sign when we're to meet again.'

Bent over his unconscionable feet, he stole away amongst the trees, and a few minutes later Rogers moved oft slowly in another direction, towards the lights of the Drovers' Arms. His thoughts as he strolled were not very favourable to his fellow criminal.

'Let me once get my hands on that gold,' he muttered, 'an' I'll bolt for 'Frisco.

CHAPTER XVII.

DICK remained very subdued throughout the next day; his head was full of the oppressive secret, and he had no heart for new enterprises. At school his mates found him taciturn and uncompanionable, and Joel Ham was astonished at his obedience and industry. Harry Hardy returned home on the Wednesday evening, and visited Mrs. Haddon's kitchen that night. His head was swathed in bandages, and he was pale and hollow-eyed. Dick felt strange towards his friend and shrank from conversation with him, but listened eagerly when Harry described his experiences in the mine on the night of the attack.

'I'd stopped the pump for a spell,' he said, 'an' presently thought I heard sounds like someone working in the 'T' drive. I crept quietly to the mouth of the drive, an' could see a man with a candle crouched down at work on the floor. I was making towards him when another darted out of the darkness beside me, an' brought me a fearful lick on the head. I staggered back into the main drive an' had a sort o' confused idea of running feet an' loud voices, an' then came another welt an' over I went. They must have dragged me up above the water level, an' I ought to thank them for that, I s'pose.'

'An' you couldn't recognise either of them?' asked Mrs. Haddon.

'No, I haven't the slightest notion who it was hit me, an' the figure of the other was just visible an' no more. I could swear to nothing except this.' He touched his head and smiled.

'The cowardly wretches!' cried Mrs. Haddon, her bosom swelling with indignation.

'They're all that,' said Harry, 'but this is something to be grateful for. Can't you see what it means? It means that everyone is ready to believe Frank's story now, an' a broken head's worth having at that price, ain't it?'

'You're a good fellow, Harry,' said the little widow softly. 'Do you think they might let Frank go now?'

'No, worse luck, not without further evidence; but the company'll probably go in for a big hunt, an' that may be the saving of him.'

This latter piece of news gave Dick further cause for agitation, and his mother's distress grew with his deepening melancholy. She was alarmed for his health, and had been trying ever since the return from Yarraman to induce him to drink copious draughts of her favorite specific, camomile tea, but without success; the boy knew of no ailment and could imagine none that would not be preferable to camomile tea taken in large doses.

On the following morning at about eleven o'clock a visitor called upon Mr. Joel Ham at the school, a slightly-built skinny man in a drab suit. He carried a small parcel, and this he opened on the master's desk as he talked in a slow sleepy way, the sleepiness accented by his inability to lift his eyelids like other people, so that they hung drowsily, almost veiling the eyes. After a few minutes Joel stepped forward and addressed the Fifth Class:

'Boys, attend! Each of you take off his left boot.'

The boys stared incredulously.

'Your left boots,' repeated the master. 'This gentleman is— eh—a chiropodist, and eh—come, come!' Joel Ham slashed the desk: the boys hastened to remove their left boots, handed them to the stranger, and watched him curiously as he examined them at the desk. The astonished scholars could see little, but the man in drab had two plaster casts before him and he was deliberately comparing the boys' boots with these. When he came to Dick's boot he turned carelessly to the master and said:

'This is our man.'

'Richard Haddon, the first boy on the back seat.'

The chiropodist did not look up.

'Boy with red hair,' he said. 'Mixed up in that Cow Flat road affair. Evidently an enterprising nipper, on the high road to the gallows.'

Joel Ham drew thumb and forefinger from the corners of his mouth to the point of his chin, and blinked his white lashes rapidly.

'No,' he said, quite emphatically; 'I don't often give advice—sensible people don't need it, fools won't take it—but you might waste time by regarding that boy's share in this business from a wrong point of view. If he has had a hand in it—and I have no doubt of it since his foot appears—think of him at the worst as the accomplice of some scoundrel cunning enough to impose upon the folly of a romantic youngster stuffed with rubbishy fiction, and gifted with an extraordinarily adventurous spirit.'

This was perhaps the longest speech ever made by Joel Ham in ordinary conversation since he came to Waddy, and it quite exhausted him. The stranger yawned pointedly.

'Where does he live?' he asked.

'Third house down the road. Mother a widow.'

'Right. You might make an excuse to send him home presently. You are a discreet man, Mr. Ham.'

'In everybody's business but my own, Mr. Downy.'

The stranger took up his parcel and marched out, and the boots having been restored to their owners work was resumed. About twenty minutes later Dick was called out, and Joel presented him with an envelope.

'Take that note to your mother, Ginger, will you? Stay a moment,' he said, as Dick turned away. He took the boy by the coat and blinked at him complaisantly for a moment.

'When in doubt, my boy, always tell the truth,' he said.

Noting a puzzled expression in Dick's face, he condescended to explain.

'When you're asked many questions and want an answer, tell the truth. Lies, my boy, are for fools and rogues—remember, fools and rogues.'

Dick set his lips and nodded; and the master, after regarding him curiously for a moment, actually patted his head—an uncommon exhibition of feeling on his part that caused the scholars to gape with wonderment.

When Dick reached his home he was astonished to find his mother seated in the front room with her handkerchief to her eyes, crying quite violently. Opposite her sat the man in drab, swinging his hat between his knees and looking exactly as if he had just been awakened from a nap. The man walked to the door, locked it, and then resumed his seat.

'Now, my lad,' he said, 'attend to me. My name is Downy. I am a detective, and I have found you out.'

The admission was not a wise one; it blanched Dick's lips, but it closed them like a spring-trap.

'I have found you out,' continued the detective. 'He has been arrested.' The detective emphasised the 'he,' and watched the effect. Dick stood before him, white and silent, his heart beating with quick blows, and his blood humming in his ears, 'Who? Who? Who?'

'The man who went down with you has been arrested, my lad, and now you must tell me the whole truth to save yourself. He says you hammered Harry Hardy on the head with an iron bar, and if you do not clear yourself I must take you to gaol.'

Dick answered nothing; his eyes never moved from the green bee on the wall even to glance at his mother sobbing in the corner.

'Come, come, come!' cried Downy impatiently, 'it's no good your denying that you were in the mine on Sunday night. You came home covered with slurry, marked with blood, and very frightened. Your mother admits that, and we have found your footprints in the clay of the Silver Stream drives at both levels. Besides, the man says you were there. Now, tell me this, and I will let you go free: who has the key of the grating over the mouth of the old Red Hand?'

'Oh! Dickie, my boy, my poor boy—why don't you answer?' sobbed Mrs. Haddon.

The detective tried again, threatened, pleaded, and cajoled, and Mrs. Haddon used all her motherly artifices; but not one word came from the boy's locked lips. Dick was possessed by a vivid hallucination; he seemed to be standing in the centre of a whirlwind. Downy and his mother were dim figures beyond, seen through the dust; and like shreds of paper whirled in the vortex, visions of Miss Chris's face, netted in fair hair, passed swiftly before his eyes, and the expression on each face was beseeching and sorrowful. Nothing could have dragged the truth from him at that moment.

Downy stood up and hung over Dick, scratching his head in a despairing way.

I'm sorry, ma'am,' he said, 'but I'll have to take him.'

'He's shieldin' some villain,' moaned Mrs. Haddon.

The detective took the widow aside and whispered with her for a few minutes, with the result that she dried her eyes and was much consoled.

Dick was taken away in Manager Holden's trap and lodged in gaol at Yarraman; and when the news leaked out, as it did towards evening, Waddy had a new sensation, and quite the most startling one in its experience. Before the women went to bed that night they had found Dick guilty of robbing the Silver Stream of thousands of ounces of gold and perpetrating a murderous assault on Harry Hardy. The news brought Joe Rogers and Ephraim Shine together at their secret meeting-place in the corner paddock—Rogers much disturbed and puzzled, Shine shaken almost out of his wits.

'I'm goin' to bolt, I tell you!' cried the searcher.

Rogers gripped him roughly.

'Bolt,' he said, 'an' you're doomed—done for. Hell! man, can't you see you'd be grabbed in less'n a day? With that mug an' that figure you'd be spotted whatever hole you crept into.'

'I know, I know; but it'll come anyhow—it'll come!

'Not so sure, unless you blab in one of these blitherin' fits. What does that kid know? Nothin'. He's found our gold, an' he's hid it away. He wants to keep it, an' you know what a stubborn devil he is. This is just a try on, an' they'll get nothin' out o' Dick Haddon. If they do they get the gold, an' we're all right if we don't play the fool.'

Rogers's reasoning was very good as far as it went; but the discovery of the boy's footprints in the drives had been kept a close secret, or even he might have admitted the wisdom of bolting without delay.

Dick spent a day and two nights in the cell at the watch-house in Yarraman. Public report at Waddy was to the effect that every influence short of torture had been used in the effort to induce him to divulge the truth, and not a word had he spoken. His mother and Mrs. Hardy and Harry had all visited him in the cell, and had failed to persuade him to open his lips. His callousness in the presence of his poor mother's distress was described in feeling terms as unworthy of the black and naked savage. All this was much nearer the truth than speculation at Waddy was wont to be; and when Dick was restored to his home in the flesh on Saturday at noon and permitted to run at large again without let or hindrance, Waddy was amazed and indignant, and Waddy's criticism of the methods of the police authorities was scathing in the extreme.

The boy was driven home by the sergeant, the same who had been commissioned to quell the Great Goat Riot.

'He's looking pulled down,' said the trooper, delivering him into his mother's arms. 'It's the confinement. Let him run about as usual, Mrs. Haddon; let him have lots of fresh air, particularly night air, and he'll soon be all right. At night, Mrs. Haddon, the air is fresh and healthy. Let him run about in the evenings, you know.'

Mrs. Haddon was very grateful for the advice and promised to act upon it. But Dick was a new boy; he remained in doors all Saturday and Sunday, wandering about the house in an aimless manner, trying to read and failing, trying to divert himself in unusual ways and failing in everything. He presented all the symptoms of a guilty, conscience-stricken wretch; and his mother, who had been priming him with camomile surreptitiously, began to lose confidence in that wonderful herb.

Meanwhile a very interesting stranger had made his appearance at Waddy; he was believed to be a drover, and he was on the spree and 'shouting' with spontaneity and freedom. His horse, a fine upstanding bay, stood saddled and bridled under McMahon's shed at the Drovers' Arms by day and night. His behaviour in drink was original and erratic. He would fraternise with the man at the bar for a time, and then go roaming at large about the township in a desultory way, sleeping casually in all sorts of absurd places; but Waddy had a large experience in 'drunks' and made liberal allowances.

Miss Chris called in at Mrs. Haddon's home on evening shortly after tea. She had not been to chapel, and was anxious about her father, who had absented himself from his duties as superintendent of late and whose behaviour had been most extraordinary when she called on him on two or three occasions during the week. She was afraid of fever, and sought advice from Mrs. Haddon, who unhesitatingly recommended camomile tea. Then Dick's ailment was discussed and Chris, much concerned, went and sat by the boy, who cowered over his book, too full to answer her kind inquiries. She put an arm about him and talked with tender solicitude; she sympathised with him in his troubles, and was angry with all his enemies, more especially the police, whose folly amazed her. Here a large tear rolled down Dick's nose and splashed upon the open page, and when she pressed him to tell all he might know and not to suffer abuse and shame to shield some wicked villain, he quite collapsed, and sat with his head sunk upon his arms, sobbing hysterically. This was so unlike the boy that Christina was quite amazed, and her eyes travelled anxiously to and from Dick's bowed head and his mother's distressed face. Then the women, to give him time to recover himself, sat together talking of other matters—Harry Hardy mainly—and Dick, ashamed of his tears, crept away to bury his effeminate sobs amongst the Cape broom in the garden.

Dick had not sat alone more than a minute when he heard a sharp whistle from the back. It was Jacker Mack's whistle and at first Dick did not respond, but sat mopping his tears with his sleeves. The whistle was repeated three or four times, and at length he determined to meet Jacker, thinking there might be some news about the reef in the Mount of Gold. He passed out through the side gate, and along to the fowl-house at the corner, behind which he expected to find his mate sitting. But when he reached the corner a pair of strong arms snatched him from the ground, and he was borne away at a rapid pace in the direction of Wilson's paddock. His face was crushed against the breast of the man who held him, in such a way that it was impossible for him to utter the slightest sound.

Across the flat in the shallow quarry he was thrown to the ground, and for a moment he caught a glimp of his captor in the darkness, a powerfully built man, wearing a viator cap that covered the whole of his face and head, with the exception of the eyes.

'Let one yelp out o' you an' I'll crush yer head with a rock!' whispered the man ferociously.

Dick was blindfolded and gagged, and his arms and legs were tied with rope, his enemy kneeling on him the while and hurting him badly in his brutal haste.

The boy was caught up again and thrown on the man's shoulder, and the journey was continued at a trot. He knew when the bush was reached, because here a fence had to be climbed. He tried to understand what this adventure might mean, but his thoughts were all confused and the gag made breathing so difficult that once or twice he feared he was going to die.

When at last the man stopped and Dick was dropped to the ground, they had travelled about a mile and a half into the bush. He heard the sound of timbers being moved, and presently was caught up again; after much fumbling and an oath or two from his companion the latter withdrew his support, and Dick felt himself to be dangling in the air from the rope that tied his limbs. Now the bandage was pulled from his eyes, and the boy, after staring about through the starlit night for a few moments, terrified and amazed, began to realise his position.

'Know where you are, me beauty?' asked the big man who stood before him, and who spoke as if with a pebble on his tongue.

Dick knew where he was. He was hanging over the open shaft of the Piper Mine, another of Waddy's abandoned claims, suspended from one of the skids by a stout rope.

'Look down,' commanded the man.

Dick obeyed and saw only the black yawning shaft. 'Know she's deep, don't yer? There's three hundred feet o' shaft below you there. That's the short road to hell. Now look here.'

He flashed the bright blade of a large knife before the eyes of his prisoner; then, seating himself on a broken truck near the shaft he began deliberately to sharpen the knife on his boot. The operation was not in the least hurried—the man was desirous of making a deep impression.

'There,' he said at length, 'that's beautiful. Feel!' He cut the skin of Dick's nose with a touch of the keen edge. 'Now, listen here. I'm goin' to take this bandage off yer mouth, 'cause I've a few perticular questions to ask an' you must answer 'em, but understand first that one little yell from you, an'—' He made a blood-curdling pretence of cutting at the rope above Dick's head. 'You'd go plug to the bottom an' be smashed to fifty bits!'

The man removed the gag and reseated himself on the old truck. As he talked he toyed with the ugly knife, making occasional passes on the side of his left boot resting on his knee.

'Look here, young feller,' he said, 'if you tell me lies down you go, understand? D'ye believe me?' he asked with sudden ferocity.

'Yes,' whispered Dick.

'Well then listen, an' answer quick an' lively. Where's the bag of gold you stole outer that big tree beyond the Bed Hand?'

Dick's heart jumped like a startled hare. He recognised his enemy now in spite of his cap and his disguised voice. It was Joe Rogers.

'D'ye deny takin' it?' asked the man sharply.

'Yes,' said Dick, cold at heart and quaking in every limb.

'Damn you for a young liar! Fer two pins I'd send you straight to smash. I know you've got that gold stowed somewhere. Where?'

The boy gave him no answer, and Rogers sprang to his feet, and tickled him again with the knife.

'You whelp!' he said hoarsely. 'I'd think ez much of slaughterin' you ez I would of brainin' a cat. Speak, if you want to live! Where's that gold?'

Dick was convinced that the man would be as good as his word, but he still lingered, casting about helplessly for an excuse, a hope of escape.

'Blast you, won't you speak?'

Dick felt the knife cut into the rope above his head, and shrieked aloud in a paroxysm of terror.

'Stop, stop! I'll tell!'

'Tell then, an' be quick. That's one strand o' the rope gone; there's two more. Speak!' He raised the knife threateningly.

'It's under that big flat stone near the spring in the Gaol Quarry.' The lie came almost involuntarily from the boy's lips in instantaneous response to a new impulse. But he was doomed to disappointment.

'Good!' ejaculated the man. 'Now, you go with me. I don't trust you; you're too smart a kid to be trusted.' As he spoke he twisted the gag into Dick's mouth again. 'No,' he cried with a sudden change of intention, 'you'll stay where you are. You're safe enough here. While I'm away think o' what's below you there, an' pray yer hardest in case you've lied to me, because if you have you're done fer. I'll kill you, s'elp me God, I will!'

Rogers took a bee line through the scrub in the direction of the quarry, leaving Dick hanging over the open shaft. The Gaol Quarry was not more than half a mile off, and Rogers ran the whole of the distance. He made his way clumsily down the rocky side from the hill, falling heavily from half the height and bruising himself badly, but paying no attention to his injuries in the anxiety of the moment. He found the big flat stone after a minute's search, and succeeded in turning it only after exerting his great strength to the utmost. There was nothing underneath. Yes, there was something; a snake hissed at him in the darkness and slid away amongst the broken rock. Rogers fell upon his knees and groped about blindly, but the ground was hard. There was no sign of the gold anywhere, and not another stone in the quarry that answered to the boy's description. Possessed with a stupid blundering fury against Dick, Rogers turned back towards the Piper. He breathed horrible blasphemies as he ran, and struck at the scrub in his insensate rage. He was a man of fierce passions, and meant murder during those first few minutes-swift and ruthless. He reached the Piper breathless from his exertions and wild with passion. He did not even pause to resume his disguise, but ran to the shaft, cursing as he went. There he stopped like a man shot, his figure stiffened, his arms thrown out straight before him; his eyes, wide and full of terror, stared between the skids rising from the shaft to the brace above.

Dick Haddon was not there. The space was empty, the rope's end moved lazily in the wind.

The revulsion of feeling was terrible: it left the strong man as weak as a child, it turned the desperate criminal into a mumbling coward. Rogers staggered to the shaft and examined the rope. It had broken where one strand was cut; the other strands were frayed out. The gold-stealer fell upon his knees and tried to call, but a mere gasp was the only sound that escaped his lips. He remained for a minute or two gazing helplessly into the pitch blackness of the shaft; then, recovering somewhat with a great effort, he rose to his feet, untied the remainder of the rope from the skid and dropped it into the shaft, and turning his back on the mine fled away through the paddocks towards Waddy. As he issued from the bush a quarter of an hour later, and crossed the open flat, a slim figure slipped from the furze covering the rail fence and followed him noiselessly at a distance.

CHAPTER XVIII.

WHEN Rogers reached his hut he sat for some time in the dark, thinking over his position. It had been his intention all along to make his escape from the district the moment he succeeded in recovering the gold, and now, in his horror at the consequences of his last act, he was incapable of cold reason. His one desire was to get away as far as possible from the scene of his crimes. He lit a candle, and the drunken drover, peeping through a crack, saw him spread a blanket on the floor and set to work hastily to make a swag. The drover watched him for a minute and then sped off in the darkness. Shortly after this Rogers was startled at the sound of a shrill and peculiar whistle. Jumping up on the impulse of the moment, with the quick suspicion of a criminal, he snatched his gun from a corner and stepped out. Standing in the light thrown from his hut door, he heard the tramp of horses' hoofs and a voice calling:

'Stand and deliver! You are my prisoner!'

Joe slipped into the shadow, sheltering himself behind the chimney, and saw two troopers riding at him. Instinctively his gun was lifted to his shoulder.

'Bail up!' he cried. 'A step nearer an' I fire!'

The troopers spurred their horses. Rogers clinched his teeth, his eye ran along the barrel, he covered the leading man and fired. The trooper was flung forward on his horse's neck, his arms dangling limply on each side. His horse sprang to a gallop, and a minute later the man slid over its shoulder and fell, rolling almost to Joe's feet as the animal rushed past.

The second trooper fired a revolver, and the bullet chipped a slab at the gold-stealer's ear. Rogers had him covered, and his finger was on the trigger when the gun was whirled from his hands and a man who had stolen up from the back closed with him. The newcomer was slim, and Rogers felt that he might break him between his hands if he could only get a proper grip; but the drunken drover—for it was he—was as sinuous as an eel, and a moment later Joe was on the broad of his back with the 'darbies' on his wrists and a trooper kneeling on his chest, while the drover, transformed into Detective Downy, stood over them, mopping his face with his big false beard.

The wounded trooper had recovered somewhat, and was on his hands and knees, with down-hanging head, in the light of the open door.

'How are you, Casey?' asked the detective anxiously.

'Aisy, sor. I'm jist wonderin' if I'm dead or alive,' said the trooper in a still small voice, watching the blood-drops falling from his forehead.

'Then the devil a bit's the matter with you, Casey.'

'Thank you, sor,' said the trooper, with a trained man's confidence in his superior. 'Thin I'd best git up, p'raps.' And he arose and stood dubiously fingering the furrow plowed along the top of his head by the gold stealer's bullet.

'Get him into the hut,' said Downy, indicating Rogers with a nod; 'and hobble the brute—he's dangerous.'

Rogers, sitting on the edge of his bunk, handcuffed and leg-ironed, gazed sullenly at the detective.

'Well,' he said, 'an' now you've got me, what's the charge?'

'A trifle of gold-stealing,' replied Downy, 'and this,' indicating Casey's bleeding head. 'To say nothing of the murder of your accomplice.'

Rogers blanched and glared at the detective, his face contorted and his eyes big with terror.

'Shine,' he murmured, 'd'ye mean Shine? It's a lie; he's not dead!'

Harry Hardy, who had just come upon the scene and was standing in the doorway, cried out at this.

'Great God!' he said. 'Then it was Ephraim Shine after all!'

'Pooh!' cried Rogers, 'it was a trick to trap me into givin' his name. You needn't 'a' troubled yerself. I don't want to shield him—damn him!'

'Do you know where this Shine's to be got at?' asked Downy, appealing to Harry, who had been working in concert with the detective ever since his appearance in Waddy.

'Yes,' was the reply. 'I know his house. He'll be easily taken.'

'Then go with the sergeant. Take Casey's horse. It'll be with the other. Here,' he threw Harry a revolver. 'Case of need, you know, but no shooting if it can be avoided.'

Harry thrust the weapon in his belt, and a minute later he and Sergeant Monk rode off in company to take Ephraim Shine in the name of the Queen.

Meanwhile Dick was not at the bottom of the Piper shaft, as Rogers concluded in his haste. Joe had not left the boy half a minute when a second man made his appearance on the other side of the shaft. This was Downy, in his drover disguise. The detective, whose sole object in assuming the disguise was to watch Dick, believing that the boy would be sure to communicate with the real thieves, had witnessed his capture by Rogers and had followed in the latter's tracks; and now, after being entertained and instructed by the words that had passed between Rogers and his captive, he cut Dick down, quickly frayed the end of the rope between two stones, and cut away Dick's bonds, throwing the rope and gag into the shaft.

'Now, my lad,' he said sternly, 'after that man. Take me the nearest track to the quarry you spoke of as quick as you can cut, and don't make noise enough to wake a cat or I'll hand you over to him when we get there.'

Dick did as he was bid; and they were in time to overlook Rogers as he searched amongst the stones, and to overhear some of the language that announced his failure. At this stage the detective, who had retained his grip of Dick's wrist, whispered:

'You can go now, but you must take a message from me to Harry Hardy. Go straight to his house and say, 'Downy says "Ready."' Can I trust you?'

Dick nodded.

'You're a plucky lad,' said Downy, 'and I'll take your word. Off you go, but make no noise.'

Dick crept quietly along the grass till he was well beyond hearing, and then ran down by Wilson's ploughed land and out into the open country. He understood that the career of Joe Rogers as a gold-stealer was drawing to a close, and the knowledge brought him a certain sense of relief in spite of the fact that he quite realised Shine's danger, and was more than ever devoted to the searcher's daughter, more than ever pleased with the idea of her hearing some day how faithful and bold he had been, how true a knight to his liege lady.

He burst into the room where Mrs. Hardy and Harry and Mrs. Haddon were seated, hatless and breathless, and filled his friends with alarm.

'Please, Harry, Downy says 'Ready!'' blurted Dick.

Harry sprang to his feet and made for the door.

'That mens he's discovered something important, mother.' he said as he passed out.

Dick followed, leaving the women astonished and curious, slipped away around the fence enclosing Harry's home, and made off towards the other end of the township. His intention was to warn Ephraim Shine of the danger that threatened. He did not doubt but that Rogers, if he fell into the hands of the troopers, would tell all.

There was a light burning in Shine's skillion, and Dick's knock was answered by Miss Chris, who wore her hat and was on the point of leaving for her home at Summers'.

'I want your father,' said Dick quickly. 'The troopers 'r' after him. Tell him to bolt.'

'Dickie—Dickie, whatever do you mean?' cried Christina, greatly agitated.

The next moment she was thrust aside and Shine appeared, showing a drawn gaunt face, the skin of which looked crinkled and yellow in the candle light, like old parchment.

'What's that?' he gasped. 'Who wants me?'

'You're found out,' said Dick, drawing back, shocked by the ghastly appearance of the man. 'They're after Rogers. They've got him by this, I expect, an' they'll soon have you if you don't make a bolt fer it.'

Shine uttered a wailing cry and Dick turned and fled again, afraid of being seen in the vicinity of the searcher's abode by Downy or any of his men. Looking back he saw that the house was now in darkness, and surmised that Ephraim had taken advantage of his warning to escape into the bush.

When Harry Hardy and the trooper rode up to Shine's house half an hour later, they found the place deserted. The door was on the latch, and the interior gave no indication of a hurried departure, but the searcher was nowhere to be seen.

'It's all right,' said Harry, 'he'll be somewhere about the township. I'll take a trip round an' see if I can hit on him, if you'll stay here an' keep watch.'

'Right,' said the sergeant, 'but you'd best drop in on Downy and let him know. If our man gets wind of what's happened he'll skedaddle.'

'If he doesn't we'll nab him at the mine at one.'

Harry found that Downy had disposed of his prisoner, having converted the cellar at the Drovers' Arms into a lock-up for the time being, and smuggled Joe Rogers in so artfully that McMahon's patrons in the bar were quite ignorant of the proximity of the prisoner and of the presence of the guardian angel sitting patiently in the next room, tenderly nursing a broken head and a six-barrelled Colt's revolver.

Harry and Downy searched Waddy from end to end in quest of Ephraim Shine, and saw nothing of him. Downy interviewed Christina without betraying his identity or his object, but could get no inforination of any value; and when the missing man failed to put in an appearance at the Silver Stream to search the miners from the pump coming off work, the hunt was abandoned for the time being.

'He's got wind of my game and cleared,' said Downy, 'but we'll have him before forty-eight hours have passed.'

'But how could he know?' asked Harry, impatient to lay Shine by the heels.

'May have heard the shots. May have been hiding anywhere. But, never fret, we'll round up your friend, my boy. Men of his make and shape are as easy to track as a hay waggon.'

In the early hours of the morning Downy drove his prisoner into Yarraman, and that day's issue of the local Mereury contained a thrilling description of the capture of the Waddy gold-stealer—a description that created an unprecedented demand for the Mercury, and quite compensated the gifted editor for, the heartburnings he had endured over the bushranging fiasco.

Waddy was dumbfounded when the Mercury came to hand, and horribly disgusted to think the stirring incident described had happened right under its nose, without its having the satisfaction of witnessing the least moving adventure or catching even a glimpse of the prisoner. Joe Rogers a free man was a familiar and commonplace object, but Joe Rogers handcuffed and leg-ironed in the custody of the law was a person of absorbing interest, and

Waddy would have turned out to a man and woman to give him an appropriate send-off.

There, before their eyes, set forth in the columns of the Mercury, were the details of Detective Downy's ruse, and valuable remarks enlarging upon the almost superhuman astuteness of the officer in question; the story of Dick's capture by Rogers, the flight to the Piper shaft and all that happened there, the fight between the gold-stealer and the troopers, the shooting of Casey, the overthrow of Rogers, and the hunt for Ephraim Shine; all these things had happened in a small township within the space of a few hours, and Waddy, that had always found its Sunday nights hang so heavily on its hands, had been cheated out of every item of the bewildering list. It was a shame, an outrage. Detective Downy was voted a public enemy, and his name was execrated from the chapel yard to McMahon's bar.

The only satisfaction available to the people was in going over the ground, and they flocked to Joe's hut and congregated there, discussing, arguing, and predicting; examining with owlish wisdom the bullet mark on the hut chimney, and counting the blood spots on the worn track near the door where the hero Casey bled in defence of his country's laws. Of course, 'the boy Haddon' was a favourite theme, and now Dick appeared as a public benefactor. The matter of the stolen gold had yet to be settled, but the most generous view of this business was popular, and the confidence in Richard Haddon was complete. The women declared emphatically and without a blush that they had always believed in the honesty and intelligence and brave good heart of the boy. To be sure he was a bit wild and a little mischievous—but, there, what boy worth his salt was not? and, in spite of everything they had all seen long ago that Widow Haddon's young son was a good lad at bottom. His conduct in deluding Joe Rogers in the face of so terrible a danger reflected credit upon Waddy, and Waddy gratefully responded by being heartily proud of him. A crowd marched to Mrs. Haddon's back fence expressly to cheer Dick; and cheer him they did, in a solemn, matter-of-fact way, like a people performing a high public duty. Dick was not in the least moved by this display of feeling, but his mother was delighted and kissed him heartily, and responded on his behalf by shaking a towel out of the back window with great energy and much genuine emotion.

CHAPTER XIX.

THE detective had asked Harry to keep careful watch upon Dick, but the boy betrayed no inclination to roam, and when he did venture out it was to call upon Harry himself. Dick's spirits had recovered marvellously, and if it were not for an occasional fit of sadness (induced by thoughts of Christina Shine) he would have been quite restored to his former healthy craving for devilment, and eager to call together the shareholders of the Mount of Gold with a view to arranging further adventures. Harry, too, no longer felt the ill effects of his injuries, and intended returning to work in the course of a few days. The recent discoveries had served to lighten his heart, and yet thoughts of Christina welled bitterness; but his mother was happy in the confidence that at last justice would be done and her son restored to her.

Dick found Harry moodily smoking in the garden, and addressed him through the fence.

'What d'ye think?' he said, with the air of one propounding a conundrum.

Harry was not in a guessing mood; he gave it up at once and Dick took another course.

'I got somethin' p'tickler to tell you,' he said.

'Have you, Ginger?' Harry was quite alert now. 'About this gold-stealin'?'

'No—o, not quite about that. I'm goin' to tell all that to Downy, but it's somethin' jist as p'tickler—about a reef we found.'

'A reef? Nonsense, Dick. How could you find a reef?'

'By diggin' fer it, I s'pose. What'd you think if I said we fellers' ye got a mine—a really mine—me an' Jacker Mack, an' Ted McKnight, an' Billy Peterson, an' Phil Doon? What'd you say, eh?'

'I'd say you didn't know what you were talking about, Ginger, my boy.'

'But if I took you down the shaft an' showed you the reef, an' showed you stone with gold stickin' in it—suppose I done that, how then?'

'Where is this reef?' asked Harry, becoming impressed by the boy's earnestness.

'Tellin's!'

'But didn't you come to tell me?'

'Come to tell you we'd found it, an' to ask what to do, so's no one can jump it. We want it took up on a proper lease, all right fer me an' the rest o' the fellers, an' we'll let you stand in.'

'I can't take up a lease unless I know where the reef is, can I?'

'Well, it ain't far from the Bed Rand.'

'Nonsense, Dick! The bottom must be over three hundred feet deep there. You couldn't cut a reef any shallower than that.'

'On'y we have.'

Harry sat for a moment lost in thought. He had suddenly recalled old talk about mysterious indications of a shallow reef in that locality, a reef the existence of which would have been in open opposition to mining traditions, and contrary to all locally known theories of scientific mining. He remembered hearing of a shaft that had been put down by a few believers, in defiance of local derision; he recalled, too, the eccentric and unheard-of drive thrown out by the Red Hand in some such absurd quest, and his respect for the boy's opinion grew into something like conviction.

'It's very queer, Dick,' he said; 'but if you'll show it to me I'll do all I can for you.'

'That's good! You see we're all in it. We're the Mount of Gold Quartz-minin' Company—me an' Jacker an' them—but it's on'y a make-believe company, an' I'd like Mr. McKnight, an' Mr. Peterson, an' Mr. Doon to come, an' the detective cove too, cause there's somethin' else there—somethin' else p'tickler too.'

'Very well, we can go an' see McKnight an' Peterson, but they'll laugh at us.'

'When they laugh we'll show 'em this,' said Dick, producing a lump of quartz.

Harry took the stone in his hand; it was not larger than a hen's egg and of a dark colour, but studded thickly with clean gold, and as he gazed at it his pipe fell from his mouth and his eyes rounded. He pursed his lips to whistle his astonishment, and forgot to do it; he lifted his hand to scratch his head and it stuck half-way; he turned and turned the stone, stupid with surprise.

'By the holy, your fortune's made if there's much o' this!' he blurted at length.

'Think there's heaps of it,' said Dick coolly.

'When can we go to it?'

'When the detective cove comes, an' I've told him 'bout somethin'.'

'Somethin' good for us, Dick?' asked Harry anxiously.

Dick nodded his head slowly several times.

'Well, if this don't lick cock-fighting. Have you told your mother?'

'No,' said Dick.

'Nothing about this either? How's that?'

'Oh,' said Dick with a man's superiority, 'she wouldn't understand. She don't know nothin' 'bout minin', you know.'

Harry looked down upon his young friend curiously for a moment.

'D'you know,' he said, 'you're a most amazing kind of a kid?'

'How?' asked Dick shortly.

'Why in the way you get mixed up in things.'

''Tain't my fault if things happen, is it?' asked the boy in an injured tone.

'S'pose it ain't,' replied Harry with a grin; 'but they all seem to come your way somehow. Look here—it can't matter now—tell me how you came to be in the Stream drive that night?'

Dick kicked up a tuft of grass, bored one heel into the soft turf, and answered nothing.

'Come on, old man, I won't turn dog.'

'I'm goin' to tell it to Detective Downy first. 'Twasn't nothin' much anyhow. I jes' went down.'

Dick would say nothing more. He found himself on the side of the law for the first time, and felt he owed a duty to Downy, whom he regarded as almost as great a man as Sam Sagacious. Downy had come to his rescue in an hour of dire peril, Downy had trusted him and taken him into his confidence to some extent, and he was determined to do the fair and square thing by the detective, at least so far as he could do so without interfering with his sacred obligation to handsome, unhappy Christina Shine.

The detective returned to the township in the afternoon to prosecute the search for Ephraim, of whom nothing had yet been heard. In the presence of his mother and Mrs. Hardy and Harry, Dick faced the officer to tell his story; but he found it hard to begin.

'Well, my lad,' said Downy, 'you're going to tell all you know?'

Dick nodded, abashed by his new importance.

'Out with it then. You were in that drive?'

'Yes.'

'You went down with Rogers and Shine?'

'I didn't.'

'Very well, my boy, how did you go?'

'Went by myself. Out of a drive what I know into the Red Hand workin's, an' down the Red Hand ladders.'

'But why? Go ahead—why?'

'To—to drag Harry out o' the water.'

There were three distinct gasps at this, and even the detective's eyelids went up a trifle.

'Go on, Dick.'

Now having started, Dick told his story in full. The incidents were not told consecutively, and he needed considerable cross-examining before the tale was properly fitted together and his audience of four had grasped the full details. Then Mrs. Hardy arose from her seat and moved towards him somewhat unsteadily; knelt by his side, took him in her arms softly and quietly, kissed him, and said in a very low voice:

'God bless you, Richard; God bless you, my brave boy.'

This, for some reason quite incomprehensible to the boy, caused a lump to swell in his breast and gave him an altogether uncalled-for inclination to blubber; but he swallowed it down with an effort, and then his mother hugged him in that billowy energetic way of hers. After which Harry took his hand and shook it for quite a long time without speaking a word. The detective alone was undemonstrative.

'Now,' said he, 'what about this gold? You hid it?'

'Yes. In our shaft.'

'Look here, Master Dick, why have you kept all this so quiet? Why did you go down that mine in stead of running for help? Come, there is something at the back of all this; out with it!'

Dick's lips closed in a familiar way, and their colourlessness indicated a stubborn defiance of all argument and persuasion.

'Did you want to steal the gold yourself?'

'No,' cried the boy angrily.

'Then you were afraid of something. By heaven! I have it. You rip! 'twas you gave warning to Ephraim Shine. You deserve six months.'

'Shame!' murmured Mrs. Hardy.

'"Tisn't fair!' expostulated Dick's mother. Dick's lips were closed again, and he stared defiantly at the detective.

'Well, well,' groaned Downy, 'this is the most extraordinary thing in boys that I have ever encountered, but he's a mass of grit— for good or bad, all grit. Shake hands, Dick.'

Dick brightened up, and shook hands cheerfully.

'You're quite sure about that gold? You hid it securely?' queried the detective.

'Yes, I buried it under the reef quite safe.'

'And nobody knows of this hole but yourself?'

'Yes, Jacker knows, an' Ted, an' Billy Peterson, an'—'

'Bless my soul, the whole township knows! We won't get an ounce of that gold—not a colour. We'd better make the search at once, Mr. Hardy. You'll need a rope and tools, I suppose. Hunt up the men you spoke of as quickly as possible, will you?'

Harry and Dick started off together in quest of McKnight. He was on the night shift, and they found him in bed. Harry explained. McKnight was scornful and profane.

'What—that boy Haddon again?' he cried. 'Now what's his little game? What devilment's he up to?

'But this looks all right,' Harry expostulated.

'All right, my grandmother's cat! You'll be findin' quartz reefs in a gum-tree next.'

'You ask Jacker an' Ted,' put in Dick resentfully, hurt to find his well-intentioned efforts so ungraciously received.

'Ask Jacker, is it? If Jacker comes playin' any of your monkey tricks with me, my lad, I'll make him smell mischief, I tell you.'

'But hang it all, Mack! you might as well come an' see. I own the chances o' finding a shallow reef in that locality look blue, but you know there was talk o' something of the kind years ago.'

'Yes, talk by fellers that didn't know a quartz lode from a load o' bricks or a stone wall. Get out, I'm sleepy.'

'Show him the specimen,' said Dick.

Harry handed it over.

'The boy says this is from his show. How's that?' he said.

McKnight took the stone indifferently, cast his eye over it, and then sat up with a jerk. He moistened the stone here and there, glared again in a strained silence, and one leg shot out of bed. He weighed the specimen in his hand, and the second leg followed. Then McKnight fell to dressing himself; he literally jumped into his clothes, and as he buttoned his vest all askew, he gasped:

'Hold on there—I'll be with you in two twos!'

'Wouldn't break my neck about it, old man,' said Harry sarcastically, 'p'raps the boy made that specimen out of a door knob an' a bit of brick.'

'Did he, but—That's just the same class o' stone as the specimen Henderson found in the back paddock twelve years ago, that sent everyone daft after a reef there. Come on.'

McKnight was now much the most eager of the three, and led the way at a great pace to Peterson's house. Peterson was more easily convinced, and in a few minutes the four joined Downy at Mrs. Hardy's. The detective had borrowed a coil of rope, the necessary tools were provided, and the party set off. The five no sooner appeared on the flat with their burdens than they were sighted by many of the people of Waddy, now eagerly on the lookout for adventure, and before they reached the bush they had quite a mob at their heels, fed by a thin stream of men, women, and children hurrying to witness the newest development of Waddy's latest and greatest affair.

Dick led the men into the Gaol Quarry, and at the spring turned and pointed the way through the scrub growth under which he and his mates always crawled to get at the opening leading into the Mount of Gold.

'In there,' he said, 'agin the wall.'

Harry and McKnight broke a passage through the saplings and ti-tree.

"Tween them two rocks,' said Dick; 'low down under the fern.'

'Yes,' cried Harry, 'here we are! Let's have the hammer, Peterson.'

Harry broke away projecting pieces of stone, widening the aperture, and Dick and the detective joined them at the opening.

'I'll go first,' said the boy. 'I can go down the ladder we made, but it mightn't bear a man.'

Dick went below and lit a couple of candles. Nothing had been touched in the drive, and he peeped into the shaft and saw that the loose dirt there was as he left it. Harry joined him in a few minutes and McKnight followed. The men came down on the boys' curious ladder, but with a rope about their waists, paid out from above. Downy was the last to go below, Peterson remaining on the surface to keep the crowd back from the entrance.

McKnight seized a candle, crawled to the extremity of Dick's diminishing drive, and examined the place curiously.

'It's right,' he cried, 'right as the bank. She's a dyke formation, I should say, an' rich. By the holy, we're made men—made men, Hardy!

Detective Downy was too deeply interested in his own quest to pay much attention to the miners.

'Now, my lad,' he said, 'where are we?'

'The bag's there under them lumps.' Dick held his candle low, throwing its light into the shaft. Downy dropped from the slabs placed across from drive to drive into the bottom, and going on his knees threw aside the lumps of mullock indicated by the boy. Dick followed him holding the candle, and watching his movements, anxiously at first, and then with terror. He flung himself down beside the detective, and plunged his hand amongst the rubble, then ceased and faced the detective, mute, despairing.

'Well, well,' cried Downy in alarm, 'what is it?

'Gone!' whispered Dick.

'Gone? Are you sure? We have not searched yet.'

'It's gone!'

'You may have made a mistake. Hardy, Mc Knight, lend a hand here.'

'No good,' said Dick, 'it's gone.—it's stolen. I put it right here, coverin' it with this flat junk an' a lot o' small stuff. I know—I know quite well.'

Harry and McKnight went into the shaft with shovels, and turned over the dirt stowed there to the depth of two feet, but the bag was gone.

'Show a light here,' Downy said suddenly, looking up at Dick from the slab on which he was seated above the two workers. He took the candle and examined the edge of the slab closely.

'You said the bag containing the stolen gold was made of hide.'

'Yes,' said the boy, 'green hide—just a calfskin bag, with the hair on.'

'Humph! Then here is proof that part of your story is true anyhow.' He held up a little tuft of reddish hair.

'Rogers had a skin bag, a red-an'-white one. Used to use it fer haulin' in the shallow alluvial at Eel Creek. I've seen it at his hut often,' said McKnight. 'But, I say, mister, if you' take the advice of an old miner you'll get out o' this just as quick as you can lick. See, the timber's been taken out o' this shaft, an' it's a wonder to me it ain't come down in a lump an' buried them kids long since. It's damn dangerous, I tell you.'

'Very good,' said Downy. 'First have a look into these drives and then we'll clear. Show me how you got through into the Red Hand workings, Dick.'

Dick led him along the drive and pointed out the little heap covering the opening where he had broken through.

'Do you think that dirt's been touched by anyone since you piled it there?' asked Downy.

'No,' said Dick, 'it seems jist the same.'

'Then the thief did not come that way.' The detective scattered the heap and examined the rough edges of the opening carefully. 'No cow hair there,' he said. 'We must hunt for that skin bag somewhere up aloft, Dick.'

When Dick reached the surface he found Hardy, McKnight, and Peterson standing apart from the crowd, with elate faces, talking earnestly.

'She's a rich dyke,' McKnight was saying, 'an' she'll go plumb down to any depth. We must get the pegs in at once, an' apply fer a lease. She just misses Silver Stream ground, an' the ole Red Hand is forfeit long ago. Boys, it's a fortune fer us.'

'Remember Phil Doon's a shareholder, too; his father's got to be in it,' said Dick.

'To be sure, lad, to be sure; all honest an' fair to the boy pioneers.'

Dick felt little enthusiasm about the Mount of Gold just then, for the loss of the bag of stolen gold troubled him sorely. He feared that Detective Downy regarded him as a liar and a cheat.

CHAPTER XX.

After coming up Downy examined the opening in the rock critically.

'Do you think a man might have made his way through that hole before you broke the edges down?' he asked Harry.

'Well, yes, with some crowding I think he might've.'

'Yet the boy said he had to squeeze his way through. Did you notice if the opening had been enlarged recently? Were there indications of recent breakages?'

'Yes, the stone had been broken in places. I s'posed the boys did that.'

'Perhaps. Here, Dick.'

Dick was quite sure neither he nor any of his mates had increased the opening. They kept it small because it was easier to hide; besides, he said, it was more fun having to squeeze through.

'Which of your mates took that bag?' asked Downy sharply.

'None of 'em.'

'Why are you so positive?'

"Cause I know they wouldn't be game.'

'Afraid of the darkness or the mine?'

'No, afraid o' me.' Dick squared his shoulders manfully.

'Get out—why should they be afraid of you?'

'Wasn't I legal an' minin' manager an' chairman o' the directors? If one did what I told him not to he'd get the sack an' a lickin', too.'

'Oh, he would, eh? Well, you'd better give me their names anyhow. And now,' he continued after jotting down the names of the shareholders of the Mount of Gold, 'show me the track you took when you dragged the hide bag through the quarry.'

Dick went back over his tracks, and Downy followed slowly on hands and knees, rescuing a hair or two from the edges of the rock or from a bramble here and there.

'Fortunately that bag of yours shed its hair freely, old man,' he said. 'here's corroborative evidence anyhow. The bag went down all right—now let's see what proof there is that it came up again.'

He returned to the hole in the rock and commenced another search, with his nose very close to the ground, moving slowly, and peering diligently into every little cranny amongst the stones. At length, after travelling about ten yards in the direction of the spring in this fashion, be called sharply:

'Hi, Dick What were you doing with that bag here?'

'Never had it nowhere near here,' answered Dick.

'Come, recollect; you put it down for a spell.' 'Didn't,' said Dick. 'Went straight along the side, an' dropped it into the shaft.'

'But look—there's hair on the top of this rock and a tuft on the corner. Mustn't tell me a cow would roost there, my lad.'

'Don't care—'twasn't me.'

Downy sat on the rock for a moment in a brown study, and the crowd, which had made itself comfort able in one end of the quarry and up one side, sat in awed silence, watching him closely, like a theatre audience waiting for some wonder-worker to perform his feats of magic.

The detective did nothing astonishing. After collecting a portion of the hair he deposited it carefully in his pocket-book, deposited the book just as carefully in his breast-pocket, and then climbed out of the quarry and marched away towards the township; and the crowd, relieved from the restraint imposed by the law as personified in him, gathered about the stone and examined it wisely, discovering a much longer and more significant sermon in it than Downy had ever suspected, and finding marrow-freezing suggestiveness in the marks of rust upon the face of the rock, which were declared by common consent to be bloodstains. Waddy confidently expected the gold-stealing case to culminate in the discovery of a particularly atrocious murder, and Ephraim Shine was selected as the probable victim. It was held by many that so good a man as the superintendent had seemed to be could not reasonably be suspected of consorting with a sinner like Joe Rogers with criminal intentions, and the idea that he had been murdered by the real thieves under peculiarly shocking circumstances was held to be more feasible, and was, in addition to that, highly satisfactory from a dramatic point of view.

The investigations of the people stopped short at the entrance to the shaft, where Peterson mounted guard and warned them off in the name of the law, and meanwhile Hardy and McKnight were pegging out the land preparatory to applying for a lease.

Downy went straight from the quarry to Shine's house, and, much to his surprise, found the missing man's daughter there. Christina had altered much during the last few hours: her face was now quite colourless, grief had robbed it of its sweet simplicity, and the buoyant ingenuousness had fled from her eyes. A new character was legible there, a strength of will more in keeping with her fine presence. The almost childlike sympathy was gone, and in its place was a trace of suffering and evidence of the deeper forces of her nature. The detective eyed her keenly, with surprise and interest, and saluted her in his most respectful manner.

'You have had the—eh, misfortune to meet me before, Miss Shine,' he said.

Christina merely bowed her head.

'I am Detective Downy. I have a warrant for the arrest of Ephraim Shine. I wish to search the house.'

'Yes,' said the girl quietly, and stepped from the door to make way for him.

Downy entered and commenced his search at once. He examined the whole place minutely, foolishly it seemed to Christina, who stood by the door apparently impassive but following all his movements with her eyes. He was particularly careful in overhauling a coat that her father had worn, and having gone through the three rooms he walked out and round the house. There was no place near where a man might hide but in the tank, and that was full of water, as he cautiously noted. He faced Christina for a moment, as if with the intention of questioning her, but changed his mind, wished her 'Good day,' and moved off.

Up to six o'clock next day nothing had been heard of Shine; he had disappeared in a most astonishing manner. The police of the whole country were alert to capture him, and it was thought that escape for him was impossible, if only on account of his physical peculiarities, which should have made him a marked man anywhere in Victoria or in either of the neighbouring provinces. Sergeant Monk and several troopers were stationed at Waddy, and were kept busy hunting in the old mines and all the nooks and corners of the district. Harry Hardy joined in the hunt throughout Tuesday. He had a feverish desire for employment—occupation for his mind which, in spite of the efforts he made to dwell upon the villainies of Ephraim Shine and the wrong he had done Frank, and the good reasons he had to hate him, would revert again and again to Christina; and then a wish, a cowardly wish, traitorous to his brother, cruel to his mother, and false to himself, stole into his heart, and he felt for one burning moment a hope that the searcher might escape for her sake, for the sake of sweet Chris, whose victory over him he acknowledged and nursed in secret with a wealth of feeling that amazed him, with a passion he had never dreamed himself capable of. He fought this wish furiously, as if it had been a tangible thing: grappling with it, choking it in his heart, and stirring up in his soul a wilder hatred for his enemy.

Harry saw Chris for a moment on the morning after the arrest of Joe Rogers; the change in her startled him, his love flamed up, and pity tore at his heart strings. His triumph must mean suffering and shame for her. Had he stood alone he would ten thousand times rather have borne what misfortune might have fallen to his lot than see her shamed and sorrowing. It was thoughts like these that rose up to make him his brother's enemy, and they were conquered in sweat and agony; and since his loyalty to his own kin could only be maintained at a fever heat, he stood forth as the most bitter and implacable foe of Ephraim Shine.

Coming from Mrs. Hardy's gate on that night at about nine o'clock, Dick Haddon collided with a breathless boy running at top speed in the direction of the Drovers' Arms, and the two went down together. When Dick had quite recovered he recognised the other, whom he had gripped with 'vengeful intentions, as Billy Peterson.

'Lemme go,' cried Billy. 'Quick, can't yer! I'm goin' fer the troopers.'

'Who for?' asked Dick, hanging to his friend.

'Find out.'

'Oh, right you are; but you won't go, that's all.'

'Well, I'm goin' to tell 'em that Tinribs is up at his house.'

'How d'yer know?'

'I was sneakin' round to get a shot at a cat, an' I heard 'em. Lemme go 'r he'll be gone, you fool.'

'Won't,' said Dick, masterfully. 'You ain't goin'.'

'Who'll stop me?'

'I will.'

''Tain't in yer.'

A struggle commenced between the boys and rapidly merged into a stand-up fight. When Harry Hardy appeared on the scene, attracted by their cries, he found the combatants locked in a fierce embrace, each clinging desperately to a handful of the other's hair and hammering vigorously at his opponent's ribs. Harry pulled them apart as if they had been terriers.

'Here, here, what's all this about?' he cried.

'Dick stopped me goin' fer the troopers,' said Billy indignantly.

'The troopers?'

'Yes, fer Mr. Shine. He's up in his house. I heard him—he was talkin' to Miss Chris in the dark.'

'Stop!' said Harry; but Billy, who had broken away, picked up his heels and ran.

Harry did not linger, but turned and sped off to wards Shine's home, leaving Dick cowering against the fence. The young man had no defined intention—he did not know what he should do if he found Shine in the house. His divided interests left his mind confused at the crucial moment, but he did not relax his speed until he was within a few yards of the searcher's door. Then, to his astonishment, he found lights burning in the house, and Christina confronted him in the doorway as he was about to enter. He drew back a step and his eyes sought the ground. He stood panting and speechless.

'What do you want, Harry?' she asked.

Had she been bitter or angry it might have been easier for him, but her voice was low and kindly, and he was abashed. He was compelled to force himself to his purpose, as he might have pushed a backing horse at a stiff fence.

'I want your father. He is here.' His voice was harsh and strained.

'My father is not in here.'

'He has been seen. Let me pass.'

'No, Harry, you have no right.' She barred the way, tall and calm and strong.

'No right? No right to take the man who has gaoled my brother—who would have murdered me?' His blood had mounted to his head; he had put aside his love as something that tempted him to evil, put it aside by an almost heroic effort of renunciation. 'I will have him,' he cried; 'the would-be murderer, the thief.'

'No,' said Christina firmly facing him.

'Then he's here—he is here?

'No.'

'You lie thinking to save him, but the troopers are coming.' He pointed back into the night. From where he stood the back door was visible, and he watched it intently.

'The troopers are the officers of the law. I can not deny them, you I can. Harry, you are fierce and cruel—fierce and unforgiving.' The reproach was not spoken fretfully; it was quite dispassionate, but it struck him like a blow and he bent before it, conscious of its injustice but not daring to deny it. They remained so in silence for a few minutes, and then heard the rush of the troopers' horses coming up the grass-grown back road at a gallop.

'They're coming,' said Harry in a low voice.

Christina neither stirred nor spoke, and Monk at the head of four horsemen swept up to the house.

'To the front, Donovan and Keel,' cried Monk. 'He may make for cover in those quarries if he bolts.

Casey, stay here. Managan, follow me.'

He dropped from his horse and led the animal to Harry, to whom he threw the rein. Christina did not attempt to bar his passage, and he and Managan passed into the house. Chris stood by the door jamb, facing Harry, erect and pale; Harry leant against the big galvanised-iron tank, absently fondling the head of the trooper's horse. Suddenly, a moment after the troopers had entered the house, he heard right at his elbow the sound of something striking upon the iron of the tank inside. He started forward with a low cry, and his eyes flew to the face of the girl. She, too, had heard the sound, and their eyes met. The terror in hers told him that he had discovered the truth.

'He's there,' he whispered.

Christina staggered back, supporting herself against the wall, and fell into a seat under the window, the light from which streamed upon her fair hair and illumined her as she sat, crushed by her misery into an attitude of profound despair, her head bowed upon her breast, her clasped hands thrust out rigidly be yond her knees.

Harry stood silent and motionless, his eyes fixed upon the grief-stricken figure of the girl, his brain in a tumult. His heart was driving him to forget everything but that he loved her, to take her in his arms and swear to shield her and cherish her, come what might. At this moment Sergeant Monk came from the house.

'Not a sign of him,' he said. 'Did you see any thing of him, Hardy?

'Not a glimpse,' answered Harry mechanically.

'Did you go inside?'

'No; Miss Shine refused admittance.'

'Why are you here, miss?' asked Monk, turning sharply to Christina.

'I am here because it is my home,' she answered unsteadily.

'But don't you live with the Summers family?'

'People may not care to shelter the daughter of—of one suspected of robbery and almost murder.' The girl's head sank lower still and a convulsive sob shook her frame; but she controlled herself with a brave effort of will and sat immovable.

Monk's horse was nosing in the bucket under the tap of the tank, and Harry stooped and turned the tap. The water ran swiftly, filling the bucket in a few seconds. While the horse drank the sergeant gave whispered orders to Casey; and Christina, with steadfast eyes and locked fingers, sat waiting for Harry to speak the dreaded words, wondering at his silence. Monk moved round the house, peering into all the corners, and came to the tank again. It stood on a small platform raised on four uprights, and all was open underneath. The sergeant examined it. He climbed to the top, removed the lid and, striking a light, looked in. The tank was full of water.

'I am going to hunt over the quarries,' said the trooper in a low voice, as he mounted. 'Donovan and Keel are taking a run in the paddock, Casey will try the houses about here. You might keep your eyes open, Hardy. Perhaps that boy was mistaken, but we mustn't miss a chance.'

Harry nodded, scarcely comprehending what the man said, and Monk rode off leaving the two alone. For a minute or more they continued in the same position; then Harry stole to Chris, and kneeling in the shadow by her side took her hand firmly in his.

'He is there,' he whispered.

'What are you going to do?' she added in a strange voice.

'Why don't you get him away?'

'Away?' she murmured vaguely.

'Yes, yes; I will help you.' His left arm clasped her closely, and his breath was on her cheek.

She turned her face towards him, and there was a new hope in it, another spirit in her glorious eyes.

'You are not going to give him up.'

'I can't—I can't do it!'

'Thank God!' she murmured, and there was some thing more than relief for her father's sake in her tone. He had made a revelation that filled her with a passion of joy which for a moment drove out the fears and anxieties that had possessed her heart.

'I love you—I love you, dear,' he continued in a voice ardent, caressing; 'an' I can't bear to see you suffer.'

She let her face sink to his and kissed him on the mouth, and he clasped her to his breast and held her, repeating again and again expressions of his devotion that love made eloquent. Her pale face turned to him seemed luminous with the ecstacy of the moment. For a brief sweet minute she abandoned herself to that ecstacy and forgot everything beside.

'I have always loved you, my darling! my darling!' she whispered—' always. That night at the gate I thought you cared and I was happy, but afterwards I was afraid. I thought you might hate me for his sake, and I was wretched.'

'I did try to, Chris—I tried to hate you. I was a fool. I couldn't do anything but love in spite of myself, an' now I'll help you, dear.'

'No, no, no, Harry; no—you must not!' She put him from her with her strong arms. 'It is wrong. I cannot let you. It is right that I should fight for him—he is my father. He has been a good father to me, and I have loved him and believed in him. It is my duty to fight for him, but you must not, my dear love. In you it would be a wrong, a crime.'

'He is your father—I love you!

'Yes, yes, and oh, I am glad you love me; but you must leave me to do what I can alone. It is not your duty to help him. Think of your mother, your brother, your own honour.'

'We can save Frank now without this.'

'You cannot be sure of that, Harry—you only hope so.'

'Am I to tell the troopers, then?'

'No, no—oh, no; I am not brave enough to say that! I cannot bear to think of you as his hunter, his bitterest foe. 'Twas that thought made my shame and my sorrow so terrible a burden; but I can carry it better now.'

'My poor girl! my poor girl!'

He bent his lips to the white hand upon his shoulder and kissed it tenderly.

'God bless you, Harry!' she faltered, tears springing to her eyes. 'I know how generous you are. As a boy you had a big brave heart, and I admired you and loved you for it; but I can take no sacrifice that might bring more sorrow upon your mother, that might wrong your brother and bring shame to you.'

'But Frank's innocence will be known. Dickie Haddon heard them as good as admit it.'

'Yes, I know the story. I made Mrs. Haddon tell me all, and I know that they left you to drown; and now for my sake you would save him, run the risk of being discovered assisting him to escape from justice—and the risk is great, dear. Think what it would mean if that became known, how it would blacken poor Frank's case. People would say they had all been in league to rob the mine; you would be despised, your mother's heart would break. Harry, that must not be. The shame is mine now; you and yours have borne enough. I cannot drag you into it again. I cannot have your precious love for me made a source of danger and dishonour to you. No, no; I love you too well for that—much too well for that, dear.'

She spoke in little more than a whisper, but there was the intensity of deep feeling in every word.

He drew her to her feet and into his arms again with tender reverence, and softly kissed her tired eyelids. She was only a girl, and the strife of the last two days had told upon her strength. It was sweet to rest so, knowing and feeling his strength, confident of his devotion.

'But I love you—I love you, Chris,' he said.

'Yes, you love me and I love you.' Her hand stole to his neck. 'Ah, how happy we might have been!'

'Might have been? We must be happy—we must!' he said vehemently. 'I love you, an' your sorrow is mine, your trouble is mine. I won't let anything interfere. I must help you!'

'No, Harry, I will not take your help. You do not stand alone. Before I would have you do that I would tell the truth myself. My father is ill; he may never get away. I think he will not. What would be left to me if he were taken after all, and you were known to have assisted him in his endeavours to elude the police? I could not bear it. No, no, dear, you must leave us alone to that. Promise.'

They were standing in the darkness by the wall. He drew her more closely to him and his only answer was a kiss.

'If he does escape,' she said, 'I will go into court and tell what I know, if it will help your brother. Perhaps I ought to tell the truth now in justice and honour, but I cannot desert my father. There is something here will not let me do that,' She pressed a hand to her bosom.

'No, you can't do that. I'm sorry for you, Chris. It's a hard fight. I want to fight with you. By Heaven! you don't know how I could fight for you.'

Her head had fallen upon his breast again; he felt her sob, and broke into vehement speech—passionate assurances of love half spoken, ejaculations, fierce endearments, tender words—then was as suddenly silent again, and stood over her with his lips amongst her hair until her mood passed.

'I will come tonight,' he whispered, when at length she ceased weeping.

'No,' she said, and she was strong again. 'In asking you to be silent I make you false to your people. I do ask that, but no more. Harry, you must not come again. Promise me you will not.'

'You'll come to me—we'll see each other?'

'No, dear. Better not, till this terrible business is over.'

Chris, I can't part like that.'

'You must, you must. Would you make it harder for me? Would you give me a new burden of shame and grief?'

'I'd die for you! There's nothing I wouldn't do for you!'

'Then do this, my true love. Promise me you will not come here again.'

'Will it be for long?'

'No, it cannot be for long. Promise me. Promise me. Promise!'

'You know if he's-taken an' tried I will have to give evidence against him.'

'I do,' she answered, shuddering.

'An' that'll make no difference to our love?'

'I will always love you, Harry.'

'This trouble's making a great change in you, Chris,' he said yearningly. 'You're pale and ill. It'll wear you out.'

She felt herself weakening again, but summoned all her resolution and stood true to her purpose.

'I can bear it,' she said. 'I must! Promise me. Harry, the troopers are coming—your promise!'

'I promise.' He held her a moment caught to his heart, they exchanged a long kiss, and she slipped from him and into the house.

CHAPTER XXI.

A MINUTE later, when Casey rode up out of the darkness, Harry was sitting alone by the window.

'You've seen nothing?' he said.

'Divil a see,' replied the trooper. 'It's sartin to me he ain't within fifty moiles av us this blessed minute.'

'It doesn't seem likely he'd hang round here, does it?'

'The man ud be twin idyits what ud do it, knowin' we'd be sartin sure to nab him, Misther Hardy.'

Harry was not disposed to smile, indeed he scarcely heeded Casey's words; he thought he detected a faint sound of weeping within the house, and his heart was filled with a passionate longing to stand by his dear love in defiance of everything. Casey, looking down upon him, noted the convulsive movements of his clenched hands, and said with a laugh:

'Sure, 'twould be sorrer an' torinint fer that same Shine if you laid thim hands on him now, me boy.'

Harry started to his feet and commenced to fondle the trooper's horse, fearing to follow the train of thought that had possessed him lest he should betray himself. Shortly after Sergeant Monk returned.

'No go,' he said. 'Anything turned up here, Casey?'

'Niver a shmell av anythin', sor,' answered the trooper.

'Well, we can raise this siege, Hardy. That boy was mistaken, sure enough.'

'If he wasn't having a game with us,' answered Harry.

'Urn, yes; that's likely enough among these young heathens of Waddy. But Downy will be here again in the morning; we'll see what he makes of it.'

Harry followed the police as they rode away, and returned slowly to his home. His anxiety for Chris's sake, and his profound sympathy for her, did not serve to quell the wild elation dancing in his veins, the triumphal spirit awakened by the knowledge of her love and fired by her kisses.

Chris, sitting alone in the house, her face buried in her hands, felt, too, something of this exultation; but she nerved herself to look into the future, and saw it grim and starless. She saw herself the daughter of the convicted thief, the thief who had only narrowly escaped having to stand his trial for murdering her lover; the thief who had shifted the burden of his guilt on to the shoulders of an innocent man, the brother of her love. Could she ever consent to be Harry's wife after that? she asked herself with sudden terror. Then she shut out the thought, and her heart sang: 'He loves me! He loves me! 'and there was joy in that no danger could destroy.

Detective Downy was in Waddy again on the following morning, his trip to Yarraman having been taken with the idea of interviewing Joe Rogers in prison and endeavouring to worm out of him some intelligence that might assist in the discovery of Ephraim Shine. But Rogers either knew nothing or could not be persuaded to tell what he knew, so the effort was fruitless.

After hearing the story of the previous night, Downy sent for Billy Peterson and questioned him closely; but the boy insisted that he had told the truth, and was quite positive it was the searcher's voice he heard. The detective was puzzled.

'You made a close hunt about the house?' he said to Sergeant Monk.

'In every nook and corner.'

'Yet there must be something in this boy's yarn. Shine is certainly in hiding somewhere near here. If he had made a run for it he must have been seen, and we should have heard of him before this. There might be a dozen holes in those quarries into which a man could creep. We must go over them. Don't leave a foot's space unsearched.'

The troopers spent several hours in the quarries, moving every stone that might hide the entrance to a small cave, and leaving no room for a suspicion that Shine could be lying in concealment there. For a Dick, who, in consideration of the seriousness of recent events with which he had been directly concerned, enjoying a week's holiday, superintended the hunt from the banks; but he wearied of the work at length, and crossed the paddocks to join the men busy in the new shaft. Harry Hardy, McKnight, Peterson, and Doon were sinking to cut the dyke discovered by the Mount of Gold Quartz-mining Company. The mine had been christened the Native Youth; Dick, as the holder of a third interest, felt himself to be a person of some consequence about the claim, and discussed its prospects with the elder miners like a person of vast experience and considerable expert knowledge, using technical phrases liberally, and not forgetting to drop a word of advice here and there. It might have been thought presumptuous in the small boy, but was nothing of the kind in the prospector and discoverer of the lode.

The big shareholder did not disdain even to assist in the work, and it was a proud and happy youth, clay-smirched and wearing 'bo-yangs' below his knees like a full-blown working miner, who marched through the bush with the other owners of the Native Youth at crib-time. Being their own bosses the men of the new mine went home to dinner, and dined at their leisure like the aristocrats they expected to be.

Prouder still was Dick when he discovered brown haired, dark-eyed little Kitty Grey loitering amongst the trees, regarding him with evident admiration and awe. He felt at that moment that he needed only a black pipe to make his triumph complete, and had a momentary resentment against the absurd prejudice that denied a boy of his years the right to smoke in public. Kitty had scarcely dared to lift her eyes to her hero for some time past: the wonderful stories told of him seemed to exalt him to such an altitude that she could hope for nothing better than to worship meekly at a great distance. She was braver now, she actually approached him and spoke to him, yet timidly enough to have softened a heart of adamant; but Dick, stung by a laughing comment from McKnight, would have passed her by with an exaggerated indifference intended to convey an idea of his sublime superiority to little girls, no matter how large and dark and appealing their eyes might be. Then she actually seized his hand.

'Don't go, Dickie,' she said, 'I want to speak to you. Miss Christina sent me.'

Kitty was a member of Christina Shine's class at the chapel, and was one of half a dozen to whom Miss Chris represented all that was beautiful and most to be desired in an angel. The mention of Christina's name served to divest Dick of all pretentiousness.

'What is it, Kitty?' he asked eagerly.

'She wants you. She says you're her friend, an' you'll go to her,' Kitty spoke in a whisper, although the men were now well beyond earshot.

'Yes,' said Dick; 'I'll go now.'

'No, not now,' said Kitty clinging to his sleeve. 'She says have your dinner an' then go. An' oh, Dickie, she's been crying, an' she's all white, an'—an'—' At this the little messenger began to cry too.

'Is she?' said Dick, sadly. 'When my mine turns out rich I'm goin' to give her a fortune.'

'Oh, are you, Dickie?' said Kitty, beaming through her tears.

'Yes,' answered he gravely; 'and then she'll marry Harry Hardy an' be happy ever after.'

'My, that will be nice,' murmured Kitty, much comforted.

'You ain't a bad little girl.' He felt called upon to reward her. 'You can walk as far as the fence with me if you like.'

Kitty was properly grateful, and they walked together to the furze-covered fence.

'Please don't tell anyone you're going to see her, Miss Christina says,' whispered Kitty, at parting.

'Right y'are,' Dick said, delighted with the mystery. 'I say, Kitty, I think p'raps I'll give you a fortune too.'

'Oh, Dickie, no; not a whole fortune, I'm too little,' cried Kitty, overwhelmed.

'Yes, a whole fortune,' he persisted grandly; 'an' maybe I'll marry you.'

'Will you, Dickie, will you? Oh, that is kind!'

'Here.' He had turned over the treasures in his pocket and found a scrap of gilt filagree off a gorgeous valentine. 'Here's somethin'.'

Kitty thought the gift very beautiful, and accepted it thankfully for its own sake and the sake of the giver, as an earnest of the fortune to come; and went her way happy but duly impressed with a sense of the responsibilities those riches must impose.

Harry Hardy had loitered behind his mates on the flat, and when the boy caught up to him again he turned to him with nervous anxiety.

'What did that girl want with you, Dick?' he asked. 'I heard her mention Miss Shine's name.'

He noted the set, stubborn look with which he was now familiar fall upon the boy's face like a mask, and he questioned no more on that point.

'Dick;' he said earnestly, 'you'll help her if you can. She's all alone, you know; not a soul to stand by her, not a soul. You might get a chance sometimes to make things easier for her. Would you?'

'My word!' said Dick simply.

Harry wrung his hand, and Dick, looking into his face, was puzzled by its expression; he looked, Dick thought, as he did on that Sunday morning when he wished to flog the superintendent before the whole congregation.

'You're a brick—a perfect brick!' said Harry.

'I'd do anythin' fer her,' Dick replied.

'Thanks, old man. I'll never forget it.'

It did not surprise the boy that Harry should thank him for services to be rendered to Miss Chris; he thought he understood the situation perfectly, and it was all very sad and perfectly consistent with his romantic ideas of such matters.

'Look here, Dick,' said Harry, before parting, 'I owe you an awful lot, my life, p'raps; but for every little thing you do for her I'll owe you a thousand times more—a thousand thousand times more.'

Dick's wise sympathetic eyes looked into his, and the boy nodded gravely.

'You can swear I'll stick up fer her,' he said.

Dick, whilst feeling quite a profound sorrow for Christina Shine, derived no little satisfaction from the position in which he found himself as the champion of oppressed virtue and the leal friend of a devoted young couple, the course of whose true love was running in devious ways. This was a role he had frequently played in fancy; but it was ever so much more gratifying in serious fact, and he took it up with romantic earnestness, a youthful Don Quixote, heroic in the service of his Dulcinea.

At dinner he favoured his mother with the latest news from the mine and glowing opinions on its prospects; and Mrs. Haddon, more than ever suggestive of roses and apples, beamed across the table upon her wonderful son, perfectly happy in the belief that Frank Hardy would presently be released, that their fortunes were practically made, and that she was the mother of the most astonishing, the cleverest, the bravest, and the handsomest lad that had ever lived. Dick's claims to beauty were perhaps a little dubious, but it must be admitted that local opinion, as expressed in local gossip a thousand times a day, went far to justify Mrs. Haddon's judgment on all the above points.

Dick escaped immediately after dinner, and went straight to Shine's house. Fortunately the troopers, in response to information received, were searching a worked-out alluvial flat about a mile off, and Downy was pursuing a delusive clue as far as Cow Flat, so his visit excited no particular attention.

The appearance Chris presented when she admitted him shocked the boy, and stirred his heart with tenderest pity. Her eyes were deep-set in dark shadows, her cheeks sunken, and there was a peculiar drawn expression about her mouth. She who had always been a miracle of neatness was negligently dressed, and her beautiful hair hung in pathetic disorder. She seated herself and drew Dick to her side.

'Dick,' she said, 'I am in great trouble.'

'Yes,' he answered, 'I know—I'm sorry.'

'And you are my only friend.'

'No fear, Harry Hardy'd do anythin' for you.'

'He cannot, Dick; it is impossible. He is generous and noble, but he cannot help me. Dick,' she drew him closer to her side, and held his hand in hers, 'tell me why you would not speak about the gold-stealers and that crime below. Was it because of me—because you wanted to spare me?'

'Yes,' he whispered.

'God bless you! God bless you, Dickie!' she said catching him to her heart and kissing his cheek. 'I guessed it. I do not know if it was right, but it was brave and true, and I love you for it.'

'Don't cry,' Dick said consolingly; 'it'll all come out happy— it always does you know.' This was the philosophy of the Waddy Library, and Dick had the most perfect faith in its teachings.

'Thank you, dear. I am going to ask you to do something more for me. I am afraid this is not right either. I know it is not right, but we cannot always do what is right—our hearts won't let us sometimes. Will you help me?'

'Yes,' he said valiantly, and would have liked nothing better at that moment than to have been called upon to face a fire-breathing dragon on her behalf.

'I want you to go to Yarraman and buy these things for me.'

She gave him money and a list of articles with the help of which she hoped to effect a disguise for her father that would enable him to leave the district. It was a very prosaic service, Dick thought, but he undertook it cheerfully.

'I want you to tell no one what you are going for. Catch the three-o'clock coach near the Bo Peep, and answer no questions.'

'I know a better way'n that,' said the boy, after a thoughtful pause. 'Mother wants some things from Yarraman. I'll get her to let me go fer 'em this afternoon.'

'Yes, yes; that is clever. But you won't tell.'

'Not a blessed soul.'

'And when you get back it will be late—bring the things to me as secretly as you can. The troopers would be suspicious if they saw you—be careful of them.'

Dick had no doubt of his ability to deceive the whole police force of the province, and undertook the mission without a misgiving, his only regret being that it was making no great demands upon his courage and ingenuity.

'Dickie,' said Chris, kissing him again at parting, 'I hope some day, when you are older, it will be a great happiness to you to think you helped a poor heartbroken girl in a time of terrible trouble.'

The boy would have liked to have framed a fine speech in answer to that, but he could only say softly and earnestly:

'I'm fearful glad now, s'elp me!'

Mrs. Haddon was easily deceived, and Dick caught the three-o'clock coach. The Waddy coach took two hours to do the journey to Yarraman and did not start back till after eight, but this was not the first time the boy had made the journey alone, and his mother had no misgivings.

Downy returned to the Drovers' Arms late in the evening, having discovered that his supposed clue led only to a half-demented sundowner living in a hollow log near Cow Flat, and having nothing whatever in common with the missing man. The search of the troopers had been fruitless, too, and at this crisis the opinion of McKnight as a pioneer of Waddy was solicited. McKnight's belief was that Shine was hiding away somewhere in the old workings of one of the deep mines—the Silver Stream perhaps—and he recalled the case of a criminal who got into the old stopes of a mine at Bendigo, and subsisted there for two weeks on the cribs of the miners, stolen while the latter were at work. The detective considered this a very probable supposition, and an invasion of the Silver Stream workings was planned for next morning.

CHAPTER XXII.

SHORTLY after eight o'clock on the night of Dick's journey to Yarraman the figure of a woman approached the searcher's house and knocked softly at the front door. There was a light burning within, but the knock provoked no response. The visitor knocked again with more vigour; presently a bolt was withdrawn and the door opened a few inches, and Christina Shine, seeing her visitor, uttered a low cry and staggered back into the centre of the room, throwing the door wide open. It was Mrs. Hardy who stood upon the threshold.

'May I come in, my dear?' she asked in a kindly tone.

Christina, standing with one hand pressed to her throat and her burning eyes fixed intently upon the face of the elder woman, nodded a slow affirmative. Mrs. Hardy entered, closing the door behind her, and stood for a moment gazing pitifully at the distracted girl, for Chris had a wild hunted look, and weariness and anxiety had almost exhausted her. She faced her visitor with terror, as if anticipating a blow.

'My poor girl,' Mrs. Hardy said gently; 'I suppose you wonder why I have come?'

Again Chris moved her head in vague acquiescence.

'I have heard how heavily this blow has fallen upon you, and my heart bled with pity. I felt I might be able to comfort you.'

Chris put her back with a weak fluttering hand.

'My dear, I am an old woman; I have seen much trouble and have borne some, and I know that hearts break most often in loneliness.'

'You know the truth?' asked the girl, through dry lips.

'I know Richard Haddon's story.' 'And you have not come to—to—'

'I have come to offer you all a woman's sympathy, my girl; to try to help you to be strong.'

Mrs. Hardy took the weary girl in her arms and kissed her pale cheek.

'You are good! You are very good!' murmured Chris brokenly, clinging to her. But she suddenly thrust herself back from the sheltering arms and uttered a cry of despair.

The door communicating with the next room had been opened and a grim figure crept into the kitchen, the figure of Ephraim Shine. The man was clad only in a tattered shirt and old moleskins; his face was as gaunt as that of death, and his skin a ghastly yellow. He moved into the room on his hands and knees, seeking something, and chummered insanely as he scratched at the hard flooring-boards with his claw-like fingers, and peered eagerly into the cracks. He moved about the room in this way, searching in the corners, dragging his way about with his face close to the floor.

'I'll find it, I'll find it,' he muttered; 'oh! I'll find it. Rogers is cunnin', but I'm more cunnin'. I know where it's hid, an' when I get it it'll be mine—all mine!

Mrs. Hardy stole close to the girl, and they clasped hands.

'Is he mad?' asked the elder woman hoarsely.

'He has taken a fever, I think,' answered the girl, 'and I can hide him no longer. I cannot help him now.' She sank back upon a chair and followed her father's movements with tearless, hopeless eyes.

'Rogers is a liar!' muttered Shine. 'A liar he is, an' he'd rob me; but I'll beat him. It's hid down here, down among the rocks. The gold is mine, mine, mine!' His voice rose to a thin scream and he beat fiercely upon the boards with his bony hand.

'He has been ill ever since Rogers was taken, but he only took this turn this evening. Oh! I tried hard to help him; I tried hard! He is my father. Oh, my poor father! my poor, poor father!

'Hush, hush, dear,' said Mrs. Hardy. 'We must help him on to his bed. Come!'

Each took an arm of the sick man and raised him to his feet. He offered no resistance, but allowed them to lead him to the bunk in the other room and place him upon it, although he continued to utter wild threats against Joe Rogers and to chummer about the gold, and move his hands about, scratching amongst the bedclothes.

Mrs. Hardy brought the light from the kitchen, and busied herself over the delirious man, making him as comfortable as possible upon his narrow bed. She gave directions to Chris and the girl obeyed them, bringing necessary things and making a fire in the kitchen. She seemed inspired with a new hope, and presently she moved to Mrs. Hardy's side again.

'Do you think he will die?' she asked.

'I do not think so, dear. It is brain fever, I believe.'

'How good you are—you whom he has wronged so cruelly!

She ceased speaking and gripped her companion's arm. The latch of the back door clicked, a step sounded upon the kitchen floor, and the next moment Detective Downy appeared within the room. He glanced from the women to the bunk, and then strode forward and laid a hand upon Ephraim Shine.

'This man is my prisoner,' he said.

Shine sat up again, moving his arms and muttering:

'Yes, yes, down the old mine; that's it! Let me go. It's hid in the old mine—my gold, my beautiful gold!'

'You cannot take him in this state,' said Mm. Hardy; 'it would be brutal.'

The detective examined him closely, and, being satisfied that the man was really ill and unlikely to escape, went to the kitchen door and blew a shrill blast of his whistle in the direction of the quarries. When he returned Chistina was on her knees by the bunk, as if praying, and Mrs. Hardy was bathing the patient's temples. After a few minutes Sergeant Monk rode up and joined them in the room.

'Here is our man,' said Downy quietly. Send Donovan for the covered-in waggon at the hotel. We will have to take him on a mattress.'

'Shot?' cried Monk.

'No; off his head. Send a couple of your men in here. I think I'll get my hands on that gold presently.'

The sergeant withdrew, and Downy touched Chris on the shoulder.

'It's a bad business, miss,' he said. 'You made a plucky fight, but this was inevitable. Will you tell me where he was hidden?'

Chris arose and stood with her back to the wall and answered him in a firm voice. She understood the futility of further evasion.

'He hid in the tank,' she said. 'It has a false bottom, and you get in from below.'

The detective expressed incredulity in a long breath.

'Well, that fairly beats me,' he said. 'When did he fix the tank?'

'I do not know. I had no idea it was done until the night of the arrest of Rogers.'

At this moment Casey and Keel entered.

'Stand by the man, Casey,' said the detective. 'Keel, follow me.'

Downy went straight to the tank and, creeping under it, struck a match and examined the floor above on which it rested. Two of the boards had been moved aside, and in the bottom of the tank there was an opening about eighteen inches in diameter with a sheet of iron to cover it, in such a way as to deceive any but the most careful seeker. The detective ordered Keel to bring a candle, and when it was forth coming he drew himself up into the tank and struck a light. An ejaculation of delight broke from his lips, for there at his hand lay a skin bag covered with red-and-white hair, and by its side shone a magnificent nugget shaped like a man's boot. This the detective recognised as the nugget described by Dick Haddon. There were also a pickle bottle containing much rough gold, and two or three small parcels.

The compartment in which Downy sat was just high enough to allow of a man sitting upright in it, and large enough to enable him to lie in a crescent position with out discomfort. A pipe from the roof was connected with the tap, so that water could be drawn from the tank as usual. The job had been carefully done, and had evidently cost Shine much labour. The searcher had designed the compartment as a hiding-place for his treasure, the quantity of which convinced Downy that his depredations at the mine (in conjunction with Rogers, probably) had been of long standing. The parcels contained sovereigns and there were small bags of silver and copper—a miser's hoard. The detective dropped the bag, the nugget, and all the other articles of value out of the tank, and with the assistance of Keel carried them into the kitchen. He examined the material in the hide bag, and found it to be washdirt showing coarse gold freely. The nugget was a magnificent one, containing, as the detective guessed, about five hundred ounces of gold, and worth probably close upon two thousand pounds. Nothing nearly so fine had ever before been discovered in the Silver Stream gutters, although they had always been rich in nuggets.

When Mrs. Hardy returned home an hour later, Harry had just come in from work. The shareholders in the Native Youth were so anxious to cut the stone that they were putting in long shifts. There were traces of tears about Mrs. Hardy's eyes, and her expression of deep sorrow alarmed her son.

'Why, what's wrong, mother?' he asked quickly. 'Have you had bad news?'

'No, Henry. I have been with Christina Shine.'

'You. You, mother?' he cried, in surprise. 'Not—' He suddenly recollected himself and was silent. He knew his mother to be incapable of a cruel or vindictive action.

'Mrs. Haddon told me how the poor girl was suffering for her father's villainy, and I was deeply sorry for her. I thought that under the circumstances my sympathy might strengthen her.'

'God bless you for that, mother' said Harry fervently, and his mother looked at him sharply, surprised by his tone.

'Shine has been arrested,' she said. 'The police have taken him in to Yarraman.'

'Taken—Shine taken!'

'He was captured while I was there.' Mrs. Hardy told her son the story of Shine's arrest, and Harry sat with set teeth and eyes intent for some minutes after she had finished.

'My boy,' his mother said, placing a hand upon his shoulder, 'this does not seem to please you.'

His head fell a little, and he opened and clenched again the strong hands gripped between his knees.

'And yet,' she continued, 'it confirms your suspicions. It may mean the assertion of Frank's innocence.'

'I love her!' he said with some passion.

His mother was greatly startled, and stood for a moment regarding him with an expression of deep feeling.

'You love her—his daughter?'

'With all my heart, mother.'

'Since when?'

'I don't know. Since that Sunday in the chapel, I believe.'

'And she?'

'She loves me.'

Mrs. Hardy moved to a chair, sat down with her face turned from him, and stayed for many minutes apparently lost in thought. She started, hearing Harry at the door.

'Where are you going?' she asked.

'To see Chris.' He answered in a tone hinting defiance, as if expecting antagonism; but his mother said nothing more, and He passed out.

Harry found Chris sitting alone in her father's house. A candle burned on the table by her side, her hands lay idly in her lap. He had expected to find her weeping, surrounded by women, but her eyes were tearless and the news of Shine's arrest was not yet known in the township. Harry fell on his knees by her side and clasped her about the waist. There was a sort of dull apathy in her face that awed him. He did not kiss her.

'I've heard, dear,' he whispered. 'All's over.'

'Yes,' she said, looking at him for the first time, without surprise.

'Why are you sitting here?' he asked.

'I'm waiting for Dickie Haddon,' she said listlessly. 'He went to Yarraman to buy some things to make a disguise. It is only fair to wait.'

He was touched with profound pity; but her mood chilled him, he dared not offer a caress.

'And then?'

'And then? Oh, then I will go to the homestead. I want rest—only rest, rest!'

'Did Summers know the truth, Chris?'

She shook her head slowly.

'No,' she said. 'I deceived him—I deceived them all. I lied to everybody. I used to pride myself once, a fortnight ago, when I was a girl, on not being a liar.

'You mustn't talk in this despairing way, dear. Let me take you home. I will meet Dick an' tell him.'

'Tell him it is too late, but I am grateful all the same—very, very grateful.'

'Yes, yes. Come. You are weary; you'll be stronger tomorrow an' braver.'

He led her away, and they walked across the flat and through the paddock in silence. It seemed to Harry that she had forgotten their avowals of love. Her attitude frightened him, he dreaded lest she should be on the eve of a serious illness; he had sore misgivings and tortured himself with many doubts. Her words rang in his head with damnable iteration: 'I deceived them all. I lied to every body.'

Maori welcomed them under the firs, capering heavily and putting himself very much in the way, but with the best intentions. Summers came to the verandah and greeted Chris with warmth.

'Eli, but ye're pale, lassie,' he said, having drawn her into the light.

'Take her in,' whispered Harry; 'she's quite worn out.'

'Will ye no come in yersel'?'

'No, no, thanks. Come back here, Mr. Summers; I want to speak to you.'

Summers led the girl into the house and returned after a few moments.

'What's happened tae the girl? She's not herself at all,' he said.

'Her father's been taken.'

'Ay, have they got him? Weel, 'twas sure to be.'

''Twas she who hid him, but he went light-headed with some sickness, an' the police came down on him. She feels it awfully, poor girl, being alone in a way.'

'Not alone, not while Jock Summers moves an' has his bein'.'

Harry had been fishing for this. He knew the man, and that his simple word meant as much as if it had been chiselled deep in marble.

'Good night,' he said, throwing out an impetuous hand. While he hastened away under the trees Summers stood upon the door-sill, gazing after him, ruefully shaking the tingling fingers of his right hand.

Harry returned to the skillion and loitered about for ten minutes without discovering anything of Dick Haddon, but at the expiration of that time Dick stole out of the darkness and approached him with an affectation of the greatest unconcern. His greeting was very casual, and he followed it with a fishing inquiry intended to discover if the young man knew anything of Christina's whereabouts.

'Never mind, Dick, old man,' said Harry kindly, 'it's all UP.'

'All up?' cried Dick.

'Yes, I know why you went to Yarraman; but it's been a wasted journey, Dick. Shine was arrested a couple of hours ago, an' she's broken hearted.'

Dick received the news in silence, and they walked homewards together.

'What'll I do with this?' asked Dick at Hardy's gate, producing a parcel from under his vest.

'Hide it away, an' keep it dark. Not a word must be said to hurt her.'

'Good,' answered the boy. 'I know a cunnin' holler tree. So long, Harry.'

'So long, mate.'

Dick liked the word mate; it touched him nearly with its fine hint of equality and community of interests; it seemed to suit their romantic conspiracy, too, and sent him away with a little glow of pride in his heart.

When Harry re-entered his own home he found his mother seated as he had left her. She arose and approached him, placing a hand on either shoulder.

'Well, my boy?'

'Well, mother?'

'You have seen her?'

'Yes. I've taken her to the homestead. She is dazed. It seems as if she no longer cared.'

'It will pass, Henry.'

'You think my love will pass?'

'All this seeming great trouble.'

'It'll pass, mother, if she comes back to me; never unless.'

'The sins of the fathers,' sighed Mrs. Hardy as he turned from her to his own room, like a wounded animal seeking darkness. 'The sins of the fathers.'

CHAPTER XXIII.

NEXT morning all Waddy knew of the arrest, and it was felt that the game was nearly played out. Dick's confession was published in the same issue of the Yarraman Mercury and public opinion in the township had decided against the searcher in spite of his long and faithful service as teacher and superintendent. The murder theory was reluctantly abandoned.

Harry Hardy called at the homestead to inquire after Chris before going to work, and was told that she was much rested but not yet up. At dinner-time he heard that she had been driven into Yarraman by Jock Summers to be near her father; the fact that she had left him without a word or a line seemed to confirm his worst suspicion, and again her words, 'I deceived them all. I lied to everybody,' returned to mock him. Harry had no quality of patience: he was impetuous, a fighter, not a waiter on fortune; but here was nothing to fight, and in his desperation he did battle on the hard ground.

They had cut the dyke in the new shaft at a shallower depth than Dick's Mount of Gold drive, and here Harry expended those turbulent emotions that welled within him, working furiously. Whether handling pick or shovel, toiling at the windlass, or ringing the heavy hammer on the drill, he wrought with a feverish energy that amazed his mates, who ascribed it all to an excusable but rather insane anxiety to test the value of their mine in the mill. For their part they were very well satisfied with the golden prospects, and quite content to 'go slow' in the certain hope of early affluence.

The next important piece of news the Mercury had to offer referred to Ephraim Shine, who had recovered consciousness in the gaol hospital but was declared to be dying from an old ailment. Steps were to be taken to secure his dying deposition. On the Saturday morning came the information that Shine was dead, and with this came the full text of his deposition—a complete confession, setting forth his crimes and those of Joe Rogers without reservation, and completely exonerating Frank Hardy. Rogers and Shine had been working together to rob the mine for two years. Their apparent hostility was a blind to deceive the people. They had conspired to fix the crime upon Frank at Rogers' suggestion, for the reason that his vigilance was making it unsafe for the faceman to continue his thefts, and because they hoped his conviction would arrest the growing suspicions. Shine agreed, for these reasons, and because he cherished a desire to marry Mrs. Haddon and found Hardy in the way. For a long time the pair had been content with such gold as Rogers could hide about his clothes, but his discovery of the big nugget, which he hid in the drive, gave them the idea of attempting robbery on a large scale, and for weeks Rogers had hidden such gold as he could lay his hands on in holes in the muddy floor of the workings, to be carried away when opportunity offered via the Red Hand laddershaft. That was to have been their last venture together, and Shine had intended to induce Mrs. Haddon to marry him, and then to take her away somewhere where he was unknown, and where it would have been possible to sell the gold in small parcels without exciting suspicion. Rogers had hidden the gold in Frank Hardy's boot, and Shine salted his washdirt on the creek with Silver Stream gold, and the slug he pretended to take from Frank's crib bag was hidden in the palm of his hand when he took up the faceman's billy from the floor of the searching shed.

Joe Rogers appeared before the bench of magistrates at Yarraman on the following Monday. Harry and Dick were in attendance as witnesses; Chris was also present in court, and there Harry saw her for the first time since the night of Shine's arrest. She sat beside Mrs. Summers, a stout, grey, motherly woman, and was dressed in deep mourning. Harry thought she had never looked so beautiful. But how changed she was from the simple gentle girl of a few days back! She sat as she did when he found her in the skillion after her father had been taken, with intent eyes bent upon the floor. When called upon to give her evidence she gave it clearly and fully, in a firm distinct voice, like a person without interest or feeling. She seemed to have no desire to shield the character of her father, but told the whole truth respecting him, and left the Court with her companion immediately on being informed that her services were no longer required, so that Harry was unable to speak with her. This was a bitter blow to him; he believed that she was taking precautions to avoid him, and saw in that action further reason for his suspicion that her declaration of affection had been a mistake or perhaps a deliberate deception. 'I deceived them all. I lied to everybody,' she said. The young man stiffened himself with chill comfortless pride, and made no effort to seek her out. He loved her, he told himself, but was no whimpering fool to abase himself at the feet of a woman who was careless, or might be even worse—pitiful.

Joe Rogers reserved his defence and was committed to stand his trial at the forthcoming sessions in about a fortnight's time, charged with gold-stealing, wounding Harry Hardy, and shooting at Trooper Casey.

Harry returned to his work. He made no further calls at the homestead to inquire after Christina, but heard from Dick that she had not returned to Waddy, but was staying in Yarraman till after the trial. Mrs. Haddon expressed an opinion that the poor girl felt the disgrace of her position keenly, and dreaded to face the people of the township where her father had been accepted as a shining light for so many years, and where she had always commanded respect and affection.

As the time for the trial approached Harry found himself hungering for a sight of her face again. Pride and common-sense were no weapons with which to fight love. At best they afforded only a poor disguise behind which a man might hide his sufferings from the scoffers.

The trial occupied two days. The prisoner was defended by a clever young lawyer from Melbourne, who fought every point pertinaciously and strove with all his energy and knowledge and cunning to represent Joe Rogers as the victim of circumstances and Ephraim Shine—especially Ephraim Shine—who was a monster of blackened iniquity, capable of a diabolical astuteness in the pursuit of his criminal intentions. The story of the boy Haddon was absolutely false in representing Rogers as having assisted in the theft of the gold produced. The boy was a creature of Shine's; that was obvious on the face of his evidence and the evidence of Miss Shine and Detective Downy. Shine had had the lad in his toils, otherwise why had he taken such precautions to shield the man, and why had he given him warning of the approach of the troopers? Rogers' story was entirely credible, he said. It was to the effect that Shine had confessed to him that he had robbed the mine of a quantity of gold and had been robbed in turn by the boy Haddon, who was his real accomplice. He solicited the aid of the unfortunate prisoner to recover the treasure, and offered him half the gold as a reward. The prisoner was tempted and he fell. His action towards the boy at the Piper Mine was taken merely to induce him to disclose the whereabouts of the lost booty, and the shooting at Trooper Casey was an accident. Rogers had acted on blind and unreasoning impulse in snatching up the gun on the approach of the police, believing his complicity with Shine in the effort to recover the hidden loot had come to light, and the discharge of the weapon was purely involuntary.

To give an air of plausibility to this plea it was necessary to represent Ephraim Shine in the worst possible light, and that conscientious and hard-working young lawyer spared no pains on his own part or the part of the dead man's daughter to make every point that would tell for his client; but Chris was not more moved than at the preliminary investigation. She told the truth simply, and no effort on the part of the barrister could shake her evidence or break through the unnatural calm in which she appeared to have enveloped herself. Harry saw her several times during the course of the trial, and found a desolate anguish in her white immobile face, that stirred up in his heart again a fury against fate, the law, and every force and condition that added the smallest pang to her sorrow. If he could have only interposed his body between her and all this trouble it would have been keen joy to him to have felt raining upon his flesh, with heavy material blows, the shafts directed against her tender heart; but his strength was of no avail, he could think of nothing that he might do but take that insolent lawyer by the throat and choke him on the floor of the Court. He was helpless to do any thing but love her, and every sight of her, every thought of her, added fuel to his passion.

She went to him once outside the Court with out stretched hands and swimming eyes, murmuring inarticulate words, and he understood that, she meant to thank him for the efforts he had made to spare her in his evidence on the previous day. In truth she bad been touched by the change in him, and she, too, was fighting with her love a harder battle than his.

'I'm sorry for you, Chris,' he said, 'but time will heal all this, never fear.'

She gazed at him and slowly shook her head.

'Never, Harry,' she said.

'It will, it will!' he persisted. 'Chris, you're coming back after it's all over?'

'Yes,' she said, 'I must.'

'An' you've not forgotten?'

'No, Harry, I have not forgotten anything.' There was a strain of firmness in her voice that jarred him, and he looked at her sharply; but her face gave him no comfort. A moment later she was joined by Mrs. Summers and another friend, and he left her, his heart unsatisfied, his mind shaken with doubts and perplexities.

Joe Rogers was found guilty and sentenced to twelve years' hard labour. Close upon eight hundred ounces of gold were handed over to the Silver Stream Company, and the Company, 'in recognition of the valuable services of Master Richard Haddon,' presented him with a gold watch and chain—which for many months after was a source of ceaseless worry to his little mother, who firmly believed that its fame must have inspired every burglar and miscellaneous thief in Victoria with an unholy longing to possess it, was continually devising new hiding-places for the treasure, and arose three or four times a night to at tack hypothetical marauders.

Returning from school at dinner-time on the day following, Dick found Frank Hardy sitting in the parlour holding his mother's hand. Mrs. Hardy and Harry were also there, and a few people were loitering about the front, having called to congratulate Frank Hardy on his release; for Frank had been given a free pardon in the Queen's name for the crimes it was now known he had never committed.

Dick found Frank looking older and graver, much more like his mother, whom he resembled in disposition too. He greeted the boy quietly but with evident feeling.

'It seems I owe my liberty to your devilment, old boy,' he said later.

Dick was beginning to find the role of hero rather wearisome, and would gladly have returned to his old footing with the people of Waddy, but there was nevertheless a good deal of satisfaction in appearing as a person of importance in the eyes of the Hardies, and he accepted the implied gratitude without any excess of uneasiness.

'Well, I've got to pay you out, my lad,' Frank continued. 'Your mother has been foolish enough to promise to be my wife, and that will place me in the responsible position of father to the most ungovernable young scamp in Christendom; and one of the conditions your mother makes is that I am to prevent you from saving any more lives and reputations. What do you think of that?'

'Oh, you'll make a rippin' father,' said Dick. 'That'll be all right.'

'Good. Then it's settled. We have your consent?'

Dick nodded gravely.

'Thanks for your confidence,' said Frank laughing. 'I think you'll find me a fairly good sort as step-fathers go.'

Dick had no fears whatever on that point; he and Frank had been excellent friends for as long as he could remember, and Frank had been his champion in many semi-public disagreements about billy-goats; and besides, he was a reader whose judgment the boy held in the highest respect, and that counted for a great deal.

The boy had a message for Harry, and delivered it with great secrecy at the earliest opportunity.

'She's back at Summers's, Harry,' he whispered. 'She gave Kitty a letter to give to me to give you.'

Harry tore the envelope with trembling impatient hands. It contained only a short note: 'Will you come to me at the gate under the firs tonight at eight?' and was coldly signed, 'Your true friend,

C. S.'

CHAPTER XXIV

HARRY awaited the approach of evening with burning impatience, and his heart was lighter than it had been for weeks. He thought that now the distraction induced by her father's danger, his arrest and his death, and the subsequent trials had departed, he would find her with a clear mind and responsive to his love, and it would be his pride and joy to teach her to forget her troubles and to make her happy. Harry, who up to the time of meeting Chris after his return to Waddy, had been even more unromantic and lacking in poetry than the average bush native, had, under the influence of his passion, evolved a strong vein of both romance and poesy; and the sudden development of this unknown side of his nature induced novel sensations. He thought of his previous self almost as a stranger, for whom he felt some sentiment of pity not untouched with contempt, and even when hope was feeblest he hugged his love and brooded over it secretly with the devotion of a tender girl.

He was at the trysting-place a quarter of an hour before the time appointed, but Christina was already there. Her greeting chilled and subdued him. He went towards her, smiling, elate, with eager arms, calling her name; she put him back with extended hands.

'No, no, Harry; not that,' she said, and he noticed in her voice the strength of some resolution, the firmness that had jarred upon him when last they met.

'Not that!' he repeated. Chris, you love me. For God's sake say it! You have said it. You told me so, an' it was true—oh, my darling, it was true!

He could see her distinctly: she stood in a shaft of moonlight falling between the sombre firs, and her face was marble-like; her whole pose was statuesque, all the girlish gentleness of the other days seemed to have fled from her, and her hour of tribulation had invested her with a dignity and force of will that sat well upon her stately figure. Harry beheld her with something like terror. This was not the woman he loved. His cause had never seemed so utterly hopeless as now, and yet he felt that it was not the true Chris with whom he was dealing; that the true Chris was the soft-eyed clinging girl safely enshrined in his heart.

'Chris,' he said, 'you have changed—but you'll come to me again?'

Her face was turned towards him; she shook her head with passionless decision.

'No, Harry,' she answered, 'that is all past. I sent for you to tell you that we must forget.'

'Forget!' he cried, springing forward and seizing her hand, 'how can I forget? Can a man forget that he loves?'

'You will forget. It is better, and you will live to be glad that you did.'

'Never, never! Chris, what do you mean? Why're you talking to me of forgetting—why, why?'

'Because I know in my heart that it must be. I came here to tell you so, to ask you to waste no more thought on me.'

'You do not care for me, then. Is that what you mean?'

She gave him no answer, but her steadfast eyes looked into his and their light was cold, there was no glimmer of affection in them.

'You never loved me, Chris?'

She continued silent; she had wrought herself to a certain point, to what she believed to be a duty, and she could only maintain the tension by exerting all her energies.

'What have I done to be treated like this?' he continued. 'I did all I could to spare you. I would have spared him, too, if it'd been in my power.'

'You were generous. Yes, you did all you could; for that I will be grateful to you all my life.'

'And I love you—I love you! I want love, not gratitude, Chris—your love.'

'You must forget me!

He approached her more closely, and his voice had lost its pleading tone.

'On the night of the arrest,' he said, 'you told me you had deceived all—lied to all; did you lie to me?'

He paused for a reply, but she did not speak, and he continued fiercely:

'Did you lie to me when you said you loved me? Was that a lie? Was it a trap?'

'It does not matter now, Harry; all is over, all.'

'An' you did lie to me. You lied because you thought I'd give your father up if my love was not returned. My God! you thought I took advantage of—'

'No, no, no!' she cried, 'not that. I thought no ill of you, I think none. Think what you will of me.'

'But I was fooled—cruelly, bitterly fooled. You needn't have done it, Chris. I'd rather have died than have added to your sufferings. Your trick wasn't necessary. I cared more for you than you'll ever know.'

Her hands trembled at her sides and her lips moved, but her eyes remained steadfast.

'I know your good heart, Harry,' she said in a voice almost harsh from the restraint put upon her. 'I will bless you and pray for you while I live, but I can never be your wife. You are mad to think of me. Some day you will be glad I refused to listen to you, and grateful to me for what I have done.'

'Grateful!' he cried. 'To be grateful I must learn to hate you. I'll go an' learn that lesson.'

He turned from her and strode towards the gate, but there he paused with his arm upon the bar, and presently he moved back to her side.

'I can't go like that, dear,' he said, seizing her hand again, 'nothing on earth can ever make me anything but your lover, an' nothing can make me believe you lied when you said you loved me. Your kisses were not lies. Speak to me—say that you did love me a little!'

'Goodbye, Harry,' she said in the same constrained tone.

'For God's sake be fair to me, Chris.'

'I am fair to you. Go; learn to love someone who will bring you happiness. Goodbye.'

'There is one woman who could bring me happiness, an' she stabs me to the heart. I won't give you up, I won't forget, I won't say goodbye. When this misery's gone from you, you will be your old self again, an' we'll be happy together.'

'Do not think that, Harry; you must put me out of your heart.'

'Never—never while I live!'

He looked into her strong pale face for a moment, and lifting her yielding hand to his lips kissed it.

'Goodnight,' he said gently. 'I'll come again.'

'Goodbye, Harry,' she whispered.

He hastened away, carrying his trouble into the sleeping bush. She stood for a few moments after he had gone, erect, with her hands pressed over her eyes, then walked towards the house with firm steps; but at the verandah uncontrollable sobs were breaking in her throat; she turned and fled into the plantation, and lying amongst the long grass wept unreservedly.

Harry's mind was in a tumult; he tried in vain to compose his faculties, to discover some reason for Miss Chris's action apart from the dreadful possibility that she had really never cared for him. Now that he had it from her own lips that she could be nothing to him, he refused to accept the situation. There were barriers raised between them, he would beat them down; there were mistakes, illusions, he would overcome them; he was strong, he would conquer. Anything was possible but that she had lied to him, but that her warm loving kisses were false and scheming. His heart scouted that idea with a blind rage that impelled him to hit out in the darkness. This spiritual fight tore the man of action, racked him limb from limb. Oh! to have been able to settle it, bare-armed and abreast of a living antagonist in the child's play of merely physical strife. He found tears on his cheek and this weakness amazed him, but his thoughts followed each other quickly, disconnectedly, like those of a drunken man; he went home baffled, but clinging to hope with the tenacity of one who feels that despair means death.

Next morning Harry found himself utterly miserable, but still trusting that time would serve to restore Chris her natural cheerful temperament, and bring home to her again the conviction that she really loved him, and then all would be well.

At about half-past two that afternoon Dick Haddon, in his capacity of faithful squire to the two lovers, visited the mine hot-foot, with news for his friend. Harry was below, but he hastened to answer the boy's message. He had dreamed of a sudden repentance on his sweetheart's part, and his heart beat fast as Dick beckoned him away from McKnight, who was at the windlass.

'She's gone away,' said the boy eagerly.

'Chris away? Where's she gone?'

'She's goin' to Melbourne—going fer years an' years. Mr. Summers is drivin' her into Yarraman now. She left a letter for you with mother. Thought I'd come an' tell you, 'case you might want to go after her.'

'Gone for good!' This possibility had not occurred to the young man. 'She left a letter for me? Are you sure it's for me?'

'Yes, yes; mother's got it. If I was you I'd get it at once; an' I'd—I'd—' Dick was much more excited than Harry; he was eager to spur his friend to action.

'How long have they been gone?' asked Harry, as he hastened towards the township. He felt that this was a crisis, that action was called for, but the news had confused him. He was fighting with the fear that she was taking this course to avoid him for the reason that his connection with her misfortunes had made him hateful to her. He burned to read her letter, but he had no mind for heroic schemes or projects.

'On'y about a quarter of an hour,' said Dick in answer to his question. 'They can't've gone far.'

'You're sure she was going to. Melbourne—going for good?'

'Certain sure—heard her tell mum.'

Mrs. Haddon was standing at the door when they reached the house, and Harry followed her into the kitchen.

'Give it to me, Alice,' he said. 'Quick! Can't you see I'm half mad?'

Mrs. Haddon handed him the letter, and he tore the envelope with awkward impatient fingers. The note was brief:

'DEAR HARRY,—I write this to bid you goodbye again, and thank you again for all your kindness and goodness. I am going away because I can no longer bear to live amongst people who know me as the daughter of one who was a thief and almost a murderer. Don't think bitterly of me. All that I have done I did for the best, according to my poor light. We may never meet again, but it would make me happier some day to know that you had forgiven me, and that you remembered me without anger in your own happiness.

—Your very true friend,
'CHRISTINA SHINE.'

Harry sank into a chair and sat for a minute staring blankly at the letter, and Mrs. Haddon stood by his side staring curiously at him. Suddenly she slapped firmly on the table with her plump hand and asked sharply:

'Well, Harry, well?'

He turned his blank eyes upon her.

'Do you care a button for that girl?'

'Care?' he said. 'I care my whole life an' soul for her!'

'Well, then, what're you goin' to do? "Re you goin' to lose her?'

'In the name o' God, Alice, what can I do? She doesn't want me; she is going away to be rid of me.'

'Not want you? You great, blind, blunderin' man you; she loves you well enough to break her heart for you. Can't you see why she's going away? Of course you can't. She's goin' because she thinks she's an object of shame an' disgrace; because she feels on her own dear head an' weighin' on her own great, soft, simple heart all the weight of the shame that belonged to that bad devil of a father of hers; because all that the papers, an' the lawyers, an' the judge said about the sins o' Ephraim Shine she feels burnin' in red letters on her own sweet face. That's why she's goin'; an' if she is leavin' you it's because she feels this whole villainous business makes her unfit to be your wife. Now what're you goin' to do, Harry Hardy?'

Harry had risen to his feet; his face was flushed, he trembled in every limb.

'Do?' he gasped. 'Do?'

'Do!' Repeated the widow in a voice that had grown almost shrill. 'There's a horse an' saddle an' bridle in McMahon's stable.'

Harry turned and ran from the house; and the little widow, standing at the door flushed and tearful, looking after him, murmured to herself:

'An' if you lose her, Harry Hardy, you're not the man I took you for, an' I'll never forgive you—never.'

She looked down and encountered Dick's eyes—seeming very much larger and graver than usual—regarding her with solemn admiration. The boy had conceived a new respect for his mother within the last two minutes, and had discovered in her a kindred spirit hitherto unsuspected.

'My colonial! that was rippin', mum!' he said.

CHAPTER XXV.

HARRY took French leave in McMahon's stable. He saddled Click, Mac's favourite hack, mounted him, and started down the dusty Yarraman road at a gallop. To Harry that ride was ever afterwards a complete blank. He started out with his mind full of one thought, an overpowering resolution. He would seek Chris, he would take her in his arms and defy every fear or scheme or power that might be directed against their love and happiness to part them again. That was his determination, and, having made it, he rode on blindly, pushing the horse to his best pace.

After passing the Bo Peep the road ran out into treeless open country, slightly undulating. There were a few trickling rock-strewn creeks to cross, and Harry rushed Click through them like a man riding for his life. Half an hour's gallop brought the vehicle in sight, and ten minutes later he came abreast of the buggy and brought his foaming horse to a trot. 'Stop!' he cried; and Summers, much amazed, pulled up his pair.

Harry threw himself from the saddle, leaving the horse his freedom, and, going to the buggy, seized Chris by the hand and drew her down towards him.

'Chris, I want to speak to you. You must, you must!'

He helped her from the vehicle. His attitude was stern and masterful, and Chris yielded with a sense of awe. Summers regarded the pair for a moment with pursed lips and bent brows; then a grim smile dawned about his mouth, and he touched his horses with the whip and drove slowly away down the road.

Harry and Chris stood upon the plain facing each other, the girl's hands clasped firmly in those of the man. Harry was dressed just as he had come from the mine; her neat black frock was marked with the grey dust from his clothes. He was flushed; his eyes had more of power than of love in them. She still strove, but felt his strength greater than hers, and her heart beat painfully. She whispered a pitiful protest when he drew her to his breast and clasped her closely in his irresistible arms.

'I won't let you go, my dear love—I swear I won't!' he whispered vehemently.

'You must. Oh, why do you make my task so hard?'

'I won't let you go from me, Chris.'

She looked into his glowing eyes, and struggled a little, murmuring incoherently.

'Never, Chris, never!' he continued. 'You love me! Look into my face an' deny it if you can. You can't!' he cried, with a flush of triumph.

'I have never denied it, Harry; but I must go. 'Tis because I love you—'

He laughed suddenly with the elation of a conqueror, and stopped her mouth with kisses.

'You love me, an' you'd leave me. Why? Tell me why, my darling, my dear love!'

She threw back her head and gazed into his eyes. 'I will tell you,' she said. 'I would leave you because I am the daughter of Ephraim Shine, the man whose memory is hated everywhere; the man whose crimes you and yours can never forget; the man who sent your innocent brother to prison, who whitened your mother's hair with grief, who left you to die in the waters of the mine—who was a triple thief and a hypocrite. He was my father and I loved him. I cannot do anything else but love him now, but you must hate and loathe him. Think of me as your wife—me, the thief's daughter, whispered about, pointed at. Think, as I have done, of that possible time when you might love me less because of him and the wrong he did you, when you might be ashamed to be seen with me. People don't forget crimes like his, Harry; they talk of them to their children. Think of your mother and your brother. Think, think—oh, Harry, think, for my strength is gone.'

He only clasped her closely and kissed her cheek.

'Think of your mother,' she continued. 'Harry, I would die to serve her. I would rather die than bring shame or grief into her life.'

'I love you! I love you!' he said.

'Think, think of the people pointing at us, whispering about my disgrace.'

'No, dear, you think. Think of me without you—cursed, ruined, without a care for anything on earth. Chris, there's not for me one ray of sunlight, not one smile in the world without you.'

Her forehead was bent upon his shoulder. He felt her strength leaving her, and continued with low vehement words:

'Dear, you love me, an' you think it's your duty to leave me. I tell you there's no man on God's earth here'd be so desolate. I'd rather be dead than lose you. To lose you is the only sorrow I can imagine. I care more for one smile of yours, one touch of your dear fingers, than for anything else in all the world. If you hate me an' want to ruin my life, you'll go. Chris, if you love me, can't you see what the loss of you would mean? I tried to think of it last night an' couldn't, it was too terrible. I was like a child facing a great black cavern peopled with devils.'

His words, his earnestness, brought her new light; she had not realised the depth of his love, she had thought that the blow might be heavy at first, but that he would soon learn to forget. She understood him better now; his love was like her own, and she knew that to be imperishable. She no longer struggled, but clung to him with trembling fingers.

'I did not think you loved me like that, dear,' she said softly.

'I worship you! And you, my wife, my sweet wife?'

She slid her arms about his neck and drew his face to hers.

They stood in the centre of an open plain above which the yellow sun hung gleaming like a ball of gold; there was silence everywhere: Harry's horse stood still with his nose to the ground, at a distance Summers' buggy dipped slowly down into the bend of an old watercourse, and far off in the dim simmering background there was a hazy suggestion of trees. The solitude was complete.

'Then you won't go, Chris?' he said.

'Yes,' she answered, smiling into his face, 'but not for ever.'

He drew her closer at the suggestion.

'But why must you go? Why should we part?'

'Please, please, dear, for a time. I—I want to be away for a little while, till I can bear it better—you know what I mean. Ah!' she cried with sudden warmth, 'I thought was going to be strong and brave and bear it all alone; but I was only a girl, not a heroine—my heart was crying out against it by day and night.'

'We'll be very happy, Chris, in spite of those silly terrors. 'Twas Mrs. Haddon sent me after you.'

'I'm glad. Oh, I'm glad!'

He gathered her to his heart, and kissed her again and again.

'Chris,' he said, 'you're not quite fair to the people of Waddy; not a man or woman of them thinks a mean thought of you.'

'But I cannot bear to face them. Let me go for a time, and I will come back.'

'An' be my wife?'

'Yes, if you still want me.'

'If! You'll write often.'

'Every day if you wish it, dear.'

'Every day then. Goodbye, my darling. I'll let you go, but not for long. If you don't come to me soon, I will come to you.'

The parting was long and loving, and then Harry recalled Jock Summers with a loud cooey. After Chris had been helped into the buggy the old man glanced sharply at Harry.

'Well, Maister Highwayman?' he said.

'She has promised to be my wife, sir,' said Harry.

Summers looked into the girl's brimming eyes, and his face softened.

'I'm right glad,' he said simply.

Harry rode by the trap as far as the town; then there was another parting, and he returned to Waddy like a man in a dream. That evening he told his mother that Christina Shine had promised to be his wife. Her answer surprised him.

'She is a brave, beautiful, genuine woman, and I would not have it different.'

'She said you were the best woman in the world, mother, and I believe she was right.'

'No, no, Henry; I will be content now to have you think me the second best,' said his mother, smiling.

Chris, who was staying with a relation of Summers' in Melbourne, wrote to say their parting should be for six months; but it did not last more than half that time, and meanwhile two or three matters of interest had happened in Waddy. There had been several crushings from the Native Youth, and the yields justified the highest expectations; Frank Hardy and Mrs. Haddon had been married, and Joel Ham had departed from Waddy under interesting circumstances. One evening when reading the Mercury in the bar at the Drovers' Arms, Ham looked up from his paper and addressed several members of the School Committee who were present:

'Gentlemen,' he said, 'I'll have to get you to fill my position within a fortnight.'

'What,' cried Peterson, 'throwin' up your billet?'

'I'm wanted in England,' said the master, tapping the paper.

There was a roar at this, which Joel treated with sublime indifference, but curiosity prompted Peterson to examine the paper closely when the teacher had set it aside, and he found the following advertisement:

'If this should meet the eye of Joel Hamlyn, second brother of Sir Just Hamlyn, of Darnstable, he is hereby informed of the death of his brother and of his succession to the title and estates. Any information respecting the above Joel Hamlyn will be thankfully received.' Then followed a description of Joel Hamlyn that was decidedly applicable to Joel Ham, and the address of a firm of Melbourne solicitors.

The schoolmaster said nothing to satisfy the curiosity of his committee, but was more communicative in the presence of Frank Hardy.

'I am Sir Joel Hamlyn now,' he said, grinning down at his white moleskins and broken boots. 'Just and I hated each other like brothers. He was eminently respectable, I was eminently otherwise. We parted with mutual satisfaction, but he had two boys when I left England, both of whom have since died, or there would have been no anxious and respectful inquiries for my disreputable self.'

'Well, I congratulate you,' said Frank. 'It will be an agreeable change.'

'I do not know,' said Sir Joel; 'I have got drunk on beer here, I shall get drunk on champagne there That's all the difference.'

Later, when parting with Frank for good, he said:

'I have a long journey before me, and I have got to make up my mind in that time in what useful capacity I shall figure in Darnstable teetotal circles, whether as a shining light or a shocking example—whether, in short, it is better to live respectable or die drunk.'

The people of Waddy never heard what Sir Joel's conclusion was, but they had an emphatic opinion about his end; which conclusion, however reasonable it may have been in the light of past events, let us hope was the wrong one.

Harry wrote to Chris before twelve weeks had passed: 'I can stand this parting no longer. I am coming to you.' Chris answering him said, 'Come,' and he went; and when he returned to Waddy Chris accompanied him. They were married very quietly at Yarraman a few months later, and Dick Haddon was the only absentee amongst their immediate friends who have figured in this story. When Harry and Chris were restored to happiness, his interest in them lost its keen edge, but he was considerate enough to send an apology to the bridegroom.

'Dear Harry,' he wrote, 'I'm sorry I can't come and be best man at your wedding, but there is to be a great race today—my grey billy, Butts, against Jacker Mack's black billy, Boxer, for two pocket-knives and a joey 'possum, owners up—and of course I couldn't get away.—Your mate, Dick.'

THE END

CPSIA information can be obtained at www.ICGtesting.com
Printed in the USA
BVOW04s1054171014

371243BV00001B/8/P